FALLING

.

FALLING

"Are you ogling my ass?" Christian asked, looking back over his shoulder as he entered the big kitchen. He pointed a finger at the fireplace, did some kind of small movement with it, and a fire whooshed to life.

Alec chuckled. "I am. Got a problem with that?"

"Yeah, I do, since I'm not getting to ogle yours, too."

Alec shrugged. "Next time don't be Mr. Macho Leader and rush off to be the first in line. Sometimes it pays to hang back. The view's better."

"Oh, I don't know." Christian stopped and turned to face him. "I'm not really complaining about the view from here."

Even with the flickering flames the only light in the big room, Alec could see every contour of Christian's nude body, including his hardening shaft.

He padded up to Christian and kissed him. "You keep looking at me like that and there's going to be less eating of food and more testing uses for kitchen utensils."

Christian's blue eyes grew heavy-lidded and dark with desire. "Keep talking like that and I'm thinking I'll gladly wait for the food."

FALLING

BY

M. L. RHODES

AMBER QUILL PRESS, LLC
http://www.amberquill.com

FALLING
AN AMBER QUILL PRESS BOOK

Amber Quill Press, LLC
http://www.amberquill.com

Layout and Formatting provided by: ElementalAlchemy.com

PUBLISHED IN THE UNITED STATES OF AMERICA

A special thanks to EJ, Trace, and Ing
for their patience in putting up with my last minute tendencies
as I try to cram my writing in around everything else.

And to my critique partner
for always being so willing to drop everything,
read my chapters, and get them back to me on a moment's notice,
as well as for the passing suggestion she made about a certain
something that grew into the awesome complication of
Alec having Forten's Syndrome.

Many thanks to Laura
for giving me a rundown on the basics of
Mercury in retrograde.

And last but not least, huge thanks to my husband
for helping me talk through certain knotty plot issues, and for
cooking lots and lots of dinners while I wrote.

PROLOGUE

Thirty years ago
London, England

"It's the only way, Evangeline."

"I won't leave you, Jason! I'm not going without you."

"I can't go. You know that. If I do, Rogan will follow. He'll hunt us down and then he'll use you and the baby to get to me. I won't let him do that. You're leaving and I have to stay."

Evangeline's golden-brown eyes widened and Jason's heart clenched at the sight of tears shimmering on her dark lashes. But he pushed back the welling emotion and hardened himself to it. Rogan would think nothing of destroying her in his quest to obtain the amulet, and Jason would do everything in his power to see that she and the baby lived, even if he did not.

"You have to leave, Evie. Now. Go far away, and live as an Ordinary—no magic." He picked up the hastily packed bag and draped it over her shoulder.

"No, Jason!" The tears slid down her cheeks.

"Hurry now, love. Your mother's waiting at the bottom of the hill. Together you'll be safe. And I can't know where you've gone—no one can. It's better that way." He hustled her to the door, but before he opened it, he couldn't stop himself from pulling his wife fiercely into his arms and kissing her, pouring all his love for her into it, hoping to leave a part of himself with her. She kissed him back with a desperation born of terror.

"Will we ever see you again?" she choked out. She stared up at him as if memorizing every curve of his face.

"I don't know," he answered honestly. He loved her too much to make false promises.

A sob tore from her.

"You're always in my heart, Evie."

"And you're always in mine."

He bent to kiss the soft, warm, sweet-smelling infant in her arms. Then he slipped a silver chain around the child's neck and tucked the small, round medallion under the blankets. "It's a protective charm. As long as the babe's wearing it, it should give some measure of protection from Rogan's magic." He kissed the sleeping infant once more.

"Now go," he said, opening the door and ushering his wife out into the dark of the moonless night.

She turned. "Jason—"

"Go! Now, Evie! There's no more time."

Her pale face was tortured, but she nodded. Her long hair fell forward, teasing across the baby's face. "I love you." The words were shaky with tears.

Jason's throat filled with emotion. "And I love you."

With a final, heart-wrenching look, she turned and made her way down the road.

He stood at the door long after she'd disappeared from sight.

"I'll always love you," he whispered. "Both of you." Then he reentered the house and shut and locked the door, for what little good it would do him. When Rogan arrived—and he would; it was inevitable—regular locks would not keep the dark mage out.

Jason spent the next hour weaving protective spells around the house, and then preparing the items he'd need if things went bad and he had to resort to his final plan.

There was nowhere left to run. He and his brothers had tried, but Rogan had hunted them one by one, until now, he was the only one left. The only one who could keep the amulet from Rogan. He'd done everything he could to assure its safety. And now, he would meet Rogan on his own terms, face to face, rather than allowing the power-hungry wizard to sneak up on him in the dark somewhere. It was his family's legacy to protect the amulet and keep it out of dark-magic hands at all costs.

He'd protect it with his life.

*　　　*　　　*

Two days ago
Headquarters, Bureau of Dark Magic Affairs
The countryside, Wiltshire, England

"After all this time, do you think it's possible he's found it?"

Christian Wetherly shoved his hands into the pockets of his jeans and leaned against the door jamb as he contemplated Bella's question.

Her black eyebrows were drawn into a frown, nearly hidden by her thick bangs, and she tapped a pencil in rapid rhythm against the desk top—a definite sign this new information they'd just received had her on edge.

"Has he actually found it, as in gotten his hands on it?" Christian shook his head. "No. I don't think so. Otherwise why all the murders? The Council suspects, and I concur, it's more likely he's narrowed it down to someone in the U.S. having information he needs, but he's not sure yet specifically who."

"Agreed." Jamie Hughes said. The lanky blond man, Bella's husband, sat perched on the edge of her desk. "He must think he's close to finding it, though, to risk exposure and possible capture after all these years. I can't think of anything except the lure of finally possessing the amulet that would bring him out of hiding. Not with the entire magic world ready to lynch him on sight."

Bella whacked her pencil so hard it snapped in two and part of it flew across the desk to hit Jamie's leg. He raised an eyebrow at her. She shrugged and mouthed, "Sorry." Then said aloud, "I thought the Amulet of Sulisa was lost when Jason Ansley died thirty years ago? That before he died, he secreted it some place where Rogan couldn't find it?"

"Before he was murdered, you mean," Jamie said.

"That wasn't ever proven. The London police labeled it a fire started by faulty wiring. Even our own people couldn't determine for sure whether or not magic was involved, or that Rogan had even been there."

"Oh, come on, Bella, you know damn good and well it was murder and you know as well as anyone who did it. Rogan went through the Ansley family with methodical precision looking for the amulet. Jason was the last one left alive. He and his wife and baby were killed when Rogan torched their house."

"But that's exactly what's always bothered me about the story. If

Jason Ansley was the last member of his family alive who knew where the amulet was, why would Rogan have destroyed him, and with him, his last chance at finding it?"

"Sodding dark mage, that's why. Does the word psychopath ring a bell with you? Maybe when Ansley refused to give up the amulet, Rogan went batty and killed him in a fit of rage. Wouldn't be the first time. The man likes to make things go boom and watch them burn. Do I have to remind you what happened thirteen years ago, when he was behind the massacre at the Gathering? I know Christian's not likely to ever forget it. Forty-nine mages and Ordinaries dead all because the Council wouldn't allow Rogan to attend."

"No one's arguing that he's a dangerous loose cannon," Christian interjected. "But Bella does have a point about why he'd kill Ansley when that was his last link to the amulet."

When Jamie shot him a disgusted look, Christian held up a hand in feigned defense. "I'm just saying…"

"Assuming he actually did murder Jason Ansley and his family, I've often wondered if it was because Jason destroyed the amulet," Bella said. "The Ansleys were its protectors for generations, but maybe Jason decided the best way to keep Rogan or some other power-seeking wizard from laying hands on it and using it for dark purposes was just to destroy the thing. And when Rogan discovered that fact, he murdered Jason."

"Okay, first of all, would the Council have allowed Jason Ansley to destroy the amulet? Doubtful. But even if that is the case, why would Rogan suddenly be active again after staying in hiding since the Gathering incident? If he's not looking for the amulet, then what?" Jamie asked, giving his wife a pointed stare.

Bella's brow furrowed again. "I don't know."

"And surely Jason knew destroying the amulet would mean certain death for him and his family. If the amulet was gone, there'd be no reason for Rogan to keep them alive," Christian added thoughtfully. "I can't see that he'd have risked the lives of his wife and child. And this is all assuming the amulet could be destroyed in the first place. From everything we know about it, I'm not sure it can be unmade. It's been in existence for thousands of years."

"True. But one thing we do know is that only a member of the Ansley family can activate the amulet. And with all of them dead, even if Rogan manages to find the thing, he can't use it. So, no worries. Right?" Jamie looked at Christian, then Bella, as if seeking reassurance.

"Wrong," Christian said in a low, strained voice. "There is a way."

Both his partners' gazes turned to meet his.

"Oh, no…you don't think…?" Bella's words were hoarse.

"I think Rogan's capable of absolutely anything. And we can't take a chance."

"How can he use it?" Jamie asked, looking confused.

"The Vargazian ritual," Bella whispered.

"The Vargaz—" Jamie's green eyes widened and his already pale, freckled skin grew even paler. "Isn't that a myth? I thought the ancient texts were lost when the library at Alexandria was burned in 600 CE?"

"Approximately 642 CE," Bella said. "Although that date isn't certain. And, yes, it's believed they were lost. But there have always been rumors another set of texts were hidden elsewhere in Egypt."

"They're just rumors, though. Right?"

"The Council doesn't think so," Christian said. "Over the last month three new archaeological digs have begun in Egypt. All of them funded by anonymous sources. All of them in locations that have long been suspected as the hiding place for the second set of texts."

"And the Council thinks Rogan might be behind the digs?" Bella asked.

"Like I said, with Rogan, anything's possible. I've sent Evan and Cayleigh to Egypt to investigate."

"Okay, let's say, hypothetically, that the texts discovered are the ones, and that Rogan could somehow get his hands on them *and*, miraculously, the amulet that's been lost for the past thirty years. Aren't the texts written in some ancient magic language no one can read any longer?" Jamie wanted to know.

"That's right." Bella perked up and nodded. "The Vargazian texts are rumored to have been written in Mensi, and it's a language that's been dead, even to the magic world, for thousands of years. There's no Rosetta Stone for it. No one can read or speak it."

A large knot formed in Christian's gut. "I can," he murmured.

The silence in the room was immediate as two sets of eyes turned to stare at him in shock.

"How?" Bella and Jamie asked at the same time.

He rubbed the ache that had formed in the back of his neck. Stress. His neck was the first place it always showed up. He stepped farther into the room and, with a sigh, sank into the leather chair across the desk from Bella. "I don't know exactly. It's fuzzy, but—"

"You had a dream, didn't you?" Bella asked, leaning forward and crossing her arms on the desk in front of her.

Christian nodded.

Jamie shook his head. "Damn, what's up with you and those dreams? Strange places, events, and now obsolete languages?"

"I keep telling you both— I've been telling you for years— Christian, you're having visions, premonitions," Bella said, sounding a bit too know-it-all.

Jamie rolled his eyes. "Premonitions means things that are going to happen in the future, Bell, not stuff that happened thousands of years ago."

She glared at him. "But his dreams aren't always about the past. Sometimes they're about the present or things that are to come. If the Vargazian texts have been found, and Rogan needs them to make the amulet work, then the fact Christian's been dreaming about Mensi—"

"Dreaming *in* it, actually," Christian amended.

"*In* it?" Bella looked at him like he'd just grown two heads.

He nodded, feeling oddly apologetic about having to admit to it, but that was followed by a flash of irritation. Why should he feel sorry for something he had no control over?

"This is important. You dreaming in Mensi…it's got something to do with what Rogan's up to."

"I know." Christian sighed. "That's why I think another set of the Vargazian texts really exists. I think that's what I saw in the dream— it's like I was there when they were hidden."

"Any other clues about location then? Something that might help us narrow down which of the three archaeological digs will yield the texts?"

"No. Unfortunately, all I saw was that they're underground in a vault or a tomb."

"Where are these dreams coming from?" Jamie asked. "And why's Chris being singled out for them? Have you got some secret destiny we don't know about, mate?"

"The hell if I know."

Bella scowled at them both. "This is important, and it's not a coincidence, Christian. You can't take this lightly."

"Do I look like I'm taking it lightly? It's not like I'm thrilled about this, but I don't believe in coincidence anymore than you do. Which is why we have to find out what Rogan knows. The Council's tasked us to do that very thing."

"And if Rogan's anywhere close to finding the amulet…" Bella said, her dark eyes wide.

"We have to get it first," Christian finished for her. "I'm going to the States, see what the American cops are up to and what they've discovered about the murder victims. The Americans don't keep a registry of mages like we do here, so although the Council's positive Rogan's involved in these deaths, right now we're not even certain if the people killed were magic folk, Ordinaries, or some of both. Maybe the American police know something that can tell us why Rogan's targeted specific people. It's possible they've uncovered something that links the victims."

He stood. "Jamie, check in with Evan and Cayleigh. I'd like to have all three of you in Egypt, one per archaeological site, to see what you can turn up."

Jamie nodded. "I'm on it."

"Bella, see what you can pull together on the Ansley family. How they managed to protect the amulet for generations, who the family members were, who they married, children…anything and everything in their history that might help us. Let me know what you discover."

"Okay."

Jamie gave Bella a quick kiss and left. Christian turned to follow.

"Christian?" Bella's voice held a note of concern that gave him pause.

He looked back at his long-time friend and colleague. He, Bella, and Jamie had met at university, instantly recognized the aura of magic on each other, and become fast friends. They'd been through more together than most people—Ordinary or magic—could ever imagine. And even though he was now in charge of the Bureau and had a dozen other operatives working for him, he was nothing without the two of them. He valued their opinions beyond all others and trusted them with his life.

"What's on your mind, Bell?"

"You look out for yourself on this mission, Christian. I don't have to tell you that Rogan's the most powerful dark mage to surface in a century. And if he finds out you're there in the States interfering with his plans…"

"I know. I'll be careful."

"Extra careful. You know how he feels about you. You're the only one who's ever come close to capturing him and he'll never forgive you for that. He'll kill you if he gets a chance."

Christian grimaced at the memory of that horrific day so many years ago. The day Rogan had savagely killed mages and Ordinaries at the Gathering. Christian had been nineteen. Green as hell when it came to just how powerful a user of dark magic could be, and ignorant enough to think he could stop a mage who had vast years of experience he didn't.

"I won't let him close enough," he assured her.

"I'd feel better if someone went with you. I'll go."

"No, I need you here. No one else can dig up information like you can and you know it. And information on the Ansley family is imperative. If we do manage to get our hands on the amulet before Rogan—assuming it still even exists—we're going to need to know how to protect it and keep it from him. The Ansleys were masterful in protecting it. So masterful I'm not sure even the Council knows how they managed to keep it safe for centuries.

"And besides, I can't exactly walk into a police precinct in the U.S., tell them I'm a mage who hunts bad mages, and by the way, what can you tell me about the murders that have been committed because I'm certain they were done by magic." He smiled at the scowl she was giving him. "I'm going to have lay low and do this undercover, with as little magic manipulation as possible. It's solo work. If more than one of us shows up, it'll look too suspicious."

She sighed. "Damn it. I hate it when you get all practical. Okay, just be safe. And don't hesitate to ask for backup if you need it."

"I will. Don't worry. This is a fact-finding mission only."

She sighed again, dramatically this time. "If only I had a quid for every time you or Jamie have told me that. Do you see these?" She lifted a lock of her short dark hair.

"See what?"

"Look closely. Gray hairs. And every one of them was put there by you and Jamie and your macho need to show off your derring-do. I don't want any more of them. Don't give me anymore," she said pointedly. "Go do your fact-finding, but don't take risks. And get your arse back here safe and sound."

"Yes, ma'am. Harridan," he shot over his shoulder as he headed for the door. Then he ducked and chuckled when he felt a ball of crackling energy fly over his head.

"You'll pay for that comment, Wetherly!" she called. But he heard laughter in her voice.

As soon as he was out in the hallway, however, he sobered. The reality of the situation settled over him like a lead cloak.

FALLING

Rogan was on the prowl again. And possibly seeking the Amulet of Sulisa. Even if they did find the amulet before he did…nothing good could possibly come of any of this.

CHAPTER 1

Present day
Shelton, Illinois, United States

"Are you shitting me?" Alec Anderson dragged a hand through his hair and shook his head as he stared at his boss, Martin Shanahan.

The usual mid-morning buzz of the metro police division rattled around them on this Tuesday morning, but all Alec cared about at the moment was confirming that he hadn't just heard the captain correctly. He'd had several nights with minimal rest and last night, the few hours of sleep he'd managed to snatch had been riddled with more of the unsettling dreams that had plagued him since this current murder case had begun. With all these damned homicides hanging over his head, having to escort a visiting cop was the last thing he needed added to his plate.

"How the hell did we end up having to participate in some kind of police exchange program anyway? I don't have time to hold a visitor's hand, Martin."

"I know you don't, and I tried to argue for you. But when I spoke with the chief yesterday evening, he specifically requested you. Something about the British cop being a homicide guy himself, and since this latest messy case is in your hands, he felt like it would be good experience—that maybe the man would learn something from you and vice versa."

"Lucky me." Alec grimaced. "I've got piles of paperwork to wade through today and witnesses to interrogate. I don't need some stranger breathing down my neck."

"Let him help you with the paperwork and the investigation. The cops in this international exchange aren't supposed to just observe, they're supposed to work. So put him to work for you. Delegate."

Alec grumbled under his breath and stared up at the stained ceiling, then ran a hand raggedly through his hair again. "I suppose I have to waste part of my day picking him up at the airport, too?"

"No, the chief said he'd made his own arrangements. I expect he'll come here to the station when he arrives."

Shanahan's gray moustache twitched and he smoothed his fingers over it, trying to hide the smile Alec knew lurked behind it. But his gaze was genuinely sympathetic. "It's just for a few weeks. Hang in there. You can cope with anything for a few weeks." Shanahan gave him a friendly pat on the back, then turned and headed down the hall toward his office.

Alec stared at the captain's broad backside. If Martin weren't such a good friend to him, and he wasn't so damned tired, he might have followed and tried to argue further. But it'd be useless. When the chief said jump, they all jumped.

"Up to my ass in unexplained murders and now I have to baby-sit some tight-assed, stuffy Brit," he muttered.

With another sigh, he spun around, hoping he might have a few hours to wade through work before the guy arrived.

But he stopped short when he discovered a dark-headed stranger standing not ten feet away. The man was staring directly at Alec with an expectant look on his face, as if Alec were exactly the person he was looking for.

A curl of dread slid through him as he had a sudden feeling he knew who the man might be…and what he'd no doubt just heard. But before he could get out an apology, the man's lips turned up and his startlingly blue eyes sparkled with humor. "I believe I'm your tight-assed, stuffy Brit."

Alec cleared his throat, not sure what to say in response, but finally settling on a simple, "God, I'm sorry." He gave the man an apologetic half-smile. Hell, what else could you do when you'd been caught red-handed being a rude asshole?

The stranger shrugged, still smiling. "I've been called worse things."

He appeared to be around Alec's age—early thirties—and had a low-key, no muss, no fuss kind of look to him, with tousled dark brown hair that was longish on top and shorter on the sides and in back, and appealing, but not classically handsome features. He wore jeans, a black turtleneck sweater, and a leather bomber jacket. Alec suddenly realized he'd automatically presumed he'd be stuck with some suit-wearing, uppity schmuck, and the visitor was hardly that. He didn't, in point of fact, appear stuffy at all—in looks or attitude. His accent wasn't brassy and neither was his voice. It was more like smooth whiskey. A martini—shaken, not stirred. *Bond. James Bond.*

Oh, for crap sake. Alec gave himself a mental shake. He was tired and it was showing. The guy was hardly Bond. Much too casual. And if he understood correctly, a cop, not an agent. Still, there was something striking about him. Alec sensed… He couldn't put his finger on what it was. A magnetism? Or maybe a shimmer of confident power?

The man stepped forward and held out a hand. "Sorry to have snuck up on you like that. Christian Wetherly."

Alec grasped his hand, and was shocked at the unexpected jolt of awareness that coursed through him at the firm, warm contact. It was so unexpected it rattled him for a moment and there was a pause before he managed to get his mouth open and remember to speak. "Alec. Alec Anderson." The handshake ended, but Alec continued to feel a tingling in his palm. "And I really am sorry for what you overheard. It's been a stressful couple of weeks, but that's no excuse."

"I understand. Your chief gave me a brief rundown on the case you're working."

Well, hell. The chief certainly hadn't wasted any time.

"Have you found anything linking the victims?"

"Nope. They're from all over the city. Some men, some women. We can't link their lifestyles or income brackets."

If he was going to be stuck with the man for the next few weeks, Martin was right…he might as well put him to work. And at this point, Alec wasn't too proud to admit this case had him stymied. He was willing to listen to any possible theories. So he continued. "At first we wondered if it was a killer who preyed on older folk—the first three victims were all over age fifty. But then the fourth was forty-one, blowing that theory all to hell. The last three were back into the over-fifty group. Still, that forty-year-old throws the profile for a loop."

Christian looked thoughtful for a moment. "The chief also told me no one's been able to determine the cause of death in any of the victims. That's…odd."

"That's right. No obvious marks. No trace of poisons. The first two weren't even considered homicides initially…it's like the victims just keeled over dead. It was thought they might have eaten the same bad food or had a reaction to medication, except the coroner ruled that out. But when it became a pattern and several more victims showed up dead over the next week, we had to take notice."

Alec began walking toward his cubicle, and motioned the British cop to join him. "What moved the case firmly into homicide territory, though," he continued, "were the witnesses."

"Witnesses?"

Alec's desk faced the back wall of the small cube, giving him a view of the gray, carpeted wall covered with bits and scraps of paper, newspaper clippings, and other assorted odds and ends collected over the past three years he'd been in this particular office. He sank into his desk chair, grabbed up a folder, swiveled around, and motioned the man into the other chair that occupied the office. As he passed the folder to Christian, their fingers brushed and again Alec was shocked at the subtle ripple of electricity that moved between them. What the hell was up with that?

"There have been three separate witnesses who've seen or heard odd things at the time of the victims' deaths."

"Odd things?" Christian leaned slightly forward and his blue eyes shimmered with intensity.

"One woman was walking her dog down the street where one of the victims lived on the night he died. She said she saw strange, flickering lights inside the victim's house. Another witness, who lived in an apartment next to a victim, heard a loud pop, but not like a gunshot. He said it was more like a big balloon popping. And, for the record, we found no evidence a gun had been fired at the crime scene. Then last night, the victim's husband swore he saw a floating ball of light just seconds before his wife screamed, looked absolutely terrified, then slumped dead in his arms. He saw no other person in the room. Only the baseball-sized light floating a few feet from them. When his wife screamed and died, he heard what he described as a 'bang' and the light disappeared."

"Disappeared?"

"Flickered out of existence. And before you say anything, yeah, I know this all sounds crazy. I'm just telling you what the witnesses claim to have seen. Maybe they all share the same delusion, but, for now, their accounts are all we have to go on."

13

He picked up the orange foam basketball from the corner of his desk and shot it at the hoop Velcroed to the cube wall. It swished through the small net and he caught it before it fell to the floor. He returned it to the desk and studied Christian, certain he'd show either shock, disbelief, or utter amusement at what Alec had just told him. But oddly, the man only stared back, his dark eyebrows drawn together as if in thought, and he didn't looked shocked at all.

"So how come you're not laughing hysterically at me like the coroner did when I told him this story?"

Christian blinked as if pulling himself back to the here and now. "Let's just say I've seen some strange things in my day."

"Uh-huh. Don't tell me you believe in ghosts or paranormal activity?" Alec couldn't stop the smile that quirked his lips.

Christian smiled back, but didn't answer.

Which, to be honest, barely registered with Alec, since he was more taken aback at the effect the other man's smile had on him. He shifted in his chair, not at all pleased to discover he was feeling any kind of attraction to this stranger. Any kind of attraction to anyone. A stab of guilt shot through him, effectively sweeping away any remaining fascination.

"You okay?" Christian asked.

"Yeah, sorry." He shook his head. Damn, this was the second time the man had caught him speechless. "Like I said, stressful couple of weeks. Haven't had a lot of sleep. So, any wild theories about what might be going on here?"

Christian leaned back in his chair. "Maybe. A couple. But too wild to share at the moment."

Alec arched an eyebrow. "No offense, but I was told you're here to work, not just observe. So if you've got something to add or any ideas of what might be happening, I'd expect you to tell me just like I'd expect anyone else here in the homicide division to do."

The other man nodded solemnly. "Point taken. And the moment I come up with anything even halfway believable, I'll let you know."

Alec studied him, not sure if Christian was being evasive or just honest. But lingering exhaustion finally made him decide it didn't really matter right now. "Sorry to jump right into business here without a lot of social pleasantries, but—"

"I understand. You've got work to do."

Alec nodded. "I'm going to go re-interview the witness from last week—the one who heard the noise in the apartment. See if we missed anything the first time. Want to tag along?"

"I do."

Alec grabbed his jacket off the back of his chair and led the Englishman through the maze of the department.

"I'm assuming with the strict airline regulations that you probably weren't allowed to carry a piece with you," he said.

"Piece?"

"Weapon? A gun? Do you want to stop at the armory and get one? I'm sure they'll loan you one to use during your stay." He pushed the button for the elevator and the door opened immediately.

"No, thanks. I don't carry one," Christian said.

When they'd entered and Alec had pressed the button for the ground floor, he turned to look at the other man. "Cops in England don't carry guns?"

A small, flitting half-smile curved Christian's mouth. "I don't. I've never really had a need for one."

"O—kay." He turned back to stare at the silver door in front of him.

It's not like he'd drawn his own weapon on the job more than a handful of times, and he'd never fired it in the line of duty aside from practicing at the range. Most cops didn't. But after so many years on the force, he felt naked without his Glock riding against his side. It gave him a sense of security, false though it might be.

The elevator ride seemed to take forever, when in truth it was probably less than thirty seconds. Alec was acutely aware of the other man standing at his side. Acutely aware they were nearly evenly matched in build and height—probably both right at six-feet and within a few pounds of each other. He was also very aware of a warm tingling energy radiating from Christian, the subtle, musky scent of his aftershave, and the fact that, whether Alec liked it or not, his jeans were beginning to feel uncomfortably tight across his groin.

Shit. He didn't need this. Didn't want it.

He had an insane, though thankfully brief, moment of wondering if Christian was even his type. With some men it was easy to spot one way or the other. He couldn't tell yet with Christian. Although the fact his body was responding to Christian's close proximity was a sign. He didn't usually find himself attracted to straight men.

Get over it. Even if the man was gay, the last thing Alec needed in his life was a relationship. *It's too soon. Still too soon.* The twinge of guilt and sadness curled through his gut again.

When the elevator doors slid open, it was all Alec could do not to breathe a sigh of relief. Yet, at the same time, some small part of him immediately missed feeling the other man's closeness.

*   *   *

Rather than exiting through the main doors of the station, they went out the smaller side entrance. The damp, December chill filled Christian's lungs, and with the low gray clouds scudding overhead, the weather wasn't unlike what he'd left at home a few hours ago. It smelled like it might snow before the day was over. He zipped his coat while Alec led him toward a black Jeep Wrangler parked on the street nearby.

As he climbed in the passenger side, he couldn't help but smile at the irony of the situation. He wanted information, and the impatient part of him wanted it now. Yet, in his guise as a police officer, he was forced to slow down and go at the pace of an Ordinary. At home and on most of his assignments, he seldom had reason to drive or use a vehicle for transportation. Normally, if he knew the specific location he needed to go, he'd simply think where he wanted to be, then materialize there.

He couldn't say he hated the ride, though. As Alec zipped through traffic, Christian had a chance to take in some of the sights—the streets and stores decorated in red and green for the holidays, the people hustling in and out of buildings, bundled up against the cold.

But underlying all that, he once again felt the same heat he'd experienced as he and Alec stood in the elevator together. An awareness of sorts that gave him pause.

Alec Anderson had been a surprise to him. He didn't know what he'd expected to find, who he'd expected to be working with when he'd arrived in the States. But the moment he'd heard Alec's frustrated muttering, then saw the genuine surprise and instant apology in his golden-brown eyes when he'd turned around, it had stirred something in Christian—respect, and a sense that this was someone he could see himself genuinely liking, becoming friends with. The American hadn't tried to play dumb or blow off the comment. He'd owned up to it, and Christian had to admire that. He suspected if he were in Alec's shoes he'd bloody well be pissed off at having a stranger interfering in his case, too. Yet Alec had handled it with dignity.

Still, it was more than that, he admitted to himself, though this was hardly the time or place, and not something he was completely comfortable with under any circumstances. He still struggled with accepting the fact it was okay for him to find another man attractive.

All those years of denial had dug their claws in deep, and when he did come across someone he found interesting, each time, an internal battle raged between those old hang-ups that told him no, no, no, and the more liberal part of him that was sick of hiding his real feelings.

So just sodding say it then. You're attracted to him. And why not? He's damned nice to look at, a little intense at times, maybe, but he seems like a good guy, and you can't deny the heat between you.

Okay, admitting Alec was an attractive man was one thing. It was safe and something he could do from a distance. But the heat thing? That was reaching. He'd just met the man, knew almost nothing about him, and the turn-on was probably one-sided. Besides, he wasn't here for this. There were considerably bigger issues at stake.

Unable to stop himself, however, he studied the American out of his peripheral vision. As he drove, Alec ran a hand through his thick, light-brown hair that was long enough it curled against the collar of his navy blue down jacket. He had a face that tended toward lean and angular with a strong jaw, but when he smiled, it lit up his entire expression, including his eyes, and kept the planes and angles warm rather than harsh. Christian noted the tired lines around the other man's eyes and mouth. Alec had mentioned not getting a lot of sleep recently.

Christian was pretty good at reading people, and Alec struck him as being confident, capable, genuine. His tiredness led Christian to believe he also cared about helping people, to the point he put others' needs ahead of his own. Underneath the strong, capable man, however, he sensed a vulnerability in Alec. Something private and emotional that he didn't show the world.

"So you must have been flying for hours."

"Excuse me?" Alec's voice brought him out of his thoughts. For a moment he was disoriented and wondered if he'd missed something.

"How many hours does it take to get to the States from England? Did you just get in this morning? If so, you must be dead from jet lag."

"It...uh, doesn't take as long as you might think." Not that he'd know. He'd never been on an airplane in his life. The time change was always a bit rough, though, on these trips. And, as simple and quick as travel was for him, it took an enormous amount of energy to materialize someplace. The longer the distance, the more energy. Which probably accounted for why he'd been zoning out for the past few minutes.

He'd better stay focused on the job at hand and quit letting his own personal stuff interfere or he was going to give away something he didn't mean to.

Generally speaking, Ordinaries weren't aware of magic or the magic folk who lived among them. There were exceptions, of course, but the average Ordinary was usually content with the status quo, and labeled as fantasy or imagination anything that, to use a cliché, was out of the ordinary. So, generally speaking, when those in the magic world lived and worked among Ordinaries, there was a certain amount of silence. Not that it was against Council law for the Ordinaries to know about magic. It was more the simple fact that mages got real tired real fast of being laughed at, shunned, or labeled as nutters, so most learned at an early age to keep their abilities and talk of magic society to themselves when in mixed company. Therefore, telling Alec it had taken him less than five minutes of travel to get to the States wasn't an option. Not if he wanted to earn the man's trust.

Yeah, great way to earn his trust...by lying to him.

Usually when he did undercover work this like, the evasions and lies never gave him pause. So why, with Alec, did it suddenly bother him?

"Why don't you tell me some more about this murder case?" he said, tamping down the odd attack of conscience. "How many victims now?"

Alec shook his head. "Too many. Seven as of last night. And we can't get a bead on where the killer will strike next. Hell, to be honest, I'm not even sure we have a bonafide killer."

That piqued Christian's interest. "What do you mean?"

"I phrased that wrong. Clearly there's a killer, but something about this case just isn't...normal. Not that murder's ever normal, but this one feels different. I mean, how does a human being kill another human being without leaving any marks or evidence of how the kill was made? Even with the witnesses, sometimes I still wonder if we're completely off base here and this isn't the work of a someone but rather a something."

"Something?"

He let out a tired sigh. "I don't know. I don't know what I mean by that exactly. Just a gut feel. Like there's...I don't know...something out of the ordinary at work here."

A strange ripple shot through Christian, causing the hair on his arms and the back of his neck to stand on end. It was like a physical reaction to what he thought of as his magic sixth sense. And that usually only happened...

No. Impossible.

Alec glanced at him and gave him a half-grin. "Wouldn't it be easier to believe all this if there were such a thing as paranormal activity? Flickering lights, floating balls of light, strange noises, people dying from what looks like sheer terror. Jesus, we could just call *Ghostbusters,* or better yet, Gandalf or one of his cronies and let him do some mystical, magical thing to track down the killer."

Christian offered a weak smile in return. "Yeah, wouldn't that be something."

CHAPTER 2

Nothing new turned up after questioning the witness. Not that Alec had expected it to, but he'd had to try. And he had to admit, it had been helpful to have Christian along. The Brit had thought to ask questions that hadn't occurred to him. At one point he thought he'd seen an "Ah-ha!" flicker through Christian's gaze as the witness spoke, but it had been short-lived, and seconds later, Alec wasn't sure that's what he'd seen at all, or if it was just Christian blinking. In any case, they'd come away with no more information than before, and it was back to square one.

"There has to be some sort of connection between the victims," Christian said when they were back in the Jeep. "Something the killer looks for in each one of them."

"We've pulled the complete backgrounds on all the victims, but we're so short-staffed at the station right now with all the other whacked out activity going on that we haven't had a chance to dig through them yet."

"Other whacked out activity?"

Alec groaned. "You know that old story about how things get crazy during a full moon? Well, that's what it's like. Except, according to the calendar, it's not a full moon."

"What kind of stuff?"

"An increase in crime in general—burglaries, muggings and such. The narcotics division has had its hands full with a completely bizarre number of drug busts—as if the druggies and dealers have decided they don't even care about hiding what they're up to. There's also been an increase in emergency room activity over the past couple of weeks. That's just stuff I know of for sure, but one of the guys in the department is married to a social worker who runs a homeless shelter in town, and she says the number of people seeking shelter has doubled this month. We've had a cold spell, but she claims this is above average for even the coldest nights of the year. Plus, there've been more fights at the shelter than usual. Probably due to overcrowding, but with all the rest of the weirdness, who knows."

He thought he heard Christian mumble, "This isn't good."

"No, it's not good. We have an old-timer in the department who says he remembers something like this happening once before, when he first went to work on the force. A month where crime was up and people acted crazier than usual. That time it happened during the summer and since they'd had record high temperatures, they chalked it up to people being cranky because of the heat. Not exactly hot this time, though."

He chuckled as he remembered something else. "One of the gals in dispatch is convinced it's an astrological thing, Mercury in retrograde or something. But then one of her cronies argues that if it was Mercury in retrograde there'd be electronic communication and transportation problems, too."

"Mercury's not in retrograde right now."

Alec turned to him and gave him a raised eyebrow look.

"Long story. Don't ask."

"Oh, no. I can't help it. I have to ask. Give me the short version if you have to, but you can't make a comment like that and leave it hanging."

A smile teased the corners of Christian's mouth. "Let's just say my mum's kind of interested in astrology and some of it rubbed off."

"Uh-huh. Okay. Well, good. 'Cause for a moment there I thought you were going to tell me that not only do British cops not carry guns, they also study the planets and stars in cop school." He shot Christian a teasing grin.

"Not real big on the woo-woo stuff, are you?" There was humor in the question.

"I believe in what I can see and touch and hear. I can't do my job based on the intangible. The only way to catch bad guys and keep 'em caught is to stick to the facts." He sobered. "Which is why this damned case is driving me mad."

"Not enough tangibles and facts?"

"Not even remotely. I mean, how the hell does one explain a floating ball of light? We've got our science guys working on it, and right now they're convinced our witness is a crackpot."

"But you don't think so?"

He felt Christian's gaze on him. Alec remembered the look on the victim's husband's face as he'd told the story. "No," he said slowly. "The man last night saw something. Something that scared the hell out of him, and he wasn't faking it. If you'd seen his eyes…"

"Would it help to talk to him again, do you think?"

They'd stopped at a traffic light and Alec turned to look at his new, temporary partner. It was strange… He hadn't worked closely with anyone like this since Drew, hadn't wanted to. But having been forced into letting Christian tag along, he had to admit, he'd missed having the companionship, having someone to toss ideas around with. He waited for the tell-tale guilt to hit him at the thought, but it didn't. And he had to wonder what that meant.

"We could try. Let me see if I can get us in." He pulled his cell phone out of its case on his belt and punched in a number.

"Get us in?"

"Remember when I said the science guys thought the witness was a crackpot? Well, they're not the only ones. Our witness, the victim's husband, was admitted to the hospital's psych ward last night for observation for a few days. His story was a little too over the top for the medics, I guess, and that, combined with the fact he was panicky and paranoid, made them decide he needed help."

When he'd made arrangements with the doctor in charge for a brief visit, Alec shut his phone and slid it back into its case.

"The poor man. His wife is killed and they stick him in the mental ward," Christian said, shaking his head.

As traffic began moving again, Alec had to concentrate once more on the road, but Christian's sympathetic response gave him another clue about the kind of man he was.

Someone it would be very easy to fall for.

This time, as if on cue, a knot of guilt formed in his gut.

He sighed. Would it ever get better? Would he ever be able to move on? But then he realized, with a jolt of surprise, that this was the first time he'd ever had such a thought. For the past eighteen months he'd let his sorrow ground him, remind him of what he'd lost. It hurt like hell and God knows he didn't want to hurt. But he'd never consciously thought about moving on before. Hadn't wanted to.

He shot a quick glance at Christian, who was staring out the side window, watching the light snow fall and appearing lost in thought. What was it about this man that had him suddenly wondering what it might be like to get on with his life?

* * *

The psychiatric ward at the hospital was brighter and cheerier than Christian had been expecting. Foolish as he knew it was, he'd had visions of the asylum from *Dracula*. Even so, as a nurse unlocked the ward door and led them through the corridors, he was still struck at the sadness of a man witnessing his wife's murder, then being taken away because the police and medical establishment thought he'd lost his mind. It reminded him all too much of similar things that had happened over the centuries to magic folk when they spoke openly about who they were. Throughout history they'd been harassed, tortured, even murdered because they were different. And though some might say the modern world had been kinder to them, atrocities still happened.

"Here we are," the blond, athletic-looking nurse said, opening the door to a room. "The doctor says you can have ten minutes with him, but you're not to unfasten him. We had to sedate him and restrain him last night to keep him calm. We'd like him to stay that way," she said briskly, ushering them in.

She crossed to the bed and patted the gray-haired, older gentleman on the shoulder. When his eyes blinked open and his bleary gaze settled on her and the two men, she said, "Frank, these two police officers have come to talk with you."

She turned back to Christian and Alec. "If you have any problems with him, buzz me and I'll be here in a jiffy."

Alec looked at Christian, gave a subtle head shake, and sighed, as if to say, "There's no way we're going to get any coherent answers with him drugged like this."

Christian nodded, again feeling a twinge of sadness at the man's situation.

"Mr. Sandell," Alec said, pulling up the one uncomfortable-looking chair provided and sinking into it.

The older man slowly turned his head to follow Alec's movement.

Alec took his thin, age-spotted hand, careful Christian noticed, not to disturb the IV line going into it. "I know it's been a tough couple of days for you so we won't bother you for long. I'm very sorry for your loss."

The elderly man wasn't completely out of it and understood what Alec was saying to him because tears pooled in his rheumy eyes. Christian had the urge to go to him and offer comfort, but he suspected Frank Sandell was already overwhelmed, and he didn't want to add to it since he was a stranger and Alec had talked to him once before. So he maintained his spot against the wall just behind and to the left of Alec, and let Alec handle the interview.

Which he did with an amazing gentleness that impressed Christian. He traveled a lot for his job, met a lot of people…most of them mages, but certainly some Ordinaries, too. Yet no one he'd met until now had so quickly filled him with as much respect and such a deep awareness as Alec did. Non-magic though he might be, Alec was anything but ordinary.

The old gentleman recounted what had happened in a weak, halting voice tinged with, Christian was surprised to note, a faint British accent. The old man had to pause periodically to gather his emotions. He and his wife had been married fifty-one years, or would have been next month.

Everything went smoothly until he got to the part of the tale where he noticed the ball of light floating only a few feet from them as he and his wife lay in bed reading, then his wife had screamed in terror and died in his arms.

"It wanted to tear her up!" he shouted, his voice surprisingly loud.

"It's okay, Mr. Sandell," Alec soothed. "What wanted to tear her up?"

"The creature!"

"Creature? I thought it was a light?"

A niggling sense of familiarity crept through Christian and he tensed, waiting to hear what else the man might say.

But instead of responding, the elderly man let out a guttural growl and began thrashing on the bed, trying to free himself and shouting obscenities.

"You're just like them! They won't listen, they don't believe me! Sons of bitches all of them! I know what killed my Mary. I know. I know!"

Alec had stood and was gently but firmly pressing the old man back down onto the bed. "Mr. Sandell, it's okay, I believe you. Shhh, I believe you."

The man, with a surprising strength, jerked one of his arms free of the Velcro restraint on the bed.

Christian saw it and, catching himself just in time before he used magic to resolve the situation, quickly moved around the bed to grasp the flailing arm in mid-air just as the man was about to hit Alec. He restrapped the thin wrist to the bed rail, hating that it had to be done.

"I know what killed her! I know!" the old man shrieked.

"Maybe we should call the nurse," Christian suggested.

But Alec, his eyes never leaving the old man, shook his head. "No, it's okay."

As Christian watched, Alec closed his eyes, seemingly oblivious to the man's thrashing and growling, then, almost as if in a trance, Alec settled both hands on the old man's chest.

The twisting and thrashing almost immediately decreased and the invectives trailed off.

"Shhh, breathe," Alec crooned in a soft voice, still with his eyes closed. "That's it. Just breathe slowly."

Ripples of astonishment coursed through Christian as he watched. Alec's coaxing, soothing voice radiated calm, but to Christian, it was also electrifying. His magic sixth sense kicked in again, and the hair on his arms stood up beneath his sweater and jacket. Every inch of his skin tingled and he was shocked to realize warm, dizzying arousal grew deep within him.

He'd never felt anything like it, had never reacted so strongly to anything. It was like the energy Alec was projecting swirled around him, through him. Yet he saw no shimmer of magic on Alec. And if what Alec was doing was magic he should see that. He studied the other man closely…but, no. Nothing. So what in bloody hell was it?

When the old man had relaxed completely, Alec opened his eyes, smiled at the gentleman, then squeezed his hand again.

"Thank you," Frank whispered.

"You're welcome."

"I need to sleep now."

"Okay, you rest."

But Frank clutched his hand. "The creature…you won't see it until it attacks. Be careful. It'll be there when you least expect it." Then his eyes fluttered closed and his breathing fell into the deep rhythm of sleep.

Alec frowned and looked up at Christian, clearly puzzled. "The creature?" he said softly.

It took all Christian's self control not to respond. Because the last few words the old man had spoken had cemented the killer's identity for him. Alec hadn't been wrong earlier when he'd wondered if it was a some*thing* and not a some*one* doing the killing. Oh, it was Rogan pulling the strings, no doubt. But he'd called in some help, of the most malicious kind.

He had to get in touch with Bella and let her know what was going on here.

But before he did that, he had some questions.

When he and Alec had exited the hospital, Christian stopped in the courtyard. Alec, who'd only been a step ahead of him, stopped as well and turned back to look at him.

"What happened in there?" Christian asked, ignoring the cold air and the flutter of snowflakes on his cheeks.

Alec didn't ask to what he was referring. Instead, he tensed, then his shoulders slumped in resignation. He met Christian's gaze steadily. "Yeah, I know I'm a hypocrite. All my talk of only liking tangibles and facts, and then that. The truth is, I can't explain it." He shrugged. "It's something my grandmother used to do when I was young, when I was hurt or upset. I don't know why it works. It just does. But if you tell another soul at the police station about it, I'll deny it with every breath in my body because I'm not about to listen to any shit over it. And the same goes for you—no shit."

He shoved his hands in his jacket pockets, turned his back on Christian, and stalked away.

Christian stared after him, still feeling the lingering effects of the energy that had flooded him in the hospital room, and still not understanding why he'd felt it or what Alec had done. It had been healing magic of the most powerful kind. Except it hadn't been. Alec hadn't had a magic aura at any point, and if it was really magic, he should have. Christian would have seen it.

But he'd definitely *felt* something.

He jogged after the other man and caught up to him just as he reached the Jeep.

"Alec."

Alec stopped near the front of the vehicle. Without turning around he said, "I mean it, Christian. Not a word." His voice was tight, as if his exhaustion had finally caught up to him.

Without thinking, Christian laid a hand on his shoulder. Too late, he realized it was probably too familiar a gesture, but Alec didn't stiffen or pull away, so Christian didn't either. In spite of the cold and the layers of clothing, he felt heat radiating off Alec's back, and the slow burn of desire began inside him again. He tried to ignore it, but couldn't. That wasn't what this was about, though.

"I'm not going to give you any shit, and you have my word no one you work with will ever hear about it from me. I just wanted to say that if the nurse had come in, they probably would have shot him up with more drugs and taken away even more of his control. What you did in there…it was a damned compassionate, decent thing."

There was a pause. Then Alec slowly turned around to face him. Christian dropped his hand and took a step back, not wanting to crowd him or make him feel like he was coming on to him. They were eye to eye and Christian realized they were the same height.

"Thank you." The words were spoken quietly.

Christian nodded.

An electric heat seemed to pulse between them, and for a split second he was certain he saw a raw and poignant hunger glistening in Alec's golden-brown eyes. Something deep inside Christian vibrated in response.

But then Alec shuttered it as effectively as if a window that had been briefly opened was suddenly pulled closed. A slight frown marred the skin of his forehead. Regret?

Christian dragged in a deep breath, forcing his own thoughts back on track. But the hum in his body wasn't so easily silenced. As Alec moved away and around to climb in the driver's door, and Christian did the same on the passenger side, a brief look passed between them. And in that instant, he knew that in the short time they'd known each other, a spark had definitely been lit.

CHAPTER 3

The afternoon and a good chunk of evening passed by in a blur of paperwork and phone calls for Alec. He and Christian hadn't spoken again until they were back at the station and then their only conversations had been case related. True to his word, Christian hadn't mentioned the scene in the hospital room again. And it seemed as if they'd both chosen to ignore the heated moment and glance they'd exchanged in the parking lot.

Well, maybe ignore wasn't the right word. At least for Alec. The instant replay of it had been running through his mind for hours. He knew he hadn't mistaken the look in Christian's eyes. Whatever it was he'd been feeling since he'd first met Christian this morning…Christian was feeling it, too.

The problem was, Alec wasn't sure what to do about it. And that's what had been torturing him ever since. It had been a relief to glance at his watch, discover it was after eight o'clock, and call it a night. He and Christian had parted ways outside the station. He'd offered to give the British cop a ride to his hotel, but Christian had refused, saying he liked to walk and it wasn't far. So he'd been spared having to ride in close quarters with the man again. As on edge as he was, he was afraid he'd either shut him out or come onto him, and he wasn't sure which would have been worse.

As Alec's Jeep crawled through traffic toward his house, he couldn't stop thinking about it. The truth was, he liked the man. A lot. And not just in a sexual attraction kind of way. So he didn't want to shut him out. But he also didn't know if he wanted to come on to him and start something he wasn't sure he could follow through with. He didn't know if he was ready for that.

He could just have a fling, he rationalized. Keep emotions out of it and get laid with an intelligent, good-looking man. There were certainly worse things in life. And with Christian only being here for a few weeks, and the vast distance between England and the U.S., it could have a definite and clean end to it.

Except one-night-stands and flings had never really worked for him. The few he'd had when he was younger, before he and Drew got serious, had never really left him feeling satisfied. It just wasn't his thing. He liked sex as much as the next guy, but he wanted the relationship with it.

It had been a long time since he'd felt the way he'd felt today with Christian. The companionship, having someone to work with, but also the flutter in his chest and the stirring in his groin. He hadn't realized how lonely he'd been, how empty, until Christian had laid a hand on his shoulder in the parking lot and he'd felt warmth seep into him. And then, when they'd been face to face, the expression on Christian's face had reached through the ice that had built up on his heart and given him a sneak peek at what he'd been missing. He'd suddenly craved it with all his being. But then the ache of missing Drew and the guilt at allowing himself to feel something with someone else had swallowed him and ended the moment.

But he hadn't forgotten it.

He parked in front of his dark house, locked the Jeep, and made his way up the sidewalk to the porch steps, his booted feet crunching in the snow. The snow had stopped falling, but several inches covered the ground. Just enough he was going to have to shovel in the morning to keep the mailman happy.

He and Drew had bought the small, older rancher the first year they'd lived together. It had needed work, but Drew had been the fixer-up type, had loved every second of sanding and staining the kitchen cabinets, retiling the bathroom, and pulling up the ratty carpet to reveal hardwood floors beneath. He'd had the patience of Job, never rushing, and perfectly okay with the fact that it had taken him the better part of three years to finish most of the projects. He'd worked on it during his days off from the department. The last thing on his list had been to build a deck in the back. He'd died before he'd had a chance to start it.

Alec unlocked the front door, entered, tossed his keys and the thick file folders he'd brought home with him onto the coffee table in the living room, and tugged off his jacket and gun. Without bothering to turn on any lights, he crossed into the kitchen and pulled open the fridge. With this case, he'd been working such long hours he hadn't taken the time to get groceries. The proverbial cupboard was getting pretty bare. He grabbed a carton of milk, checked the date, opened it and sniffed it just in case, then finished it off in a few swallows. Nothing else in the sparsely-filled refrigerator looked appealing—or edible.

He slapped together a quick pb and j sandwich and ate it on his way back to the living room, where he flipped on the TV and the light next to the couch. With a news program droning in the background, he opened the first folder, determined to make his way through some of the victims' background information before he went to bed.

He awoke a little after midnight with a crick in his neck, the TV still on, and the folder and papers scattered across his lap, the couch, the floor.

"Damn it." He had a vague memory of reading a couple of pages on the first victim and then that was it. He'd probably fallen asleep only a few minutes after he sat down.

Grumbling, he powered off the TV, turned off the light, and made his way to bed, stripping out of his clothes as he went.

But once there, he was annoyed to discover he couldn't close his eyes. Details of the murders, the old man's frenzied shouting about how no one would believe him and then his odd comments about the "creature" chased through Alec's head. Over and over, around and around…and none of it making any more sense now than it had earlier in the day.

He batted at his pillow, kicked off the covers, then pulled them back on when he got too cold. He needed the sleep…his mind just wasn't cooperating.

But when his thoughts turned to Christian Wetherly, his mind was the least of his problems. He remembered again the way Christian's hand had felt on his shoulder, the way his blue eyes had darkened with desire, how heat and electricity had pulsed between Christian and him as they stood close together.

As it had earlier in the day, Alec's body reacted. His balls grew achy, his cock stirred, and no amount of tossing and turning helped alleviate it.

Finally, when he couldn't stand it any more, he got up. "Cold as arctic hell outside and I have to take a frigging cold shower!"

But he opted for a hot one instead, hoping the heat would be soporific, help him relax so he could get to sleep.

As he soaped himself, he cupped his balls with one hand and slid his other along his erection. Memories of how many times he and Drew had showered together right here, touching and teasing, hot, slippery hands working over and into hot, slippery body parts coursed through him.

He closed his eyes and tried to pull Drew up in his memory, imagining his large, muscular body shimmering with water droplets, his bulging pecs and biceps, his short blond hair clinging to his head, his laughing hazel eyes making promises Alec knew he'd keep.

Drew had been built like a linebacker, several inches taller than Alec's six-feet, and thirty pounds heavier. He'd been a mischievous, playful lover at times, and other times had liked it hard and fast, even a bit rough. Alec had never really gotten into the rough stuff much, but he'd always played along because it had been a big turn-on for Drew. On more than one occasion he'd let Drew tied him up or handcuff him and do things to him that he hadn't ever let anyone else do. Things that made him squirm uncomfortably if he thought about them too much.

But the times he'd liked best were when their joinings were slow and truly intimate. And probably because those encounters hadn't happened as frequently as the playful or frenzied ones, after Drew died, Alec had found he'd missed them the most.

It was one of those he focused on now, trying to remember how it had felt to have Drew's big hands roaming his body, sliding over his shoulders, then moving down his chest and abs until his palms brushed against Alec's shaft and his fingers teased whorls in the wet, dark curls surrounding it.

With his hands, Alec traced the same path. He imagined he could hear Drew murmuring to him, telling him how much he loved watching Alec's cock grow harder and harder and rise up to meet his touch.

Alec closed his eyes and let himself drift in the fantasy. He could almost....*almost* picture Drew kneeling in front of him. A twinge of sadness crept through him that the memories were beginning to fade around the edges, that he couldn't quite see Drew in Technicolor anymore. It was more like watching him through a soft-focus lens now, in watercolor tones. But the hands on his cock felt good and it was easy to loose himself once again in the fantasy they were Drew's.

One hand fondled his balls, while the other curved around his erection, tugging on the skin behind the head in a slow motion. The heat of the shower, the hot water pounding on his back, and the slick, foamy soap only added to the pleasure.

He imagined Drew's tongue laving his swollen cockhead, felt the tip grinding against the slit, then following the contours of the sensitive ridge on the underside. He thought he was prepared for what came next, but when his length was surrounded in the moist heat of a sucking mouth, he groaned.

"Damn, that's good," he murmured, amazed at how real the sensation was.

He could almost feel a warm hand snake around to cup his ass and draw him closer, while the other stroked the base of his cock in counterpoint to the incredible suction on the head. Then, just as he thought he couldn't take it anymore, the devouring mouth began to move up and down on him, drawing him deep until he felt his ultra-sensitive tip brush against the back of a throat, slowing sliding him out until only his cockhead remained in the heat, then swallowing him again. Over and over, hot mouth working his hot, slick shaft.

The sensation was ecstasy. And hell. He didn't remember Drew ever being this gentle, yet at the same time didn't remember it ever feeling quite this sensuous either. Maybe it was because it had been so long since he'd been with someone, or maybe because his old memories truly were fading so he was making up new variations that had never actually happened, but he'd never felt so overwhelmed with sensation before.

A burning tingle built in Alec's balls and his cock pulsed with excitement. He wanted it to go on and on, but his body craved release. He tried to thrust faster, but the hand—no, now it was two hands on his ass—restrained him, held him in place, forcing him to accept the slow, thrilling torture. He slid his fingers into the thick, damp hair of the man who seemed to know intuitively how much pleasure he could stand and just how to keep him hovering at the edge in a delicious way.

The motion increased; so did the wet suction, until Alec's entire body vibrated and low moans escaped him. "Oh, God…"

One of the hands released his ass and moved back to the front, to stroke his balls, then tickle beneath them. Alec bucked in response. His body was on fire, and his entire existence zeroed in on the amazing mouth working his penis in a way it had never been worked, and the teasing fingers at play at the very root of him.

And then he was over the edge, his body convulsing, cum jetting from him in hot waves until he was spent and weak-kneed from satisfied exhaustion.

Eyes still squeezed tightly closed, he slumped against the wall in the shower and tried again to picture his fantasy lover's face. But when he did, he went rigid with shock. It wasn't Drew's hazel gaze staring up at him….instead, the eyes were a brilliant sapphire blue, and they were filled with a sizzling intensity that washed over Alec in rippling waves.

"Christian," he whispered.

"We belong together, Alec."

The softly spoken words reached into a part of Alec that had been barren for months, and filled him with a longing so deep he could barely breathe.

Alec's eyes fluttered open, and the moment they did and he came back to the reality of standing in the shower, the shower Drew had painstakingly tiled, where they'd played and loved for three years, a knot formed in his stomach.

How could Christian Wetherly have invaded his fantasies like that? Brazenly pushed Drew aside, and taken over?

No, damn it. He didn't want this. He wasn't ready to let go of Drew yet, wasn't ready to move on. *It's still too soon.*

But when he closed his eyes and tried to recapture Drew's image, he could no longer see it. Only the thick waves of dark hair, the warm planes and angles of a new and expressive face, and the startling blue eyes that seemed to see into his soul.

Drained and confused by what had just happened, Alec rinsed off, shut off the water, and stepped out of the shower. He toweled off, pulled on clean boxers, and sought out the refuge of bed again. He flipped on the bedside light and picked up the framed picture of himself and Drew that sat on the nightstand. Running his thumb across Drew's face, he tried to memorize it all over again, hating that he hadn't been able to call up his features only a few minutes before.

Maybe it was his exhaustion and the stress of the murder case that were wearing him down, making him emotional and needy. Probably. But whatever the cause, he couldn't afford to be less than his best right now. Couldn't afford distractions. And from the moment he'd turned to find Christian Wetherly standing behind him at the station this morning, the man had been a distraction.

It was time to put a stop to it. Time to keep his mind on his job, and hold the British cop at a professional distance as he should have from the start.

He turned off the light and slid under the covers. Right now he didn't have time for the emotional roller coaster ride of another relationship. Didn't want it. In a few weeks, Christian would return to England and Alec could get back to his regular life. In the meantime, he'd keep Christian busy on the case and make sure no other knowing, heated glances passed between them and, more importantly, no more sexual fantasies surfaced.

But as he finally drifted off to sleep, the last thing he remembered were the words Christian had spoken.

"We belong together, Alec…"

*   *   *

Christian jolted awake from what he'd thought was a dead sleep. He was damp with sweat, but when he pulled the covers off, discovered it was a bit more than that.

Still breathing hard, he moved to a sitting position. He hadn't had a wet dream since…well, bugger, in a long damn time.

And it hadn't been just any wet dream either, he realized, as memories of the dream surfaced and tingles of recognition spread over his skin, giving him goose bumps.

Alec.

He'd just had the most vivid dream he'd been giving Alec a blow job. He could remember the sleek feel of the other man's wet skin under his hands—they'd been in the shower together—smell his soapy-clean scent mixed with the heady musk of his arousal. And a hell of an arousal it had been, too. Alec's cock had been thick and veiny and pulsing under his hand, then growing even larger in his mouth…

"Bloody hell." Christian scrubbed a hand over his face. He rose and padded to the bathroom.

He could even remember the salty-sweet flavor of Alec's cum, and the way the other man had shuddered against him and groaned when he lost it. He'd been hard as a rock himself, and when Alec spilled his seed, Christian had done the same.

"We belong together, Alec."

It had been his voice saying that. But where had he come up with such a thing? He barely knew the man.

"It was just a dream," he chided, staring at himself in the bathroom mirror.

So then why did the words resonate in his gut?

He shook his head. "Just a dream. Don't make it into more than it is."

He cleaned himself up and went back to bed. But no matter how he tried, he couldn't get back to sleep. Not with x-rated fantasies about Alec Anderson continuing to run through his head.

"Oh, for fuck's sake," he muttered, sitting up again. He glanced at the clock and saw it was nearly two in the morning. Here. But in England everyone would be up and about. It was a good time to make a call to Bella. He'd wanted to touch base with her right away when he got in last night, but even though it was late evening here when he'd returned to his room, it was the middle of the night at home. And he knew Bella well enough to know that if it wasn't an emergency, she wouldn't appreciate be awakened. The woman was like a shrew when her sleep was interrupted.

Of course, only having about four hours himself after being up for nearly twenty-four, and combined with the energy drain such a long distance teleportation had required, he was probably going to be a bear himself later today.

Forcing the dream with Alec to the back of his mind, he pulled on a pair of sweats and found his cell phone.

It only rang twice before it was picked up.

"Christian? Are you all right?"

"Of course I am. Why wouldn't I be? And good morning to you, too."

"Yeah, yeah, good morning." He imagined Bella smiling. "Except isn't it like 2:00 A.M. there?"

"Yeah, but I was awake anyway and wanted to talk to you."

"Have you found anything helpful about the murders?"

"Nothing linking the victims thus far. But what I do know is that Rogan's managed to either buy the services of a guiller or he's figured out a way to control one and make it work for him."

He heard Bella's soft hiss of breath. "A guiller! Are you quite sure?"

"As sure as I can be without having seen one with my own eyes. But there are witness accounts that have me convinced. Odd flashing lights, popping noises, a floating ball of light, people seeming to die from terror. And one older man talked about 'the creature.' All the victims show no obvious signs of physical trauma. They're just dropping dead. It's got the local police in a quandary."

"That does sound like guiller activity. The question is, why? I mean, why a guiller? There are so many other beasts and demons out there for hire that would be easier to deal with. The guillers are some of the most primitive, vicious creatures in the magic world. And if Rogan's looking for the amulet, why's he using a guiller to kill people?"

"We don't totally understand what capabilities the guillers have because they're usually so secretive—they show up, kill, then they disappear again. But from what I know, research suggests they have the potential to read minds. If that's true, it's possible he's using the creature to get information from the victims."

"Looking for the amulet, seeing if any of them know its whereabouts. Yes, that's it I bet."

"And it's no doubt convenient the guillers are so gruesome they quite literally scare their victims to death, because then Rogan doesn't have to worry about anyone being left to talk about what he's looking for."

"No…" Bella said, as if she were lost in a thought. "I'm not sure that's…"

He could hear the shuffling of papers, then hear Bella moving around. He suspected she was probably looking for some book on the subject that she kept in the extensive library attached to her office.

"I remember reading something on guillers in an old Council article," she said. "Okay, yes, here we go. This suggests that if guillers can delve into people's minds, if one were to do so, it would probably mess up the person's mind so much the victim might never be functional again."

"What are you saying?"

"I'm saying that there'd be nothing left in the victim's minds but mush. The emotional trauma of having their brains scrambled, so to speak, would be more than most humans could cope with. They'd die. Not from the terror of seeing the guiller itself—though I suspect encountering one up close would be pretty awful—but because the human mind is a delicate thing and having it ravaged would be too horrifying for it to recover from. The dying would be almost a defensive reaction. A way to shut down the terror of being lost in one's own mind. That's how a guiller kills its victims. And it doesn't say so here, but I wonder… I bet guillers don't just kill for sport as we've always suspected. I bet they somehow feed off human minds."

"Holy mother of God."

"Christian, this is bad."

"Yeah, I'm getting that. There's more. Alec, the American police detective I'm working with, told me over the past couple of weeks things have been strange around here. An increase in crime, people on edge, fighting."

"And you think that might be related?"

"I think it's a little too convenient it's happening right now, while Rogan's active here and he's sending guillers after people. I don't believe in coincidence. I'm wondering if he's worked some kind of spell on this area. Something that might play with people's minds a bit, that might alter brain wave patterns, or mess with people's emotions."

"It's possible. Let me do some research and see if I can find anything that might cause what you're describing."

Christian had a sudden thought. "Also, if you do find something, see if it might also somehow manage to dampen someone's magic ability."

"Dampen it? Are you having trouble with your powers?" There was a note of concern in her voice.

"No, not that I've noticed." Instead of walking the several blocks from the police station to his hotel tonight, he'd been lazy and had teleported, figuring it'd take less energy to do it over a short distance than the walking itself would expend. And he'd used his magic for several small things before he went to bed. "It's...something else. Not involving me."

"O—kay."

"Just check for me, will you?" It had just occurred to him that whatever was causing the havoc around town might be blocking his ability to read Alec properly. That could explain why Christian kept feeling tingly around him, but couldn't see a magic aura. It would also explain Alec's ability to do what he'd done at the hospital. It was worth looking into anyway.

"All right. I'll check. And by the way, I'm pulling together as much information on the Ansley family as I can. They're quite the fascinating lot, let me tell you. With the amulet lost these past thirty years, and the last of the Ansley family dead, I suspect no one's had much reason to research them since then. But I discovered the Council has heaps of records about them in one of their top secret databases."

"And they let you access it?"

"Some of it. And the rest...let's just say I always was good at puzzling out particularly knotty protective charms and spells, and what they don't know won't hurt them."

Christian chuckled.

"Touch base with me tomorrow morning your time," Bella said. "But if I come up with any information on your spell theory there in the States before then, I'll call you."

"Will do. Thanks, Bell."

"Christian…a guiller? You watch your back more than ever, you hear me? If Rogan knows you're there, he could send it after you."

"I'll stay alert. I promise."

"You'd better."

"Hey, before we go…have Jamie and the others found anything yet?"

"No, he, Evan, and Cayleigh are still working on the Egypt angle. I'll let you know when they succeed."

Christian smiled. Not *if* they succeeded, but *when*. That's one of the reasons he loved working with the group of mages he did. They always found a way to get their jobs done.

"Okay, keep me posted. I'll talk to you tomorrow morning."

He pressed off their connection and tucked his phone back into his jacket pocket, then glanced at his watch. Still only 2.30 A.M. here. He sodding hated the time changes on trips like this. It wreaked havoc on his body the first few days. He was dead tired, but his internal clock was convinced it was morning and time to be up and about.

He wondered what Alec was doing right now. Sleeping probably. He needed to be anyway.

Another vision of the shower dream filled his head before he could stop it. And that led him off into wondering what it would be like to spend intimate time with the man. Wondered what it would be like to openly share a life with him—with someone *like* him, he amended. He'd only just met Alec. No way had he known him long enough to be thinking about having a relationship with him.

Besides—the same old battle reared to life again inside him—not only did he live in England and Alec here, he honestly wasn't sure that even if they did attempt to have something, he'd be able to do it openly. He tried to picture the looks on Jamie's and Bella's faces if he showed up one day with a male lover. He liked to hope they'd deal. But he was afraid Jamie in particular would get weirded out and their friendship would go down the loo. Bella…Bella, under other circumstances, would probably accept it. But because of the Kate factor, he wasn't sure she could.

The thought of losing his friendships with the two most important people in his life made him almost sick to his stomach. But so did the pretending.

He sighed. Lying back down, he draped his arm over his eyes, and willed himself to take several deep breaths and calm down. Every time he let his mind wander in this direction he ended up on edge. And he didn't need this right now. Rogan. Guillers. And God knew what else. That should be enough to keep him on the straight and narrow. That needed to be his focus right now.

If only he could banish Alec from his mind so easily. But the man was there, clinging at the edges, finding little ways to creep in no matter how Christian tried to distract himself.

An odd gnawing in his insides kept him awake until well after the sun rose.

CHAPTER 4

By Friday Alec had decided he was in hell. There'd been another murder, another over-fifty victim, but this one with no witnesses and no other clues that could help pinpoint the killer. The weather had been completely wretched, with daytime temperatures barely reaching the teens, nighttime lows in the single digits, and an oppressive, cold, gray dampness that hung over everything—including his spirits. He'd been on the go non-stop, getting home late, catching a few hours of unsettled sleep, and back on the job by the time it grew light out. And underlying it all, always, was a constant awareness of Christian.

Oh, he'd done a brilliant job of holding the man at arm's length, had kept him busy, and tried to avoid spending too much time alone with him—which had been next to impossible, considering the Englishman shared his office space and went with him whenever he had business to attend to away from the station. Still, he'd made a point of keeping all conversations case related, had allowed no room for personal talk, and above all, had made extra sure they never touched. Because if they had, he was afraid all his best intentions would go straight to…well…hell. Especially in light of the fantasies that continued to creep into his mind when he least expected. Not to mention the dreams.

Damn, but the one last night had seemed even more real than usual. And there'd been no mistaking who his partner was this time. If the deft, gentle hands on his body, so different from Drew's large, calloused, insistent ones weren't enough of a clue, the softly whispered endearments and eroticisms in the British accent left no room for doubt.

"Turn over, love."

Alec rolled onto his stomach. A blaze flickered in the fireplace of a bedroom he didn't recognize. The soft mattress and bedding cradled his nude body, and he was drowsy and comfortable. But the sensation of warm hands caressing his back and kneading his muscles caused slow ripples of growing desire in him.

"Feel good?"

"Oh, yeah." With his eyes closed and his head resting on his arms, he luxuriated in a nirvana between utter relaxation and tingling arousal. Each gentle push, each well-placed stroke of palm and fingers against his bare flesh, made him feel more alive—and more turned-on—than he'd been in months.

The hands moved lower, working on his gluts, but with the occasional brush of wandering fingertips teasing along the crease in his ass, sending shocks of electricity straight to his balls and his thickening shaft.

More. Yes, there. Deeper. *Jesus, touch me...oh, yeah, right there, he thought, willing his partner to read his mind.*

Out of pure, primal instinct, he rose to his knees, asking without words for what he wanted. And getting the response he'd hoped for.

Masculine heat moved closer to him, between his legs. Slippery with lube and hot as sin, a sleek, velvet cock impaled him, sliding into his willing body without hesitation. Alec shuddered and his muscles contracted in excitement at the invasion. He heard a soft groan of pleasure behind him, and it was echoed by his own. When his passage had fully sheathed the plundering cock, the incredible, sensual hands gripped his hips and pulled him tight against his partner's groin, holding them together, balls to flesh.

They didn't move for the longest time, and the sensation was a unique one for Alec who'd shared mostly powerful, fast, and intense lovemaking with Drew. He felt filled to bursting, and could even discern the thrum of his partner's pulse inside him. Was able to sense his own, pounding in response. The closeness was like nothing he'd ever experienced. There was an intimacy to it that went far beyond fucking as Alec has always known it.

"We belong together, Alec." The words, spoken in a hushed, reverent tone, were as intimate as the joining.

"Yes. God, yes, we do."

"Morning. You're here early."

The words startled Alec out of his thoughts and it wasn't until he blinked and found himself still standing in the break room at the station, mug clenched in hand, that he even remembered where he was. *Shit.*

With his pulse still racing from the memory of the dream, he turned to face the man who'd so thoroughly saturated his thoughts and fantasies for the past several days.

"Hey. Yeah, I thought maybe I'd catch up on some reading this morning." Alec said a quick grateful thanks to the powers that watched over him that his untucked shirt covered the obvious evidence of where his thoughts had been moments before.

Christian looked as tired as Alec felt, like he hadn't been sleeping well either. But even with the weary strain around his eyes and mouth, the sight of his dark windblown hair, and the navy blue V-neck sweater he wore over a gray T-shirt that brought out the color of his blue eyes, and most of all, the sight of his easy smile stirred a warm tingle in Alec's chest he couldn't ignore.

As Christian moved to stand next to him, picked up a clean mug, and filled it with hot water from the pot, Alec finally had to face facts.

Oh, crap. He was falling. *Falling...falling.* All the holding at arm's length in the world hadn't made a damn bit of difference. He was falling for Christian Wetherly in a big, messy, sexual, and what he was afraid was also an emotional way.

The Englishman pulled a teabag from the box on the shelf above the counter and dropped it into his mug. Then he leaned closer—close enough Alec got a whiff of the spicy, intoxicating musk aftershave he wore—and peered into Alec's mug. He grinned. And, God help him, Alec had the sudden urge to grab him and kiss him.

"I thought you Americans liked coffee?" Christian's tone was teasing, and with the close proximity between them, it took all Alec's control to stay calm and not do anything rash.

"Isn't that a stereotype?" Alec asked, surprised when a half-smile of his own emerged. "Kind of like you Brits and your..." He gave Christian's mug an exaggerated glance. "...tea?"

"I happen to like tea. And it's a time-honored British tradition. But you...?"

Alec shrugged, fully smiling now. "So sue me. I hate coffee. I like hot chocolate. You can give me crap if you want, but I am who I am."

"I respect that." Christian grabbed a plastic spoon from the overstuffed mug that held them, and deftly scooped up the tea bag, twisting the string from it around it and the spoon to squeeze out the last drops.

"Seems like a lot of work, the whole tea-making thing."

"For what's it worth, I don't usually drink it from a teabag at home. We keep loose leaf tea and one of those old fashioned items you've probably never owned—a teapot." Christian looked up from what he was doing and his eyes sparkled with humor.

Alec ignored the teapot comment because he'd fixated on a different significant word. "We?"

Was it possible Christian was involved with someone? And if so, why did a tiny flare of green-eyed monster flicker to life inside him? It shouldn't matter. Yet...it suddenly did.

"My housemates and I." But then, as if he'd suddenly just realized what Alec's thoughts were focused on, Christian's mischievous expression faded to be replaced by a glimmer of pleasurable surprise that Alec might care. "They're my best friends. Jamie and Bella. They're married...to each other."

"Ah." Alec had to avert his gaze from Christian's, afraid his relief would show. And damn it, why in hell was he relieved? It didn't matter who the man lived with.

And what was he doing here anyway? He'd sworn off personal topics of conversation earlier in the week. Business only, he reminded himself.

But his mouth had other ideas, already asking, "So where do you live?"

Christian poured sugar into his tea, then added milk from the refrigerator. "It's a big, old rambling house in the country. Really old. It used to belong to an earl, way back when. Bella and Jamie live on the third floor and I live on the second. On the first floor we share the kitchen and have office space."

"Sounds nice."

"It is." Christian leaned back against the counter and took a sip of his tea. His eyes met Alec's over the rim of the mug, still shimmering with a heat that sent little waves of awareness rippling through Alec's body. "You should come visit sometime."

A nervous laugh escaped Alec, and it pissed him off because it sounded nervous. "Yeah, me go to England. Wouldn't that be something? I'm not really a traveler." Definitely time to change the subject. "So, I'm going to go try to tackle some of the victim's background information this morning. Want to help?"

"Of course."

Alec tried to ignore the little flicker of disappointment he read in Christian's eyes at his abrupt change of subject. "After you."

Still, for all his good intentions of getting back to work and forgetting his lapse of good judgment in allowing himself to be drawn into the personal conversation, as he followed Christian back to the cubicle they currently shared, something about the sight of the tall, lean man radiated a powerful magnetism for Alec. He wanted to know more about him. Wanted to know what kind of food he liked, what kind of books he read, music he preferred, what his views on religion and the world were.

Shit. Falling so hard and fast I hope the hell I don't end up in a broken heap when I hit bottom. Because with Christian's life in England and his here, there would be a bottom. It was inevitable.

And then it occurred to him…he hadn't once thought about Drew during the entire conversation he and Christian had just shared. And not once felt guilty either.

A jolt of sadness hit him. He really was moving on, moving away from Drew and his memory.

"Alec! Christian!" Martin Shanahan called from behind them, before they reached the office. They turned simultaneously.

"What's up?"

The harried expression on the captain's face and his panting breaths, indicating he'd been in a hurry to find them, said it all.

"Damn. Another murder?" Alec asked, already knowing the answer.

Shanahan's gray head bobbed up and down. "Possibly. The call the just came in. It hasn't been confirmed yet, but one of the waiters at Café Richelieu came in early this morning and discovered their sous chef dead on the floor in the kitchen. Considering the circumstances of the other deaths, with no marks on the victims' bodies…"

"We'll check it out."

They stopped at the cubicle only long enough to grab their jackets, then were in Alec's Jeep, heading downtown within minutes.

*   *   *

It was mid-afternoon before the coroner was able to determine the sous chef had died of a heart attack, no doubt brought on by an existing heart condition and the three hundred pounds of weight the man carried around.

"Not a murder victim," Alec said, slumping into his desk chair and looking as disgusted as Christian felt. "We just spent the past eight hours chasing all over town for a heart attack victim. And meanwhile, the frigging murderer is still on the loose and we've accomplished absolutely nothing today toward finding him."

He picked up his foam basketball, but rather than tossing it into the hoop mounted on the wall, threw it with angry force, watching as it bounced off and rolled under the desk. He dragged a hand through his hair. "Fuck."

Alec wasn't the only one frustrated. The only thing Christian had been able to confirm this week was that all the victims were magic folk. It had taken interviews with family members, friends, and co-workers of the victims to piece it together to come to that conclusion—many of them hadn't a clue their recently deceased friends or loved ones were mages. He'd worked at the station with Alec until late each evening, then had spent another few hours talking to people on his own.

He'd heard from Bella, and for her part, she'd decided there was definitely some type of magic disturbance in the air, and it probably was causing the general "weirdness" as Alec called it. She suspected it had something to do with the guiller activity. The guillers had the ability to travel not only from place to place in this dimension, but apparently through space and time as well. And that caused enough ripples in the energy within a twenty-mile radius of their comings and goings to affect humans sensitive to such energy fluctuations. She had also concluded, however, that the energy fluctuations were not enough to dampen magic powers, so he was back to square one wondering about Alec's healing abilities. He still believed in his gut it was magic, but Alec showed none of the usual signs.

As far as Rogan, there had to be some connection between the victims besides just their magic abilities. He had Bella working on it from her end, but suspected the answer lay somewhere in the stacks of file folders currently teetering on Alec's desk—the victims' background information. He wished there was some way to use magic to ferret out any pertinent information, but magic had its limits. It was going to take old-fashioned time and energy to search for links.

"We need to go through those files," he said, thinking aloud.

Alec's gaze swept over them. "No shit. But it's like a circus around this place. Trying to do it here is almost a lost cause. And I've been so damned tired at night I haven't made much progress."

His eyebrows drew together as if he'd had a sudden thought. When he looked at Christian, Christian was struck by the sudden uncertainty that flickered in his eyes. But then it was masked as, Christian was beginning to learn, Alec pushed his personal feelings and reactions to the background. It seemed like the man worked overtime to suppress his emotions around Christian.

He wished Alec would quit shutting him out. It had been happening all week and he couldn't figure out what was going on. As long as everything was all business, it was fine—at least outwardly. Frankly, he'd been shocked he'd managed to draw the man into a regular conversation this morning.

Ever since they'd had the moment of connection in the car park at the hospital, Alec had withdrawn on every level except work. All Christian could figure was that he'd conveyed his attraction to Alec and it had Alec running scared. He'd been certain, from the look in Alec's eyes that afternoon, the feeling was reciprocated. But after three days of Alec doing everything possible to keep him at a distance, Christian was beginning to doubt what he'd seen. And bloody hell, maybe he'd been wrong. He was new at this picking up men thing. He didn't know the signs and signals, so maybe he'd read the situation completely wrong and Alec was straight as an arrow.

If that was the case, he wished the dreams about Alec would quit haunting him. Because in his dreams, Alec was, in every way, a very sensuous and willing partner.

He dragged in a deep breath and forced himself back to the here and now before he could be drawn into the memory of the particularly erotic and emotional dream he'd had last night.

Alec didn't seem to have noticed Christian's thoughts had wandered off. He was staring at the dingy carpet on the floor, scowling. But creases lined his forehead and he suddenly sighed, as if he were struggling over something.

"You have an idea?" Christian prodded.

Alec looked up at him and nodded slowly. "If we ever want to have a prayer of getting through this stuff, we can't do it here. I was thinking…" He hesitated and Christian wanted to shake him and tell him to just say it.

Finally, Alec said, "Do you want to come over to my place tonight? Maybe between the two of us we can slog through most of them and if I have company I might not fall asleep on the damned couch like I have the past three nights."

The vision of Alec exhausted, asleep on his couch, papers spread around him, brushed aside all his irritation at the man of moments ago.

"Yeah. Of course. I'd be happy to come over."

"Okay, then." Alec sighed again and, as Christian watched, it looked like whatever crap he'd been keeping bottled up, eased away a little, leaving him more open than he had been in days, but with a hint of vulnerability that touched Christian.

Alec glanced at his watch. "It's almost four o'clock. Let's get the hell out of here now, want to? Before something else comes up?"

Christian was already standing and sliding his arms into his leather jacket. He wasn't sure what had finally allowed Alec to open the door a crack, but he wasn't going to linger around here and miss it.

CHAPTER 5

"Hand me that one over there," Christian said without looking up from the file he was reading, pointing across the coffee table to a folder near Alec's left hand, half-hidden under the empty pizza box that was the remains from their dinner.

Alec pulled it free and passed it over to him. "Did you find something?"

"I'm not sure."

Christian took the file and opened it. He slid his finger down the first page, the second, then stopped midway down the third, but shook his head and continued on. Several pages later, he paused again. "Maybe." His dark eyebrows drew together and Alec watched as he pulled the page from the folder and compared it to a page in the other victim's file he'd been reading.

As he shuffled through several other sheets of paper, Alec noticed what elegant hands Christian had. Long-fingered, neatly trimmed nails, lightly-tanned skin. Drew's had been callused from all the home improvement work he did in his spare time, and he perpetually seemed to have scrapes or scratches across his knuckles or bruised fingernails from rough wood or wayward hammers. But Christian's were smooth and blemish-free, yet still looked strong, masculine, and capable.

A flash of the dream from last night came to him again, of just how capable those hands were. And how gentle. And how incredibly imaginative and sensual.

Shit. Snap out of it, man. It was just a dream, not real life!

48

Alec gave himself a mental shake. *Focus. Work. That's what we're here for.*

This was exactly what he'd been afraid was going to happen when he'd struggled over whether or not to invite Christian over here.

"What are you thinking?" he asked, to break the silence that was clearly giving him much too much time for his mind to wander.

"Which file are you looking at?" Christian asked.

Alec glanced at the page in front of him. "Edward Seymour. Fifty-nine years old."

"Have you come across anything in that one about him living anywhere else? Or traveling anywhere out of the US?"

"Not yet. Let me check through the rest of it."

Half an hour later he looked over at Christian, who had picked up a third folder, Mary Sandell, the wife of the man they'd talked with at the hospital, and was poring through it. "Nope, nothing mentioned about living outside the U.S.," he told Christian. "Why? What was I looking for specifically?"

Christian closed the third folder and set it aside. "Damn, nothing definitive there either, at least that I caught on my quick skim."

"Christian. What are we looking for?"

His gaze lifted to meet Alec's. "Sorry. Both of these two"—he lifted the original two folders and waved them in the air—"have been to England. One of them lived there for several years, the other traveled extensively there about thirty years ago. And remember Frank Sandell? He has a lingering British accent. His wife was definitely American, but he wasn't."

"And you think this might be a connection?"

"I don't know. You didn't see anything in the Edward Seymour file, and I didn't find anything specific in Mary Sandell's either. But that doesn't necessarily mean they didn't ever visit there. We probably don't have a full accounting of every place all these people traveled. Where they lived, yes, but not traveled."

"Two victims doesn't a connection make," Alec cautioned. "And just because Mary Sandell's husband is English doesn't prove anything either since it wasn't he who was killed, but her."

"Yes, but there are eight victims total, and we've only looked for this specific connection in four of them." He picked up the remaining folders, handed two more to Alec, and kept two for himself. "Let's see what we find in these."

Alec had to give it to him...the man had a single-minded intensity at times that was impressive.

But halfway through the second file, Alec's focus was shot to hell. The lack of sleep this week was catching up to him and he'd been doing nothing but work since six-thirty this morning.

"There was nothing in the last one and I just can't look at this one anymore. I have to take a break." He tossed his current stack of papers on the coffee table and rose. "I need another beer. Want one?"

Christian glanced up and his eyes looked as bleary as Alec's felt. "Yeah. Sure."

Alec trooped into the kitchen, opened the fridge and started to pull two bottles from a new six pack they'd stopped at the grocery store and bought on the way home, but then paused. "What the hell." He grabbed up the entire box and returned to the living room, where he cleared a spot on the coffee table with a swipe of his hand and set it down.

One of Christian's eyebrows rose and a smile that was just entirely too sexy curved his lips. "The whole six-pack?"

"It's eleven o'clock on a Friday night. We've been staring at this stuff for hours. I don't know about you, but I've had all I can take for now." He handed a bottle to the other man. "Besides, there's not enough to get tanked, just enough to relax."

Alec sank onto the floor on the other side of the coffee table and stretched his legs out in front of him.

Christian twisted off the top, put the brown bottle to his lips, and swallowed, then leaned back against the wall where he sat. "So how'd you end up being a police detective, Alec Anderson?"

"I assume you don't want the exciting rundown of how I was a uniformed beat cop first and worked my way up?"

Christian was drawing him into personal conversation again, but he decided at this point he didn't care. It was wearing him out to keep up the professional wall between them. And damn it, he'd missed having company, having someone to talk to after work hours. It had been nice not to come home tonight to another long, lonely evening in the silent house.

"Not that I'm sure it wouldn't be fascinating, but you assume correctly."

Alec swirled the beer in his bottle, watching as the foam crept up to the rim without going over. "I became a cop because Martin—Captain Shanahan—was my mentor, and my friend, at a time when I really needed one, when I was a teenager."

He could tell from Christian's expression he wanted to know more but was too polite to probe. Alec sighed and decided he might as well tell the whole story.

"My parents died when I was little—my dad when I was a baby, and my mom when I was about two. I lived with my grandmother after that, but then when I was ten, she passed away also. I was shuffled around from foster home to foster home like a lot of orphans are. Finally, when I was sixteen, the foster family I was living with enrolled me in the Big Brothers Big Sisters program and Martin became my Big Brother. He gave me a sense of purpose, focus. He encouraged me to go to college, which I did, and when I graduated, I joined the police force. I wanted to be like him."

"You're close to him then?"

"Yeah. He's really stood by me over the years. He's been a good friend. He's always treated me like I'm family."

"I'm sorry about your parents and your grandmother."

"Thanks. But it was a long time ago. I don't even remember my parents. "

"It doesn't mean you can't still miss having them in your life, though," Christian said quietly. "My dad died a couple of years ago— cancer—and there isn't a day goes by that I don't think of him."

Alec nodded, understanding all too well. He was the same about Drew. "I'm sorry about your dad. Is your mom still alive?"

"Oh, yeah. She lives in London and is doing really well. She travels quite a bit—she's in the States right now, in fact, doing some speaking engagements. But when she's home, I see her quite often." He smiled fondly. "She's always calling me and banging on about whatever book she's writing at the time."

"She's a writer?"

He chuckled, and it was a warm, rich sound that curled around Alec. "Mmm-hmm. Remember I mentioned she's kind of into astrology?"

"Yeah."

"Well, she's not really just kind of into it." Christian looked at Alec a bit sheepishly. "She's pretty much all the way into it. It's been her passion most of her life and she's had many books published on the subject. She's something of an authority in the astrological community."

A grin slid across Alec's face.

"I know. Probably sounds fairly mad to a man who likes facts and tangibles." The teasing gleam was back in Christian's gaze, and it caused a flutter in Alec's stomach.

"So, with a mom who's 'into' astrology, how did you become a cop?"

Christian took several swallows from his beer before he answered. "I suppose, in a way, not unlike you did. I had a good mentor. My dad. He used to take me along with him when he was on the job and I loved it. I spent most of my growing-up years hanging around with the operatives he worked with, and I never wanted to do anything else. I guess you could say it was in my blood."

"Operatives? That's an odd word to use."

"Ah. Yeah, well, I work for a specialized division. We do a lot of undercover work."

"I thought Martin mentioned you were a homicide guy?"

"Yeah, that's part of what I do."

Alec studied him as he finished off the last of his beer. He got the impression Christian wasn't giving him the full scoop on his job. Operatives. A lot of undercover work. Homicide was only part of what he did. A startling thought hit him. *Crap.* Maybe he hadn't been all wrong that first day when his mind had wandered into James Bond territory. Maybe Christian wasn't actually a cop at all, but an agent of some sort.

And that led him to wondering at the coincidence of Christian discovering at least two of the victims, maybe three, had a connection with England. Maybe it wasn't such a coincidence. And maybe that's why the chief had specifically assigned Christian to him…because of this case. Maybe Christian had come to the States in the first place to get information about this case?

Alec wasn't sure whether to laugh at his own wandering thoughts and write them off as the product of a lack of sleep enhanced by alcohol—although, he was barely even buzzed from the beer—or take them seriously and wonder just who Christian really was.

If Christian was here undercover, only posing as a cop, then Alec decided he wasn't ready to tip his hand yet. So far, Christian had been a help and, quite frankly, Alec knew he was batting zero on this case. A first for him. He'd never been in the position of being so frigging clueless about an investigation he'd headed-up.

No, he'd watch and wait and see what happened for now. Hell, it could just be his imagination anyway.

"You're awfully quiet," Christian said.

"Sorry. Long day. Wandering mind. So…" He had a burning

question he wanted to ask, had been wanting to ask all week, but knew if he did he might not like the answer. He also knew that by asking it, it meant he was admitting to himself his interest in Christian went above and beyond the professional. Hell, he already knew it did. But maybe it would be admitting it to Christian? Still, one way or another, it was best to get this out of the way right now.

"So?"

"So do you have anyone special in your life? A…girlfriend?"

Christian dragged in a deep breath.

Uh-oh. That maybe wasn't a good sign.

"I think I'm going to need another beer for this talk," the Englishman said. He twisted the cap off another bottle and swallowed almost half of it before he spoke again.

"To give you the short answer, no, there's no one in my life right now."

"But…?" Alec could tell there was more to this story.

Christian sighed. "I was with someone for a long time, almost four years. My friend Bella's younger sister, Kate."

Alec's heart dropped to the pit of his stomach. A woman. The answer he hadn't wanted to hear.

But it was probably better this way. Cleaner. Less messy and complicated.

Still…the way Christian had looked at him in the parking lot. He couldn't get that out of his mind. He was certain he hadn't imagined it. And the way he was looking at him right now…almost as if he were trying to tell Alec with a glance to hear him out.

So he took the cue and forged into the fray. "It didn't work out?" he asked.

"We were engaged for the last two years we were together. She was ecstatic to get married, had a huge wedding planned. But the truth was, I was terrified at the thought." Christian took another drink of his beer.

"I felt bad because I wanted her to be happy. And I didn't think I was afraid of commitment. I'm really not," he said, catching Alec's gaze. "I loved her, but…"

"She just wasn't the one for you?" Alec suggested.

"No, she wasn't. I began to realize I loved her like a friend. Like my best friend's little sister. We always had fun together, could talk about anything, but it just always felt like there should be more. Like there was something missing." His expression softened as he looked at Alec, and Alec's pulse suddenly began to race.

But then Christian shook his head and rubbed the back of his neck. "She's the one who ended up breaking it off because I kept stalling, and I still feel really shitty about that. I should have just been honest with her about my feelings and not let it drag on as long as I did. She deserved better than that."

"And there hasn't been anyone since?"

"No." There was that look again. The one that sent a surge of slow-burning heat through Alec's veins. "I guess I've been waiting for the right…person to come along."

Not woman. Person.

Before Alec could gather his thoughts from that remark, Christian asked, "So what about you? Has there ever been a special someone in your life?"

Alec should have suspected the question was coming. Should have been prepared for it. But he wasn't, and it hit him hard, like a blow to the gut, the pain nearly stealing his breath.

Oh, God, he didn't know if he could talk about this.

Yes. You can. It's time to talk about it and move past it.

"I'm sorry. Bad question?" Christian asked, looking genuinely contrite. Alec realized his expression must have given him away.

"No, not bad. Just…kind of a bittersweet one, I guess."

At the sight of Christian's furrowed brow, he knew he had to explain.

"I lived with someone, was in love with someone. We were together for three years. It was my partner from work."

"What happened with…her?"

"Him," Alec said, purposefully meeting Christian's gaze.

The other man nodded, not seeming surprised.

"Eighteen months ago, on his way home from work late one night, Drew stopped at a convenience store to get a soda. I'd gone into work early that morning, so I'd left before he had and he'd stayed to finish up some paperwork on a case he was on. When he got inside the store, he realized he'd just walked into a robbery in progress. He'd left his gun and badge in his truck, and had no way to call for backup. The perp—a young man—had a gun held to the clerk's head. Drew was too smart to interfere at that point, knowing it was likely once the kid got his money, he'd clear out, then Drew would call it in and go in pursuit.

"And that's probably what would have happened. Except another customer in the store decided to play hero. Before Drew could stop him, he snuck up behind the gunman and tried to hit him with a metal pipe he'd found in the store."

Alec stared past Christian, at the built-in bookshelves on the far wall. Bookshelves Drew had built. "I guess everything went to hell. The gunman started shooting at anything and everything. He was drugged out and on edge. He shot the clerk, killed him on the spot. Nicked the guy who'd tried to hit him from behind. Drew had thrown himself on top of a woman to protect her, and he took two bullets. He died on the way to the hospital, before I could see him."

"Oh, God, Alec. I'm sorry." Christian's voice was soft and filled with so much empathy it almost made Alec hurt worse to hear it.

"He hung on long enough to tell the medics and the cops at the scene what happened. They caught the guy who did it. He got a life sentence."

"Which is good. But you still lost the man you loved. And you didn't get to say goodbye."

Alec shrugged, trying to fight back the emotion that threatened to spill out. "We all know there are risks when we do this job."

"Except he wasn't on the job."

"No. He wasn't." And that was exactly what had made it even harder to deal with. Drew's murder had happened when least expected, when he was officially off duty. When he was supposed to be safe, and Alec wasn't supposed to have to worry about him. But Drew had always taken an enormous amount of pride in being a cop, and Alec knew no matter what the time clock at the station said, Drew had never considered himself truly off duty.

Christian reached across the table, pulled another beer from the carton, opened it, and handed it to Alec. It was the perfect response. If Christian had said anything else, Alec wasn't sure he would have been able to hold it together. The man had an uncanny ability to read him and do the right things.

Alec accepted the offered beer, doing his damnedest to ignore the little tingle of energy that surged up his hand and into his arm when their fingers inadvertently touched.

Not now, not when I've just been talking about Drew.

But he couldn't control it any more than he could control the beat of his heart.

Christian, quite adeptly, managed to turn the conversation to other things, and Alec was once again grateful to him. It gave him time to pull himself out of the melancholy that always hit him when he spoke of or thought about Drew.

They talked about mundane subjects—the weather in England, the miserable weather here this past week, hiking, which it seemed they both enjoyed, movies, the upcoming holidays.

By the time they'd finished off the six-pack, Alec was feeling mellow and surprisingly content, all things considered.

"Can I ask you a question?" Christian asked. "A personal question?" He was still sitting on the floor, back leaning against the wall, with his long legs stretched out in front of him.

Alec had moved to the couch and was slumped on it with his sock-clad feet crossed on the coffee table.

"Sure. Go for it."

Christian hesitated for a moment, then, as if deciding he might as well just blurt it out, said, "When did you know? That you were gay?"

For some reason the question caused a ripple of heat deep in Alec's groin. Or maybe it wasn't the question so much as the man who was asking it.

"I was sixteen, almost seventeen. I had so much crap going on in my life—new foster home, new teachers who were less than thrilled with my performance that year, and just general teenage angst and discontent. It was about that time I started to realize I wasn't into girls like most of my guy friends were. I mean, they were nice enough and I had several girls who were friends, but I'd never really had a girlfriend. Still, that didn't mean that much to me at the time. It wasn't until one of my friends who was a girl talked me into helping her and some of her other friends sneak into a strip club.

"The club was having ladies' night. So while the girls were oohing and aahing and squealing around me, it occurred to me as I was watching these men strut around in the almost-altogether that I was getting excited by it."

He chuckled softly at the memory. "Over the next few months I snuck back there on my own several times. At first it was to prove to myself that the first time had been a fluke and I wasn't really turned on by other men. But eventually it was because I *was* turned on and I wanted more. After that, I met my first lover my senior year of high school. It didn't last long, but it was enough to confirm that girls definitely didn't do it for me."

Good God. The alcohol really had made him mellow to have blabbed about all that. He glanced at Christian to find him lost in thought.

"What about you?" Alec asked, without thinking. "When did you know?"

At Christian's startled expression and his quick intake of breath, Alec suspected he'd just shocked the hell out of the Englishman, and instantly felt guilty for doing it. Christian had almost married a woman. Alec still had no way of knowing for certain he was interested in men.

You mean interested in you?

"I…I'm…" Christian stumbled over the words.

Alec sat up, feeling bad for causing him what was obviously huge discomfort. The man looked like a deer caught in the headlights of an oncoming eighteen-wheeler. "You don't have to answer that. I'm sorry."

"It's okay. I'm just…I'm…not really…"

"Christian, I mean it. Don't say another word. Forget I said it."

Christian's mouth closed and an emotional storm churned in his eyes. He offered Alec a weak smile. "It's getting late. I should probably go."

Alec sighed. "I really am sorry. I didn't mean to run you off."

Christian pushed himself to his feet, and Alec followed, rising from the couch.

"You didn't. It's okay."

"Yeah, I did," Alec whispered, mentally kicking himself in the ass.

"Alec." Christian placed a hand on his shoulder, and the heat from his palm burned straight through Alec's long-sleeved T-shirt. "You didn't and aren't scaring me off." He pointed at the wall clock. "Look at the time. It's almost one-thirty in the morning. I didn't realize how late it was. And we're both running on fumes here." He smiled again, and managed to make it look more or less genuine, but Alec could clearly read the angst still shadowed in his gaze.

Alec nodded. What else could he do? But he felt sick at heart to have been so callous.

"I'll drive you home."

"You don't need to do that. I like to walk and it's not that far to where I'm staying."

"It's like ten degrees outside. You'll freeze. And it can't be all that close. On Tuesday night you said it was close to work, but that's a couple of miles away."

"No, I promise, it's not far. I'll be fine."

"Christian, don't be st—"

Christian put a finger against his lips and the raw shock of feeling it there startled Alec into silence more than anything. Liquid heat instantly pooled in his groin and his balls tightened.

Christian jerked his hand away as if the contact had burned him, but he managed, somehow, to keep his composure. Better than Alec.

"Trust me," he said. "I'll be safe and warm in my hotel room in less than five minutes. I promise."

Alec swallowed hard and nodded. He was still reeling at just how deeply and quickly such a simple touch had affected him.

He walked Christian to the door, waited while he pulled on his jacket, then held it open for him. The cold night air seeped through his jeans and shirt, raising goose bumps on his skin.

Christian paused before he stepped out. "Thanks for feeding me dinner."

A soft snort escaped Alec. "Delivery pizza…real gourmet stuff." He forced a strained smile on his face. "But you're welcome. I guess I'll finish looking through those other files tomorrow. I'll let you know if I find any other England connections. Thanks for your help with that tonight."

"My pleasure." Christian took a deep breath and hesitated for a moment, but then said, "Well, goodnight."

"Night." A knot had formed in Alec's stomach. He didn't want Christian to go like this, with this between them. But he didn't know what else he could say. He'd already done enough damage and was afraid anything else that came out of his mouth at this point would just make it worse.

Christian started across the porch toward the steps. But he stopped suddenly. He didn't turn around, just stood there, facing away from the house.

"Christian?" It was so cold out, Alec's breath turned to mist.

Alec watched the other man's shoulders rise and fall. Then, he heard Christian mutter, "I'm such a stupid prick." Without turning around, he said in a louder voice, "Almost two years, although I really knew it in my heart a long time before that." There was a pause. "No one I work with knows, though. Neither does my mother. Even my best friends don't have a clue."

Alec's breath caught.

Christian finally turned to face him. "I'm sorry. I don't know why I reacted the way I did in there, trying to deny it." Then he shook his head and sighed. "Yes, I do. The truth is, I'm still not completely comfortable talking about it. It's hard for me. My dad, rest his soul, was a wonderful, strong man. But he wasn't very open-minded sometimes and he made no secret he didn't condone gay relationships. So I pretty much spent my entire adult life in denial about my own feelings. I…"

He looked away from Alec and upward, as if he were intently studying the bare-branched elm tree next to the porch. But the sorrow in his voice tugged at Alec's heart.

"I loved the man. I looked up to him. But I knew if I ever told him how I felt, he'd never accept it, and the pride he had in me would dry up and that would be that. It wasn't until after he died that I was even able to admit it to myself."

His gaze moved back to meet Alec's. "This week…since I met you, I've felt things. About you."

Alec's heart pounded. "I've felt them, too," he admitted.

Christian nodded. "I thought you did, that first day, at the hospital. But then I wasn't sure because you wouldn't ever let me in again after that. I was afraid I'd misread you. It wasn't until tonight I really understood why you kept me at a distance." His forehead creased. "I know now it's because you're not ready to be with someone again so soon. And I want you to know I'll respect that."

The heavy, tight knot in Alec's stomach seemed to grow larger, and another one formed in his throat. This was it. The moment of decision. Was he going to keep falling back on his relationship with Drew and never allow himself to live? Was he going to let Christian walk away?

"I won't be here much longer, but while I am, you have my word I won't—"

At the thought of Christian leaving, at never getting a chance to see if there could be anything between them, all indecision fled. In two steps Alec crossed to where Christian stood, cupped the other man's face in his palm, and kissed him, cutting him off mid-sentence.

Christian stiffened in obvious surprise. But then he was kissing back. Tentatively at first, as if he weren't sure Alec wasn't going to pull away any moment, but finally surrendering to it.

The first thing that struck Alec was how very different kissing Christian was from kissing Drew. There was no sense of being dominated, as there had often been with Drew. This was an equal and passionate coming together that stirred more than Alec's libido. Their mouths melded and tongues met with an odd familiarity, as if they'd kissed dozens of times before, yet it was new and thrilling at the same time.

And, my God, it was heaven. Christian's warmth—from his mouth, his tall, lean body, his hand that moved up to tangle in Alec's hair—

speared through Alec until he felt like he would melt, inside and out.

When they paused for air, Christian's blue gaze met his, full of intensity, pleasure, but also caution.

Alec stared back, a million things running through his head.

Fine lines formed across Christian's forehead and around his mouth. "You okay?"

The knot in his throat was back, nearly choking him. Alec shook his head. "I haven't been okay since you came here."

Christian's eyes widened, then he winced and his gaze filled with sad apology. "I'm sor—"

Alec pressed two fingers against his mouth to silence him. "No. I don't want you to be sorry. There's nothing to be sorry for." He slid his fingers off Christian's lips and stroked his fingertips along the man's lightly stubbled jaw. "I just want you to kiss me and make it better."

He very nearly heard Christian's heart stop beating. Or at least he thought he imagined it. Christian started to speak, and Alec knew it was going to be a protest, so he silenced him again.

"You don't understand what I'm saying. You're all I can think about. When I'm away from you, all I want is to see you again. When I'm with you, all I want is to be close to you. Every time I close my eyes, I see you, feel you, dream about you, fantasize about you. My past, Drew…I can't even picture him in my mind anymore. Thinking about you, wanting you…it's making me crazy, Christian."

Christian dragged in a slow, shaky breath. Then another.

Alec's voice was barely above a hoarse whisper. "So you see, the only cure for what ails me is…I think…you."

CHAPTER 6

There was a heartbeat where they simply stared at one another. And then Christian was pulling him close, kissing him again, this time with no hesitation, no walls between them.

They moved toward the doorway, Alec backing through it and pulling Christian with him. He toed the door shut as Christian pressed him up against the wall just inside it.

The kiss deepened, slowed, becoming less desperate and more intimate. Christian's palm slid up under Alec's shirt to stroke slow circles against his lower back. Alec worked his hands inside Christian's leather jacket and eased it over his shoulders. It fell to the floor with a soft plop of leather on hardwood.

Both sets of their hands roamed, pushing shirts up and off. Their bodies came together…smooth, muscular heat to smooth, muscular heat, and Alec groaned at how good it felt.

They kissed for long, languid minutes, savoring each other and the closeness, letting their hands wander, building a slow-burning passion unlike anything Alec had ever experienced outside of the dreams and fantasies he'd had about Christian this week.

Once again he was struck with how different this was from his and Drew's relationship. With Drew, everything had been turned on high speed and high intensity all the time. By now, Drew would have had Alec's clothes ripped off and Alec himself facing the wall, hands above his head, while Drew thrust into him and jacked Alec off at the same time, until they both came to hard and fast climaxes. Even their first time together had been like that, with Drew making no bones about what he wanted between them, and then, when Alec assured him the interest was returned, fucking Alec bent over the hood of one of the department's unmarked cars alongside Route 30 where they could have been discovered at any time.

Sex with Drew had been like an exhilarating thrill ride, like bungee jumping off a bridge into a canyon thousands of feet below. It had been breathtaking, wild, and never dull. And Drew, for all that he loved being the dominant partner, had never been selfish with Alec, always making sure his orgasms were big and fulfilling.

But this…with Christian…it was fulfilling in a different way. It spoke to a part of Alec that he hadn't even realized was needy until now. No, until that night in the shower earlier in the week.

He hadn't realized just how much he'd been craving tenderness with the intimacy. He'd loved the occasions he and Drew had shared slow, gentle lovemaking, and probably should have spoken up to Drew that he'd like it that way more often. But being with Christian stirred to life a deep-seated passion he hadn't felt with Drew even at their gentlest moments.

The realization shocked him. And sent a surge of guilt through him.

It seemed almost a betrayal to be thinking such things. He shouldn't be comparing the two men. Drew was gone and what they'd had was real and good. And now he might have something real and good with Christian, too. Good, but different. Nothing to compare.

And, yet, he couldn't help but do so. Christian's hands on his body, his mouth exploring Alec's were intoxicating, seductive, and…God help him, so damned right. Right in an elemental way Alec felt all the way to his bones.

When Alec finally had to pull his mouth free to drag in air, Christian didn't seem to need to do the same. He alternated between nipping at and pressing soft kisses against Alec's neck.

Alec closed his eyes, arched toward Christian's attention, and rested his head back against the wall, giving himself up to the slow, sensual pleasure of it. "You don't know how many times I've thought about this over the past few days," he said, stroking his hands up and down Christian's bare back, enjoying the feel of warm skin against his palms. "I've dreamed about it. About you. About being with you."

Christian paused in his kissing, causing Alec to open his eyes. When he did, it was to find Christian watching him.

"Real dreams? While you were sleeping?"

Alec nodded. "Almost every night since we met. Intimate dreams," he admitted. "Erotic dreams."

Christian's eyebrows rose. "So have I. Had dreams. About you, us."

"They were so real," Alec murmured. "I could feel you, smell you—"

"Taste?"

"Yes."

"So could I. I could even taste your…" A dark flush spread up his cheeks.

Alec stared at Christian wide-eyed. "My cum?" he whispered.

At Christian's nod, Alec's heart raced. "I could taste yours, too. And your hands…when you touch me now, they feel just like they did in the dreams."

Christian's forehead creased and he rubbed a finger against the small silver medallion that hung from a sterling chain and rested against Alec's chest. "I even remember this," he said softly, almost disbelieving. "Remember seeing it on you, touching it like this. Except I've never seen it until just now…have I?" His blue eyes rose in question to look at Alec.

Alec shook his head. "How could you…?"

"I don't know. Unless…"

"Unless?"

He shook his head. "No, it's…no."

Leaning in close, Alec feathered his lips against the hollow where Christian's neck and shoulder joined, savoring the warm, slightly salty flavor of his skin. Then he moved upward. When he reached his ear, he dipped the tip of his tongue inside it, to trace the curve of it.

Christian let out a huff of breath and buried his fingers in Alec's hair.

As he had in one of the dreams, Alec rekissed the path down Christian's neck, across his collar bone, the firm planes of his pectorals and, finally, swirled his tongue around one of Christian's flat, bronze nipples. Alec felt the other man's body vibrating against his in response.

"In one of your dreams, did I do this?" Alec asked before he took the hard nub in his mouth and sucked on it, then bit down lightly.

A low moan escaped Christian. "Yes, just like that. And I did this…"

He pulled Alec's face up and, gazing deeply into Alec's eyes, kissed him again, taking his time, sucking on his tongue until heat infused Alec, seeping into his veins, and surging in his balls.

He slid his hands around to cup Christian's ass through his jeans and pulled him close. Their groins began a sensuous grind against each other. Christian's hard length strained against the denim, and Alec ached to feel it against his own without the barrier between them.

"I want you," he said, pulling his mouth free. "Jesus, I want you. I can't believe how much."

His gaze and fingers moved toward the button and zipper of Christian's jeans, but the other man caught his hands.

Alec looked up at him, torn between wanting to jerk free so he could continue emancipating the solid length of cock he knew lay beneath the zipper, and wondering if Christian didn't want him with the same ferocity he felt.

At the expression on Christian's face, though, he knew the other man felt it, too…the powerful urge to be flesh to flesh. Yet Christian continued to hold Alec's hands.

"Are you sure, Alec? I don't want to rush you into anything."

A warm ached filled Alec's heart at the other man's sincerity. And it just made him want him more.

"Yes. I wouldn't be standing here right now if I wasn't. I've been making love with you all week in my dreams. Everything about you is familiar. As if…"

"As if the dreams were real," Christian said, finishing Alec's thought.

"Yes," Alec breathed.

"I know." His brows drew together again in the particular way Alec was beginning to see as sexy and endearing.

Before the other man could voice any other concerns, Alec pressed his lips to Christian's and showed him in the kiss how ready he was to take this step. At the same time, their fingers untwined. While Alec's moved directly to the button on Christian's jeans, popping it free, Christian's curved around either side of Alec's waist. His thumbs played against Alec's lower abdomen, teased through the line of hair that disappeared into his jeans and then, when Alec sucked in his stomach, dipped into the waistband of them and his briefs, and brushed lower, just skimming the tip of Alec's erect shaft.

Alec shuddered and his own fingers faltered for a moment on Christian's zipper.

"Feel good?" Christian murmured against his ear, brushing a thumb over the slit of his cockhead again.

"Oh, yeah." He wanted to add, "Unzip me, damn it, and touch me properly," but the truth was, there was something sexy as hell about having Christian's hand down his pants, prolonging full contact, letting the anticipation build.

That didn't stop him from resuming work on Christian's zipper, however. He was too far gone to stall.

With the zipper out of the way, he parted the flaps of Christian's jeans, eased his briefs out of the way, and found what he sought jutting from the smoldering warmth of soft dark curls. Alec's mouth went dry at the sight. It was just as he remembered it from the dreams. Long, impossibly stiff, lightly veined with a thick head already emerged past sexy foreskin. Alec's ass throbbed in anticipation of how it would feel entering him.

"You have a fucking beautiful cock, you know that?" When his hand curved around the base of it, it rose eagerly to meet his touch.

Christian groaned.

"Feel good?" Alec mimicked with a mischievous smile. It did to him.

"I think you already know the answer to that," came the hoarse response. Hungry sensuality swirled in Christian's eyes, which only made Alec's own eager lust pound all the more strongly.

Within moments Christian had him unzipped and free as well and, without hesitation, captured Alec's shaft and rubbed it against his own in Alec's hand.

As they stared into each other's eyes, their breathing came out in ragged, unison rasps. The sensation of their dicks pressed together and the searing heat tingling between them where they touched made Alec's balls ache.

"I want to be inside you." Christian's voice was low and rippled with sex. "I want to be buried inside you and feel you clenching and quivering around my cock, pulling me deeper, deeper"—he punctuated the words with gentle thrusts of his groin against Alec's—"until we're so damned close together there's no way to tell where one of us ends and the other starts."

Alec's knees nearly gave out at the words. "Jesus." His heart raced. "Yes. God yes" he said breathlessly.

Christian's mouth came down on his again, and Alec returned the kiss with urgency. Their tongues stroked and thrust, and their cocks matched the rhythm, sliding and rubbing against each other. It was slow, delicious torture, and, as he had so many times in the dreams, he wanted it to go on and on forever. But at the same time, as the heat built, he wanted more, wanted exactly what Christian had said…wanted the man filling him, thoroughly, over and over until they were both sweat-slicked and lost forever in one another.

With a sizzling look at Alec, Christian stepped back and peeled Alec's jeans and briefs down until they fell at his ankles. Alec kicked them off and Christian knelt in front of him.

He paused and looked up. "I'm clean. I haven't been with anyone since long before my last test."

Alec nodded. "Same for me. I get tested every six months for work. There's been no one since Drew."

A tiny sliver of sadness and guilt slid through him. But Christian's understanding smile and the feel of his thumb stroking over Alec's crown sent it flitting away as quickly as it had come. Panting as the feather-light brushing motion over and around his swollen head became almost too much bear, he urged, "For God's sake, suck me. Please."

Christian chuckled softly, but the heated intensity in his blue eyes stole Alec's breath. Without any further teasing or petting or lead-up, he anchored his hands on Alec's hips and swallowed his cock to the root.

Alec groaned at the suddenness of the motion. He clutched at Christian's shoulders and was grateful he had the wall behind him to hold him up. The wet heat of Christian's mouth was the best thing he'd felt in months, years maybe.

Christian held him deep, without moving, until Alec was shaking with frustrated need. "Shit. Oh, God, please…" he begged. He had the sudden urge to thrust hard and deep down Christian's throat, to fuck his mouth and find release for all the pent-up passion that had been building in him this week.

But Christian held him in place, his fingers digging into Alec's hips—not enough to hurt, just enough to let Alec know they'd get around to that in good time, but this was going to happen at the pace he set.

And that just turned Alec on all the more. He didn't have much experience at having sexual acts prolonged and was discovering, between this and the dreams, just what he'd been missing. His hips twisted and his balls throbbed, but still Christian didn't let him move.

"You're killing me," Alec rasped. "Jesus, Christian…"

Christian's sparkling eyes looked up at him and Alec watched him smile around his cock. Then he felt the softest swirl of tongue at the base of it, teasing him beyond belief.

"Argh! Please…"

Finally Christian's mouth began to move up and down on him, bringing strangled cries of relief and building passion from Alec.

He closed his eyes against the sheer blinding pleasure of the sensations rushing through him, but then let them flicker open again so he could watch. He'd never seen anything so sensual or utterly arousing in his life as watching his wet, engorged dick sliding in and out of Christian's mouth. The sight alone was enough to make him come. But he fought back the urge, wanting, as always, for it to last as long as possible. And Christian wasn't in any hurry. Just when Alec thought he was about to go over the precipice, Christian seemed to know it and he'd change his motion, move his tongue differently, slow down or speed up.

One of his hands slid down off Alec's hip to cup his balls, now slippery with saliva. Christian rubbed his fingers through it before moving lower. A slick fingertip brushed against the tight opening of Alec's passage and then pushed into it.

Alec moaned with pleasure, and closed his eyes. His hips bucked rhythmically. Out of instinct, he began to thrust his cock against Christian's throat. This time Christian didn't stop him and, in fact, he moved a hand around to Alec's ass and pressed him deeper, encouraging it. At the same time, he eased another slippery finger up inside Alec, heightening the sensation of fullness and stretching.

Alec could feel his pulse pounding in his ears. His body thrummed with desire like he'd never known, every muscle and nerve ending stretched tight in anticipation of the orgasm he knew was imminent.

When Christian's fingers curved inside him and nudged his prostate, the resulting jolts of white hot electricity carried him up that last peak and put him over the edge in a shuddering explosion. He cried out as seed erupted from him over and over, hitting the back of Christian's throat. It kept coming, in powerful bursts that made Alec's testicles ache.

By the time he was drained, he could barely stand his legs were so shaky.

Christian rose, his eyes still burning with a passion that made Alec's heart pound. He took Alec's face in his hands and kissed him. Deeply. Alec could taste his own semen and it sent another mini-quake of desire through him. Damn. How could he still be needy after what had just happened? Yet heat stirred in his groin.

He slid his fingers through Christian's soft, thick hair, angled his head, and pulled him closer, kissing him harder.

"Christ, you're good," he murmured against Christian's lips when the kiss had finally ended.

"And you taste incredible, just like I remembered. I could do that to you every day for the rest of my life and never get tired of it."

Alec's pulse hitched. "Yeah?"

"Oh, yeah."

Christian's stiff prick rubbed against Alec's abs, hot and sleek, and another burst of raw need shot through Alec, shocking him with its intensity.

With a hand on the other man's chest, he pushed him backward, maneuvering him around the coffee table, and into a sitting position on the couch. Then he dropped to his knees on the braided rug in front of him until his face was inches from that magnificent cock. Alec curved a hand around it, licked up the glistening drops of pre-cum oozing from it, eliciting a hoarse groan from Christian, then smiled up at him.

"Now it's my turn to suck you. I'm going to make you come so hard your eyes roll back in your head."

"Bloody hell," Christian murmured, his breathing coming out in soft pants already.

Still smiling, Alec prodded him to raise his hips while he worked his jeans down over them and his thighs until they pooled at his ankles where they stuck because of his boots. He didn't bother unlacing them and removing the jeans. There'd be time for that later. Right now, he wanted Christian's cock too much to bother with stripping him completely.

With one hand Alec stroked his balls, with the other he tickled below them as he pressed kissed against Christian's thighs and into the warm, soft hair around the base of his dick. He savored the slightly salty taste of Christian's testicles and their rough texture against his lips. When he began to tongue Christian's balls, laving them and then slowly, carefully drawing one into his mouth, Christian tensed.

"Alec…damn, oh, damn."

Alec smiled, loving the loss of control he heard in Christian's voice. His mouth roamed up, licking Christian's cock like a thick stick of candy, until Christian shuddered and moaned at the slow, prolonged attention.

"Watch," Alec told him, looking up to capture Christian's gaze. "I want you to watch your beautiful cock fucking my mouth and see how much I love tasting you, too."

His thoroughly heated expression filled Alec with satisfaction.

"Do you have any idea how fucking sexy it is when you talk like that?"

A slow grin curved Alec's lips. "Oh, I have an idea. Now watch…"

With Christian's volcanic stare focused on him, on them together, Alec swallowed the man's long, throbbing cock into his mouth in a leisurely, inch-by-inch motion that had Christian's shaking and his hands clutching at Alec's shoulders.

Once it was in, Alec couldn't get enough of Christian's prick, couldn't seem to cover enough territory with his tongue, couldn't get it deep enough. The pre-cum that continued to seep from his slit was addictive and, with single-minded purpose, Alec sucked and worked at the slippery shaft, eager to bring Christian off so he could get more. The low groans of pleasure Christian made and the building thrusts of his hips as he plunged his cock deeper into Alec's mouth, only brought Alec to an even more frenzied height of need.

He fondled Christian's balls, and with his other hand, circled his fingers around the base of his thick cock and squeezed. Christian's spicy, musky scent infused his senses, and he tasted better than anything Alec remembered. Damn, he'd never wanted, needed anyone like this.

"I need you, Alec," Christian moaned, once again seeming to read Alec's mind. "I need you so fucking much...oh, sodding hell!"

Christian's cock jerked, then jerked again and hot, salty seed flooded Alec's mouth. He swallowed, taking it all, craving more, feeling a rush of both satisfaction and emotion surge through him. He buried his face in Christian's damp, dark curls, deep-throating him. Christian's hands on his head held him there as he thrust one final time, shuddering against Alec while the last few drops of cum flowed from him.

Alec slowly licked him clean to the sound of Christian's ragged breathing, then sat up. Christian pulled him up onto the couch next to him and into a kiss that was filled with much more than lust. Their gazes met, Christian's surging with the same emotion Alec felt stirring in himself. After Drew he'd never thought to find someone else who could claim his body and his heart, and yet, when he'd least expected it…

"You need to know something," Christian said, cradling Alec's face in his hands. His gaze was intense, stealing Alec's breath.

"What's that?"

"I don't want to scare you or rush you, but I do want to be honest with you about this. I'm falling for you in a big way, Alec. The things I feel when I'm with you, about you…you need to know this isn't just about the sex."

Alec swallowed past the lump in his throat created by the man's sincerity and openness. "I never expected to feel this way about you. I wasn't looking for someone."

"I know."

"I'm not sorry. And I'm finding that every minute I spend with you makes me want you more and more. I'm falling, too. And not just because of the sex."

A smile crossed Christian's face. "But, damn it's good."

"Oh, yeah." Another slow burn began in Alec, and he wondered if he'd ever get enough of this man. "God, I'm not ready for you to go back to England," he voiced before he thought about it.

"I won't be going back for a while still, so let's not think about that right now, okay? I don't want to think about it."

Alec nodded, but he couldn't help wondering what would happen when it was time for Christian to go home. Would they be able to sustain a relationship over thousands of miles? How often would they see each other?

He hadn't traveled much because the truth was, as much as he enjoyed driving around town, long car or train trips, boats, as well as plane flights made him physically ill in a way doctors had never been able to explain. It wasn't the garden variety of motion sickness that could be helped by drugs or meditation or pressure points or biofeedback. He'd tried them all. And it didn't pass when the travel was over. It wasn't unusual for him to be sick for days afterward. For him travel could be life-threatening. He'd almost died on a plane ride when he was a teenager, and the thought of getting on one again scared the hell out of him.

It would be almost impossible for Christian and him to have a relationship unless one of them were willing to move to the other's country, and that brought up a whole new set of complications…one of them would have to give up his job, his home, his friends and life and move to a place with a completely different lifestyle. And again, the chances of it being Alec who'd be able to do that would be nil since he couldn't travel.

"Hey." Christian tipped his face up and looked at him, worry lines creasing his forehead.

"I'm okay. I just…I don't travel well," he admitted. "I don't know how we'll be able to see each other."

"We'll find a way." The promise in Christian's eyes and voice almost convinced Alec it might be possible. Almost.

Their mouths met again, and it didn't take long for hands to wander as well.

"Fuck, I can't believe how hard I am and how much I want you again," Alec groaned.

"In bed this time." Christian gripped Alec's cock and stroked it slowly. "I want to do things to you that would be much more comfortable in bed."

"Hell, yes. Bed is definitely in order."

He rose and held out a hand to help Christian to his feet. When they were standing, the kissing and fondling resumed and they got nowhere for several minutes.

"Weren't we headed somewhere?" Christian reminded.

Alec grinned down at Christian's jeans still wadded around his ankles, keeping him from walking. "I don't think you're going much of anywhere like that."

Christian shot him a half-humorous, half-frustrated glare, then stared down at the problem. "Bugger."

Alec burst into laughter. "Well, uh, yeah…but not until you can move."

This time Christian's lips twitched into a smile. "Smart arse." He bent over to find the laces on his boots under the denim, and Alec couldn't help but admire his lean back and the way his muscles bunched and tightened as he worked. Damn, the man was sexy. And he wanted him in bed, wanted to feel the full-length of their bodies pressed together.

He squatted down to help, but then, a thought occurred to him. He pressed his hands lightly against Christian's to stop him and looked up into his eyes.

"Wait. Not here." He didn't want any old shadows lingering around them, any more guilt feelings that might emerge from being with another lover in the bed he'd shared with Drew. He wanted this experience with Christian to be about just them.

For a fleeting second confusion flickered in Christian's eyes, but then, as if he could read Alec's mind, Alec saw understanding come over him. He smiled. "Want to go to my place?"

Alec pulled him down into a grateful kiss. "Yes. I do." He grinned, feeling suddenly free, and eager to carry on with what they'd started here. "You did say it wasn't far, didn't you?"

The return grin on Christian's face sent a new surge of desire through Alec. "I did, and it's not."

They both straightened to their full heights, with Christian pulling up his jeans and boxer briefs as he did.

"Then for God's sake, let's go," Alec said. "I'm going to make the assumption I'll be staying with you what little bit of the night is left and go grab a change of clothes."

Christian gave Alec's erect cock a gentle squeeze. "Or maybe you won't need any at all," he whispered.

Alec's breath caught in his chest. "Maybe I won't."

With one final kiss, stroke, and a sigh, Christian released Alec. "Get dressed and go get some clothes. If nothing else, you'll need something to wear to work on Monday."

"You planning to keep me busy all weekend?"

"God, I hope so."

Another grin curved Alec's lips. Unable to resist the urge, he bent over and licked the head of Christian's bulging hard-on, which jutted through the open flap of his boxer briefs, savoring the lingering salty taste of his once again seeping arousal and drawing a guttural groan from the man.

Then, sorry to have to postpone the pleasure, but at the same time looking forward to stripping Christian bare and having the time to fully explore him, Alec unhanded him, letting Christian put himself back to rights while he did the same, finding his jeans and pulling them on.

"Hurry," Christian said, tugging his sweater down over his dark head and giving Alec a pointed look that set his veins on fire.

"Damn straight. Don't move. I'll be back in less than a minute."

CHAPTER 7

Christian's body pulsed with a need he'd never before experienced with anyone—woman or man. He could still feel the lingering sensation of Alec's tongue on his cock and see the look of promise in his eyes.

But what made him laugh softly was the way his hands were shaking—like a stupid teenage prat about to have his first big sexual adventure. He hadn't been a teenager in a long damn time, and this was hardly his first adventure. Granted, his experience with men was more limited than his experience with women, but it wasn't by any means his first time with a man. Still…being with Alec gave it that heady, blood pounding, heart-racing, hand-shaking first time glow. Damn but he had it bad for the man.

He'd been shocked at Alec's response on the porch, had never, in his wildest dreams after hearing Alec tell about Drew's death, expected him to say the things he had.

You're all I can think about. When I'm away from you, all I want is to see you again. When I'm with you, all I want is to be close to you. Every time I close my eyes, I see you, feel you, dream about you, fantasize about you.

Christian couldn't have summed up his own experience this past week any better. It appeared they'd both been drowning in their need for one another.

And now…

He didn't want to think beyond what was happening between them right now. Didn't want to think about what would happen when it was time for him to return to England. Or how he was going to deal with explaining—or not—to Alec that he was a mage, and that while his real job could be considered a form of police work if one stretched one's imagination, the bad guys he hunted seldom used conventional weapons and most often had powers that equaled or exceeded Christian's own.

And even if Alec could get past the magic thing...he tried to hide it, but Christian sensed that Alec finding out Christian's job was dangerous—more dangerous even than his own—wasn't going to go over great. Alec had already lost a partner to a dangerous job and Christian couldn't promise him he'd always be safe when he went on an assignment.

He grimaced. No, that conversation was not something he wanted to think about tonight. As Bella was in the habit of saying whenever a mage opted to tell an Ordinary what he or she really was, "It's not going to go well." Because it seldom did. And right now, Christian didn't want to do anything to cause a rift between him and Alec.

He wanted Alec too much, in every way. He already couldn't think about not having Alec in his life, was already imagining what it would be like to wake up next to him in the morning, every morning. There was a connection between them that went beyond simple lust or attraction. They'd been having vivid dreams about each other, and were fucking amazing together in real life—his body was still tingling from the blow job Alec had given him, and the one he'd given Alec. The man even tasted familiar and right. Everything about them together was right. Like… *Oh, bloody hell. Like we belong together.* The words from the dreams.

He didn't believe in coincidences, so what did it mean?

But before he could think it through, a sharp cry ripped through his mind, nearly blinding him with pain. He staggered from the power of it.

Alec! Oh, God, what was wrong?

Without thinking, acting on pure, adrenaline-boosted instinct, Christian materialized in Alec's bedroom to find Alec in the grip of a hideous creature. Bluish-gray-tinged skin, thin arms and legs with inch-long black talons, eyes as black as the depths of hell, and a round, gaping maw.

In a split second glance, Christian took in the fact it had Alec by the throat with one hand, holding him up in the air. Its other hand was pressed to Alec's head with one of its long fingernails inserted deeply into his temple. Alec's eyes were open, but slowly closing.

Terror surged through Christian. "Get off him!" With his right hand, he reached out and a white-hot bolt of energy flowed from it. It hit the guiller in the back. But where it would have killed most any other creature or, at minimum, created a blackened wound, the energy merely bounced off the guiller.

It dropped Alec, however, and lunged around to face Christian.

Its eyes sucked him in, mesmerizing him. He could feel a cold dampness emanating from it, feel it drawing him closer, luring him with a nefarious control that scared the shit out of him.

Struggling to keep his wits about him and not be drawn in by the guiller's power over him, using both hands this time, he let another burst of energy, more powerful than before, surge through him and flow from his hands, hitting the guiller square in the chest.

Letting out a god-awful noise that was part scream, part growl, it morphed into a ball of blue light and then, with a popping noise, disappeared.

Shaking from the exertion of energy—he'd had to channel a huge amount of it that second time—and from shock and fear, he ran across the room and knelt next to Alec, who lay on the floor, crumpled onto his side.

"Oh, fuck. Fuck!" He rolled Alec onto his back.

Alec was still breathing, though it was rapid and light, but his eyes were closed and he didn't respond to Christian's touch or voice.

"Alec! Can you hear me?"

No response.

One-handed, he whipped his cell phone out of his pocket and hit the speed dial direct line to Bella's phone. She answered after the first ring.

"Bella, the guiller just attacked Alec. It didn't kill him, he's still breathing, but he's out, not responding. Please tell me he's going to make it."

"Christian, slow down. You said the guiller attacked Alec, the American detective?"

"Yes, damn it, I just said that. Tell me what to do for him. Do I take him to the regular hospital or does he need magic healing?"

"I don't kno—"

"Bella!"

"I'm sorry, but I don't know, Chris! Hang on, I'll see what I can find."

"No time."

As he talked to her, he checked Alec for injuries, even though he knew there would be none visible.

"I've got to get him to the hospital. What's the emergency number here? Is it 999 like ours?"

"No. No, it's…um…911. Call 911."

But as Bella spoke, Alec moaned and his eyes fluttered open.

"I'll call you back."

"Chris—"

He disconnected and dropped his phone back into his jacket pocket, then lifted Alec's head onto a pillow he pulled off the bed.

"Alec?" He held his hand and squeezed it, startled at how cold it felt in his palm.

Alec stared up at him, looking disoriented, and for a moment panic filled Christian that the guiller had done serious damage to his mind.

But then Alec groaned and lifted his free hand to his temple—which showed no mark at all from where the guiller's fingernail had been inserted.

"Christian?" His fingers laced through Christian's and squeezed back.

"I'm here. Are you okay?"

"I think so. I remember coming in here to get some clothes so we could leave, and then I heard a noise. I turned and…" He winced as if he were struggling to recall. "What happened?"

"It was the killer we've been after. It…he attacked you. Alec, are you sure you're okay?" Christian could hear the tinge of fear in his voice, but he didn't care. He'd always prided himself on his ability to stay calm in a crisis, but this was Alec and somehow that changed everything. "I was just about to call 911."

"No. I'll be all right."

He pushed himself to a sitting position with Christian's help. Then his gaze fluttered up to clash with Christian's. As Christian watched, he saw the events of the night crystallize in Alec's mind. Alec's eyes widened.

"What the hell was that thing?" he whispered, his voice raspy.

"That's not important right now. What's important is getting you some help. Let me call 911."

"No. I wouldn't know what to tell any of the cops who arrived."

"I was thinking more about your health than calling in the police," Christian said gently. "In any case, we need to get out of here. I didn't kill it. I think I just scared it off, but it might come back."

Alec stared at him. "That thing... And you...you did..." Frown lines furrowed his forehead.

Bugger. Obviously Alec had seen enough before he passed out to know the guiller appearing wasn't the only bit of unusual activity that had occurred.

"Alec, later, okay? I promise, I'll explain later. But right now we need to get out of here."

Alec's frown deepened, but he nodded. "Yeah. Yeah, okay." He grimaced and rubbed his temple again.

"Your head?"

"Hurts like frigging hell."

"We should get you to the hospital to be checked out."

"No."

"Alec—"

"No, I said. Again I ask you, what the hell am I going to tell them? They wouldn't believe me. They'd end up strapping me to a bed in the psych ward alongside Frank Sandell."

He wouldn't meet Christian's gaze now, which sent a frisson of anxiety through Christian.

"You don't have to tell them exactly what happened. They could still check you over to be sure you're okay."

"No. I'll be fine."

Finality rang in the words and Christian had to tamp down his frustration. But it didn't stop worry from eating at him.

"Can you stand?"

"Yeah."

"Come on." He draped one of his arms around Alec's shoulders and rose, helping Alec to his feet. Alec wobbled for a moment, leaning against Christian, but then pulled away to stand on his own.

Christian's anxiety built. Alec's withdrawal wasn't just because he was stubborn and wanted to pretend he was okay. There'd been a definite "don't touch me" factor to it.

Damn it. A knot formed in his stomach. Bella's standard warning that letting an Ordinary know the truth never went well came back to haunt him with a vengeance. If he weren't so concerned the guiller might return at any moment and maybe bring a few friends along, he'd try to reassure Alec and come up with an explanation right now.

And you think he'd listen at this point? He was just attacked by a gruesome, otherworldly creature that appeared out of nowhere, then you appeared out of nowhere, too, and shot bolts of lightning at it. He thinks you're a complete nutter.

The truth hit him hard, and for the first time ever he wished he wasn't a mage and could be just a regular guy. Dealing with situations like this had never bothered him in the past. But this time it was personal, and this thing between him and Alec was so new and fragile. The guiller attack and him having to use his powers in front of Alec unexpectedly couldn't have happened at a worse time.

Alec made his way without mishap into the living room, but Christian wasn't taking any chances. "Give me the keys. I'll drive. I don't think you should be behind the wheel right now." He held out his hand and, when Alec tried to protest, gave him a pointed stare.

"I'll be fine," Alec grumbled, but he picked up the keys from the end table next to the couch and dropped them in Christian's palm. "Do you even know how to drive on the right side of the road?"

"I'll manage." He handed Alec his coat and held open the door. The cold air hit him, nearly stealing his breath,

"Where are we going?"

"My hotel for now." At Alec's hesitation, Christian sighed. "Look, we need to leave here for safety reasons. My hotel's not far. We can talk there, okay? I promise."

Alec rubbed his head and winced. Then his shoulders slumped. "Okay, fine. Let's go."

But he stopped halfway down the porch steps. "Gun."

"What?"

"I need my gun and badge."

He turned and tried to brush past Christian, but Christian stopped him with a hand firmly on his chest.

Alec's gun probably wouldn't do him any good if the guiller came back and he started to say as much, but decided the better of it. "You stay here. I'll get them."

He went to the door and pretended for a brief moment to be looking for the house key on the ring of keys Alec had given him, but, with a slight wave of his hand, he used magic to unlock the door. He found Alec's shoulder holster and gun, as well as his badge, and was back at Alec's side within seconds. As he handed them over, once again a jolt of pain hit him when Alec jerked away when their hands made contact.

Damn it. How had it come to this so quickly? Was it just a few minutes ago they'd been tangled in an intimate embrace, teasing and kissing and ready to go to bed together to carry on with what they'd started?

You could do a charm?

No. Absolutely not.

But then everything would go back to the way it was before the guiller came.

No.

In general, mages weren't allowed to alter Ordinaries' memories. It was against Council law. But agents who worked for the Bureau of Dark Magic Affairs had the authority to do memory modification as needed on an Ordinary, if the agent felt it was in the Bureau's or the Ordinary's best interest not to remember seeing a magic event. And although it wasn't Christian's favorite thing to do—tamper with anyone's mind or memories—he had used it on occasion in critical situations when it would have been harmful to the Ordinary involved to remember, or if it was a top-secret assignment and the Bureau wanted no witnesses.

He could do a small modification charm on Alec so he'd remember being attacked, but not by who or what. He wouldn't remember seeing Christian materialize in the room and use magic to get rid of the attacker. He'd simply remember being attacked, then regaining consciousness with a headache he thought he got from being hit over the head or banging his head on the floor when he fell.

If he did it, he and Alec would, most likely, regain the closeness and intimacy they'd shared before the attack. And a part of him craved that like he'd never craved anything else. It would be so much simpler and there wouldn't be this growing chasm of chilly withdrawal between them.

But he couldn't mess with Alec that way. The thought made the knot in his stomach even more agonizing. There were already secrets between them, which he hated. Tampering with his memories would be the worst kind of betrayal. And it would be living a lie. More than the one he was already living.

Not to mention, he was afraid altering Alec's memory would leave him even more vulnerable to another attack because he wouldn't know what they were up against.

With another surge in his gut, Christian admitted that everything about this situation sucked. Maybe he should just tell Alec the truth. The whole truth. About everything.

Have you gone completely mad? He could almost hear Bella's voice in his mind because that's what she'd say. *Use a charm. It's less complicated. Then just watch him like a hawk and be sure he's not alone and you can be there in case the guiller attacks again.*

Torn between his job and his growing personal feelings for Alec, he couldn't find a good answer.

No traffic cluttered the streets at two-thirty in the morning so it didn't take long to get to Christian's hotel. They barely spoke on the brief trip. Alec stared out the passenger window, his fingers massaging his temple.

Worry ate at Christian when he saw what Alec was doing. What kind of damage might the guiller have done? Had it been in there long enough to cause permanent harm?

A thought occurred to him and he almost spoke it, but then swallowed it back, not certain it would be appreciated at the moment. But it kept returning, so finally he said, "Can you do the calming and healing thing on yourself? Would that help ease the pain?"

"I can't do it to myself. It doesn't work." Alec's voice was low, drained, but with a terse edge to it, punctuating the distance between them.

If what Alec did was a form of magic, Christian wasn't totally surprised. Magic had limitations and sometimes odd quirks like that.

When they arrived at Christian's hotel, he used the card key the hotel had provided to enter his room rather than do magic since Alec was standing in plain sight. They entered the room and Alec flipped on the light switch. But the moment the door was shut, he turned to Christian, his face a grim mask.

Christian knew what was coming. He dragged in a deep breath and tried to force himself to stay calm, but his stomach churned and the ache that always formed in his neck when he was under stress throbbed to life. He tugged off his jacket and draped it over the armchair just inside the door.

Alec didn't bother doing the same. He was still pale, and drawn lines stretched the skin around his eyes and mouth. But his golden-brown eyes glittered with barely restrained anger.

"I'm going to ask you again," he said. "What the hell was that thing? And don't tell me you don't know because you clearly do. And then you can tell me who the hell you really are."

Every line of Alec's body radiated tension, and in spite of his recent encounter with the guiller, Christian recognized he was a force to be reckoned with. Alec wasn't a weak-minded Ordinary who'd be easy to placate with smoke and mirrors. He was a strong, intelligent man and, in spite of the anger that rippled off him, a buzz of arousal coursed through Christian. He still wanted him…anger and all.

A charm would be so simple.

No, damn it. No charms.

In a sudden but absolute decision that he was doing the right thing, Christian chose to tell the truth. He knew he might lose Alec by doing it. But he hated the secrets between them, and it was better to be upfront now than to wait days, weeks, months, and have Alec find out anyway. By then, if he chose to leave, it would only hurt worse because they'd be even more firmly entrenched with one another, would only care more about each other.

"I'm waiting," Alec said through gritted teeth.

Christian pulled the chair out from the desk and turned it to face the bed. "Sit down before you fall down. I'll tell you what you want to know, but not until you sit. You're still weak from the attack."

He watched as Alec's Adam's apple traveled up and down his throat in a slow swallow, saw indecision, anger, hurt, but also a flicker of barely concealed longing swirl in his gaze.

Finally he sighed and sank into the chair.

"Can I get you something for your head?"

"No. Just tell me. And no bullshit. You owe me that much."

Christian sat on the edge of the bed facing Alec and scrubbed a hand over his eyes. He'd never felt so tired. Or so hopeless. He already knew in his gut this wasn't going to go well. But it was better this than to create a thicker web of lies and deceptions. He did owe Alec that much. Even if it meant he might lose him.

"The creature that attacked you is called a guiller. We don't know all that much about them except that they seem to have the ability to get into people's mind, siphon off their thoughts. The end result of their invasion is usually death."

"And I'm alive because…?" Alec's voice was tight.

"I'm not sure. Probably because I found you and scared it off before it could do any real damage." At least he hoped that was the case.

"And this creature…a guiller you said it's called…is what exactly? I mean, I live in the world of reality here, so please explain to me how something like this happens? Or, more to the point, is this some psychotic trick you're playing? Did you drug me at some point so I'd start having hallucinations like this? And if so, why would you do that? Unless you're the killer and you have something to hide."

Christian's heart stalled out in his chest. This was worse even than he'd expected. He tried to swallow past the knot in his throat that Alec would think he might be a murderer, and reminded himself Alec did live in a world very different from his, a world where something like a guiller couldn't exist outside a dream or hallucination.

"Alec…I would never do anything to harm you in any way. And you didn't hallucinate what happened. I know it sounds crazy, but there are things in this world you haven't heard of, yet they do exist. The guiller is real. It's what's been killing all the people in this town. It's able to kill without leaving any marks."

"Right…"

"It delves into people's minds, reads their thoughts. But in doing so, it sort of scrambles their brains and the people die from it. I think you have a headache because it had started doing its thing, but I stopped it in time."

"Yeah. Let's talk about that. About how you just appeared out of thin air. And then made some kind of light come out of your hands. Do you think I've completely lost my mind? Do you really think I'd buy into a delusion like that?"

Bloody hell. Here goes…

He took a deep breath. "What I told you before is the truth. I do work for a specialized department of law enforcement in England."

Alec's eyes narrowed. "You're a spy, aren't you?"

"No, not exactly. But the work I do is considered top secret in most circles. I work with a group of people who have special…abilities. We can channel the universal energy that surrounds us all, the energy that makes up all life here on Earth, and use it to make things happen."

"Uh-huh."

"Magic. We have the ability to do magic."

The dead silence in the room seemed to echo in the depths of Christian's brain. And then Alec laughed. It was a dry, bitter sound, but a laugh nonetheless.

"It's the truth. You wanted to know how I was able to show up in your bedroom, how the guiller was able to appear, and how I used my hands to channel energy that scared off the guiller…that's how."

Alec's laughter tapered off and he wiped his eyes. "I've heard enough. I'm out of here."

He started to rise, but Christian stood. "No, wait. Let me show you." He held out a hand and with a small finger movement extinguished the lights in the room. Then he did the reverse and turned them back on.

Alec had dropped back into the chair, but otherwise hadn't moved.

He simply stared at Christian with a closed expression.

Christian held out his hands. "See, no remote, no nothing. Magic." He moved his fingers again to turn the lights off and on.

"Am I supposed to be impressed by a parlor trick? What, are you a magician in your spare time?"

"I'm a mage. There's a difference. I don't do tricks or illusions like a magician. It's the real deal, real magic, with real results and consequences. A mage has the ability to channel energy and use it—for practical things like turning the lights on and off, for transportation, for protection. There are other uses as well." He gave Alec a pointed look. "Healing, for example. Some mages have the ability to heal by channeling energy through their hands."

But Alec either didn't notice or had no interest in taking the bait. He continued to stare at Christian with that same closed-off expression.

Christian sighed. "Let me give you another demonstration. I said we can use it for protection. Watch."

He held up a hand, focused, and white light surrounded him, ebbing and flowing in a perfect, shimmering sphere that completely encompassed him. He saw a flicker of surprise in Alec's eyes, but it was quickly hidden away.

"This," he said, looking at Alec through the light, "is a protection shield. We can use it for defense, much as the knights of old used their shields to deflect spears and arrows." He looked around and spied an appropriate object. "See that pencil on the desk over there? Pick it up and throw at me."

Alec didn't move.

"Come on," Christian said. "Even if you think this is only another trick, do it and humor me."

Several seconds ticked by, but finally Alec stood and picked up the pencil.

"Throw it. As hard as you can."

Alec zinged it at Christian. It bounced off the protection shield and fell onto the bed.

"Just another trick," Alec said. "It's not like a pencil was going to hurt you anyway."

"Okay, use something heavier. Something that could do damage."

Alec's eyebrows drew together.

"I'm serious. Find something heavy. Something that could really hurt me if it hit me. Or…better yet, take out your weapon and shoot at me."

At that Alec's expression turned to one of horror. "Are you frigging crazy? Jesus, Christian."

Christian remained calm, although he felt a shimmer of warmth in his chest that he'd gotten a genuine reaction out of Alec. "The shield will hold." It would take nearly all his strength to keep it up against something like a speeding bullet, but it would hold.

"No. Fucking. Way."

"Okay, okay. Find something else then. The light on the desk. It's heavy. Pick it up and hit me with it."

Alec shook his head.

"Just do it," Christian snapped. "Pick up the sodding light and try to hit me. If it breaks, I'll pay for the damages. Do it."

Alec's nostrils flared slightly and he glared at Christian, probably because of his commanding tone. But at the same time, a flicker of what looked like respect shone in his eyes as well.

For God's sake, did the man think he didn't know how to take charge if the need arose? Did he think Christian was some half-brained lackey who always took orders from everyone else?

Of course he doesn't know. He has no idea you run the Bureau.

Alec unplugged the cord, tugged off the shade, and hefted the lamp in his hands. But he paused a few feet from Christian. "You're completely whacked. You know that?"

"Hit me," Christian growled, tired of the game playing. There were too many more important things they needed to be talking about.

Alec hoisted the lamp like a baseball bat.

"Don't hold back. Do it has hard as you want. I know you're pissed at me, so feel free to take out your frustrations."

Tight lines formed around Alec's mouth. He swung. And he didn't hold back.

Christian winced as the lamp made contact with the shield, sending reverberating shocks rippling through it and into his hand from where the energy flowed. But the sphere held, as he knew it would. The bulb on the lamp, however, shattered and the lamp broke in two.

Alec dropped the remaining half he held in his hands as if it burned him. He took a step backward, then another, all the while staring at Christian in obvious shock.

Christian ignored it. "As you can see, it's great as far as it goes and can come in handy. But it has limitations. As long as I have this up, I can't use my powers on anything outside the sphere. I can't fight back. All I can do is stand here and be protected. Plus, I can't maintain the shield forever. While the shield itself is made up of energy that surrounds us and is therefore free for the taking, in order to create it and maintain it, I have to channel that energy. And that takes stamina."

He let his hand drop and the shield immediately collapsed.

"In other words, channeling energy to use for anything can quickly drain a mage if they don't know how to conserve it. We can't go around using huge amounts of channeled energy all the time or we'd collapse from exhaustion. So again, there are limitations. Turning the lights on and off requires minimal work. Holding a protection shield more so. And if something's banging on the shield, it takes even more strength to hold it in place because each time something hits it, it drains off some of the energy holding it together so we have to be able to replace that energy as quickly as possible. Teleportation requires even more stamina, and the longer the distance, the more draining it can be."

"Did you just say teleportation?" Alec had backed against the chair and was using it to steady himself. His expression said he was certain Christian really had gone mad now.

"Yes. That's how a mage can get from one place to another. It's how I entered your bedroom tonight. I think about where I want to be and then I transport there."

"Jesus, this is just too much. Too much," Alec muttered. "I…" He ran a shaking hand through his hair.

"I know. I know it's a lot and I know it sounds crazy. But it's all true."

"Show me." His voice was tight.

"Show you what?"

"Teleportation. Show me. Prove it."

"Okay." Christian thought himself just outside the door of his hotel room. He opened the door and walked back in.

Alec seemed nonplussed. "A trick. Another illusion. You're going to have to do better than that."

"Fine." Damn, he was tired. His neck ached and all this pointless magic was draining him, especially after the energy he'd had to use to fight the guiller, and the fact he hadn't gotten any sleep in almost twenty-four hours. "Why don't you tell me where you want me to go."

Alec thought for a moment. "Go to my office at the police station. Bring me back something from my desk…my foam basketball."

Christian sighed. "I'll be back in less than thirty seconds. Are you still going to be here when I return?" His gut clenched at the idea of Alec bolting off, but he knew he couldn't stop him if he chose to go.

God, he'd give anything to have this nightmare go away, to be back in Alec's living room, kissing the man and once again experiencing the amazing closeness and rightness they'd shared earlier. His heart ached with a vengeance and even though he was standing only a few feet from Alec, he'd never felt so far away from him.

He wondered if some of his misery must show on his face because Alec's expression softened and sorrow churned in his eyes. For a split second, Christian got the distinct impression Alec wanted to reach for him, touch him, and Christian's breath caught in his chest. But then Alec swallowed hard and sank into the desk chair.

"I'll be here," he said in a low voice, still looking at Christian with sad eyes, his voice hoarse with what sounded like barely restrained emotion.

Christian cleared his throat against his own battle with emotion and nodded. "I'll be right back."

He materialized in Alec's office. At this ungodly hour of the morning the place was deserted. But he couldn't find the basketball on the desk. Then he remembered Alec throwing it earlier in the day and how it had rolled under the desk. He bent over, retrieved it, and thought himself back to his hotel room, knowing it was very possible it would be empty when he arrived.

But Alec was there. When he saw Christian materialize in front him, his eyes widened. And when Christian handed him the orange foam sphere, he seemed almost afraid to take it.

"It's not going to hurt you. It's just your sodding ball like you asked for."

Christian dropped it in his lap, then collapsed onto the edge of the bed. *So damn tired.* He fought the urge to lay down and close his eyes.

Alec picked up the ball and studied it. "It really is mine…it has the chunk missing out of it." He jabbed a finger into a gouge where a bit of the foam was missing. His gaze rose to meet Christian's. Once again Christian couldn't read it, though.

"Do me," Alec said.

Christian choked on his own saliva and coughed. "Excuse me?" Visions of he and Alec sprawled nude on the bed, touching and tasting and fucking one another senseless filled his mind.

But Alec didn't seem to pick up his own erotic word choice. "Teleport me."

"Oh." The knot was back in Christian's gut, this time disappointment. He'd known Alec hadn't really meant it the way he'd heard it, but this was so far from what he wanted that it was jarring to be thrust back into reality. "I can't."

Alec's eyebrows rose and those damned tight lines were back around his mouth. "Can't? Because it's not for real and the tricks only work if you're the one doing them?"

Christian sighed and rubbed his eyes. "How long are we going to go through this, Alec? How long are you going to ask me to sit here doing magic for you like I'm your trick dog?"

He swore softly under his breath, rose, and paced to the window.

"I can't teleport you because, as I told you, magic has limitations. Every mage can learn to teleport herself or himself, and we can take inanimate objects with us. Like your basketball. We can teleport with one another. But one thing we can't do is teleport another human who's not magic. I told you, magic is hard work, it can be a huge drain, and teleporting is one of the biggest. The energy required to teleport oneself and another human who's not magic, or even an adult human who is magic but doesn't know how to use it and therefore can't help, would be so much that both the passenger and the mage channeling the energy could be killed."

He swung around to face Alec. "Mages are human, just like anyone else. We can die, just like anyone else. And if we overload our systems, push them past the breaking point…"

Christian sighed again, feeling the strain of the night tell on him. "Look, there are some things you need to know, so I suggest you listen to what I have to say. Whether you like it or not, or believe it or not, I'm going to tell you what I know about the murders that have been happening here. Then you can do what you'd like with the information. But for your own safety, you need to know this. And you also need to know some things that I suspect about you."

"What the hell's that supposed to mean?"

"Murders first. The organization I work for believes a dark mage named Rogan is responsible for the murders. He's a powerful force and has been underground for many years. We have evidence he's active again. But for you to understand, I have to start farther back in time."

Christian paced between the bed and window as he spoke. "Years ago there was an amulet that, the legends say, had the ability to enhance the powers of the mage who possessed it. The amulet itself was created thousands of years ago and its origins are unknown. Whoever possessed it was said to have power beyond imagination. The amulet itself was neutral—neither good nor bad—which meant it could be utilized either way. It was used many times throughout history to help maintain peace. But eventually it got into the hands of a greedy and power-hungry mage king who tried to use it to conquer all the lands around him. Thousands of people—mages and Ordinaries—died horrible deaths.

"The Magic Council, which has been in existence in one form or another almost since humans have lived on Earth, decided the amulet was too dangerous and it needed to be brought in and hidden. To make a long story shorter, it took hundreds of years before the amulet was finally attained by the Council—it was hidden and resurfaced dozens of times by others hungry for power before the Council was able to claim it. Once they had the amulet, however, they had to find a way to keep it safe and out of dark mage hands. So it was given to a friend of one of the Council members, a man known to be true and honorable."

"Why not one of the Council members? Wouldn't that have been better protection?" Alec asked.

Christian was startled by Alec's interest. Was it possible something of what he'd said and done tonight was sinking in? He tried not to get his hopes up. "It was decided the risk was too great for a Council member to watch over it because the temptation might always be there to use the amulet. And they didn't want it used for any purpose. Its power was so great that even if someone intended to use it for good, power itself can easily corrupt.

"So the amulet stayed hidden, passed on from generation to generation to other members of the original man's family until, after a thousand years, many of its secrets were lost, including how to make it work. The family who protected it, the Ansley family, began to develop incredible magic powers themselves over the years, probably simply from being around the amulet, and it was believed they alone had the ability to activate the amulet. But they stayed true to their task and guarded it with their lives. And there were many attempts on their lives over the years as dark mages sought the amulet. In the end, though, no matter how many Ansleys were killed protecting it, there was always at least one family member left to guard its location."

"Which"—he sighed—"brings us back to Rogan. Thirty years ago a dark mage named Rogan began to build power. He was the protégé of one of the Council members and, when he was young, it was thought he'd eventually have a place on the Council himself. But his hunger for power surpassed even his need to be on the Council, and he turned to dark magic."

He leaned against the dresser and crossed his arms over his chest as he looked thoughtfully at Alec. "Magic, you see, is kind of like the amulet—it's neutral energy that can be used for anything. Most mages use it with good intentions. But it can be used to harm, and just like in the Ordinary world, where a person can go bad and turn to stealing, extortion, rape or murder, so can a mage. They manipulate the energy to do harm. We say it's 'dark magic,' but in truth, it's the intention that's bad, not the magic itself."

Alec still seemed to be with him, although Christian could sense him fighting against his interest.

"Rogan pulled away from the Council and came up with his own agenda for how the magic world should be run. But to make his plan work, he decided he needed the amulet, and the only thing that stood between him and the amulet was the Ansley family. At that time, there were five Ansley brothers. Rogan went through them one by one, and when he didn't get what he wanted, he killed them as a threat to the remaining family members. Until only the youngest remained—Jason Ansley. He made his last stand against Rogan, or so we believe. In the end Jason, his wife, and their baby were killed. Most believe Rogan was responsible, but it was hard to prove. With Jason's death, the amulet appeared to be lost. There was no one left who knew its location, and though Rogan continued to wield what power he had for many years after that, he never could have what he ultimately desired. After a horrific massacre at a mage gathering thirteen years ago, Rogan went underground. Until now."

Christian's paced again. "A month ago we started getting reports of him, and then two weeks ago, the murders here began." He stopped and looked at Alec. "One of the things I've found while I've been here is that all of the victims were mages."

"Oh, for crap sake," Alec said, shaking his head. But Christian noticed he was still listening intently to everything he said.

"We feel certain Rogan's behind it, and it's highly likely he thinks someone here in this area knows something about the amulet. That's why I wondered about several of the victims having a connection with England. This is speculation mind you, but it's possible he thinks they might have met with someone—Jason Ansley perhaps—and Ansley told them something about the location or even passed the amulet off to one of them. We think he's using the guiller's ability to read minds to search for the information."

"I thought you said only a member of the Ansley family knew how to activate the amulet, though. If they're all dead, what's this Rogan guy think he's going to do with it?"

"A good question. Around the same time Rogan surfaced, and shortly before the murders here started, a series of new archaeological digs began in Egypt. All were funded anonymously. Each of these locations has the potential to be the resting place for a set of scrolls rumored to contain the texts of something called the Vargazian ritual."

"Which is?"

"It's a ritual that would allow the amulet to be activated." He spared the details of how the ritual itself involved human sacrifices and other horrible deeds. "We believe Rogan is behind the Egyptian excavations. We think he's looking for the scrolls. If he can lay his hands on the amulet and the scrolls that contain the text of the Vargazian ritual, he can, potentially, activate the amulet. And if that happens, I can guarantee you a lot of people are going to die. And they're not all going to be mages. Ordinaries—humans who can't do magic—will, too, because Rogan doesn't give a sodding crap how many lives he takes or who gets in his way."

"So you came here because you wanted to get more information about these people, the victims?"

"That's right. Ideally, we want to find Rogan, capture him, and make him pay for his crimes over the years. But we also need to find that amulet before he does. And right now…" Christian huffed out a frustrated breath and rubbed his neck. "Right now, we don't have a bloody clue where the amulet is, or if it even still exists. The guillers have killed the victims so we have no idea if Rogan's gotten any information from them. And we haven't found a connection among all the victims yet so we don't even know how to predict who he might go after next."

It was silent in the room for several seconds.

Then Alec finally spoke. "So, pretending for a moment that everything you're telling me is true, and I'm not even remotely saying I believe you because, let's face it, this is the real world and this whole story you've spun for me is straight from some epic fantasy novel"— his voice was low and tight—"but, in this fantasy of yours, where do I fit into the picture? I'm clearly not one of your magic people with special powers. I seriously doubt that thing showed up to attack me. It was probably there for you and I just got in the way. So why am I here listening to this fairy tale? What do you need me for and why are you trying to so hard to convince me to buy into this crazy talk of yours?

Am I just some stupid regular human you figured you could sweet talk and fuck in order to get information about the case?"

Christian's gut twisted. He really had ruined any chance he'd ever be able to have a relationship with Alec. The man hated him now.

"After what happened between us earlier tonight, the way we both felt, I can't believe you'd even ask that," Christian said softly, trying to keep the hurt out of his voice, but not being entirely successful.

Alec swallowed hard and wouldn't meet his gaze.

"As for you not being a magic person...I think that might not be exactly true. I think you do have magic abilities."

Alec did look at him now, and his eyes were filled with pain. "How far are you going to take this, Christian? Okay, you used me. And you concocted this elaborate story. But now you're trying to turn *me* into one of your fantasy characters. Is the real me not good enough for you?"

Christian sank onto the edge of the bed, numb with shock at the other man's words. "My God," he whispered. "How could you even think that?"

"You tell me."

"Alec, what I feel for you doesn't hinge on whether or not you have special abilities or the fact you're in charge of the murder investigation. I fell for you because you're a good man. Because you care about people and it shows in everything you do. Because you're intelligent and strong. And because you touched me in here." He placed a hand over his heart.

Alec rubbed his temple and grimaced. He closed his eyes briefly, but when they opened they were still filled with turmoil. "Then why do you feel the need to make me into something more than I am?"

"I'm not making you into anything. You have gifts that were yours before I ever met you."

When Alec tried to interrupt, Christian rushed on. "Like your ability to heal. What you did for Frank Sandell in the hospital—that's special, Alec. You might try to blow it off as being nothing and you might not want to talk about it and pretend it doesn't happen, but you know good and well it's an ability most people don't have. And what about the dreams? We both had similar, maybe even the same dreams all week. That's not ordinary either. Those happened for a reason, and there's a reason they were real enough that when we did finally get together we knew things about each other we shouldn't have known. It's magic. It can't be anything else."

Alec was shaking his head.

"Then tonight, when the guiller attacked you, you called me. With your mind. I heard you in my mind. That's how I knew you were being hurt and why I teleported to you. Only a powerful mage could do something like that. It's not a common gift."

"I'm not going to listen to any more of this."

"You have to listen. And you know it's true. You may not understand how you have these abilities, hell I don't understand it because I can't see a magic aura on you and I should be able to. But you know deep in your heart I'm telling the truth."

Alec ran both his hands through his hair. His face was tortured. "I can't trust anything you've told me, don't you understand that? You throw me down the rabbit hole and then you expect me to just open my arms and accept you and all the crap you feed me? It doesn't work like that. Since I've know you, have you told me anything that's true? All the things you said about your girlfriend and your dad dying and your mom being an author...are those all lies, too? People you've created to help convince me to believe in you?"

"Alec..." Christian could barely speak for wrenching pain in his chest. "I haven't lied to you about anything. My dad did die two years ago from cancer. And my mother is real. Look her up at any bookstore—Maura Wetherly."

Alec stood and Christian did as well, knowing the end was near.

"This isn't the way I thought this night would end." Alec looked at him with those turbulent golden-brown eyes Christian knew he'd have dreams about the rest of his life.

"Me either," he said softly, trying not to let the ache in his heart drop him to his knees.

Alec's gaze, sad and accusing, sliced into him, cutting him to the bone. "I thought I cared about you. I trusted you." He shook his head. "I was a damn fool."

He swung around and was through the door before Christian could stop him.

"Alec! Please, you could still be in danger."

But the man was already down the metal stairs and climbing into his Jeep.

Christian put up a hand to stop him using magic, but then let it drop back to his side. No matter how great his concern for Alec or how badly his chest ached, he couldn't force Alec to stay. It went against everything in him.

He'd told the truth. And Alec had refused to listen. There was nothing else to be done.

He'd gambled…and lost.

CHAPTER 8

Sick at heart, Christian wandered back into the hotel room. Its sterile coolness seeped into him, exacerbating the loneliness left behind in Alec's turbulent departure. He hadn't felt this alone since the night he'd sat by his father's bed and held his hand as he died. His mother had been there, too, sitting on the other side. Yet the loneliness that had settled over him, the finality of it all, of knowing his dad, his mentor, would never be in his life again, had left him desolate.

But this was different and yet even more painful. He felt Alec's loss at his very core. As if a part of him had been ripped out, leaving a void that could never be filled again. Tears burned behind his eyelids. He swiped at his eyes with the back of his hand to keep them from falling. But stopping them didn't stop the pain.

A rush of sound suddenly filled his ears and the hair on his arms and the back of his neck prickled. He swung around, hand raised, and the familiar, shimmering field of white light surrounded him.

But the figure that appeared in the room wasn't the guiller as he'd feared.

"Damn it, Bella! You scared the bloody hell out of me." He lowered his hand and the shield. "What are you doing here?"

"I was worried about you. You turned off your phone and after that last call, when you said the guiller had attacked the American, I was afraid something had happened to you."

Christian sank onto the chair so recently vacated by Alec and dropped his head into his hands, swiping at his eyes again and fighting to pull himself together so Bella wouldn't see his misery.

But he could tell from her voice it was too late.

"Christian?" Bella knelt in front of him and put her hands on his knees. "What happened? Talk to me."

He sighed. "I told him."

"Who?"

"Alec. I told him everything. About us. About magic. About the guiller and Rogan."

"Oh." The word was little more than a surprised breath of air. "Why?"

"Because he saw the guiller. Saw me materialize in the room and use magic to scare it off."

"But you didn't have to tell him. You could have—"

"No. I couldn't." He looked up to gaze into Bella's dark eyes. "I couldn't manipulate his memories that way and create even more lies."

He could see that Bella wanted to ask why not, but she kept the question to herself. Instead, she asked, "And, um, how did he take it?"

"It didn't go well." Christian dropped his head back into his hands, sick at heart and worried as hell where Alec was going and whether or not he'd be safe.

Bella picked up part of the broken lamp that lay on the floor. "I can see that. Did he get angry?"

"No. I mean, yes, but he didn't do that to the lamp. Not the way you think. It was a magic demonstration."

She laid the lamp part aside. "Christian, what happened with the guiller? How did it attack? And where?"

"We were at Alec's house—reading through some of the background files on the victims," he added hastily, uncomfortable about having Bella suspect what was really going on right before the guiller showed up. "Alec had gone to his bedroom. He'd only been gone a short while, not even a minute, and he called me. He was in pain. I didn't think. I just reacted. I materialized in the bedroom to find the guiller holding Alec with his long claw or fingernail or whatever the hell you want to call it jabbed deep into Alec's temple."

Bella gasped. "It was trying to read his mind. That's how they do it?"

"Apparently so. I zapped it, but it didn't even faze the thing. The energy just bounced off its back, didn't make a scratch. It dropped Alec but turned to me. I zapped it again, harder—in fact, with as much energy as I could pull in. I still didn't kill it. I think I just scared it off.

It morphed into a blue ball of light and disappeared."

"And this Alec? He survived?"

"Yes. I think I got there before it could do any real damage. At least I hope so. He had a terrible headache afterward, but wouldn't go to the hospital or let me get help."

"I did some looking after you called and there are only a handful of known cases where people have survived a guiller attack. They're usually so fast, in and out, that no one has time to react or stop them. But in the cases where people did survive, there were a variety of results. I suspect it depends on how long the guiller was tapped in…" She made a face and shuddered. "A fingernail embedded in the temple? Good God."

"Yeah, didn't leave a mark, though."

"Well, it wouldn't, would it? A guiller's able to bend time, shift through dimensions, do magic in its own way."

"Anyway…the survivors, Bell?"

"Oh, right. It probably depends how long the guiller's been probing into the person's mind. In one case the survivor was fine afterward, suffering headaches for a few days, but otherwise normal. In a couple of cases, the people were left with headaches and poor short term memory recall. They might remember what happened to them twenty years ago, but not what they ate for breakfast that morning or what their friend said to them five minutes before. There were a handful who began having hallucinations and delusions, talking to themselves, and had to be institutionalized because they couldn't get along in society. And then…" She winced.

"And then?" Christian probed, not liking what he was hearing.

"And then were some who went completely mad, tried to kill themselves or others. Most of them succeeded in doing themselves in. Probably because the damage the guillers did was extensive enough they just wanted to end their lives to escape the hell they were left in."

"Oh, fuck." Visions of Alec going mad until he took his own life tore through Christian's mind. He tried to comfort himself with the fact Alec had seemed okay except for a headache, but the thoughts were persistent.

"I'm sure that's not going to happen to Alec," Bella said, squeezing his legs. "I'm sure he'll be fine. Do you know where he is now?"

Christian shook his head, remembering the last words Alec had said to him in that sorrowful, betrayed voice. *I thought I cared about you. I trusted you. I was a damned fool.* "He was overwhelmed by everything

I told him. I couldn't make him stay."

He knew what Bella was thinking, that yes, he could have. But again, that would have involved using magic on Alec against his will, and Christian refused to do that.

"I'm worried the guiller might try again and Alec will be unprotected. He won't have the means to stop it, and next time it'll kill him."

"Okay, a tough question for you here. Why would the guiller have attacked an Ordinary police detective, Christian? You said you'd confirmed all the victims were magic folk. Is it possible the guiller came looking for you and just happened upon Alec first?"

"Of course it's possible. That's one of the first things I thought of, and do you think I don't feel guilty as hell if that's the case? But…there's something you should know, Bella. Alec may not be completely Ordinary."

"What do you mean?"

"There's this thing Alec can do. I watched him do it. He has the ability to use his hands for healing. At the hospital he used it on a witness we were interviewing—an older man who'd watched a guiller kill his wife. They put him in the psych ward when he started talking about floating balls of light and a 'creature.' He was strapped to the bed and they had him drugged." He grimaced as he remembered the scene. "When we were talking to him, he went a little mad, got agitated, ripped an arm free from the restraints, tried to hit Alec, started yelling about how no one would believe him and they were all sons of bitches."

Bella moved up to sit on the bed, but he could tell she was listening intently.

"I suggested we call a nurse, but Alec said no. Then he went into almost a meditative state, placed his hands on the man's chest, and within moments, the man had calmed down. I know that doesn't sound like a big deal. I wouldn't think so either if I heard someone tell about it. But I was there. And the energy that flowed from Alec was unmistakably powerful. I could feel it swirling around me, inside me." He remembered how it had aroused him, brought all his senses to life. "I swear to God it was magic. Except…"

"Except?"

"Except he didn't then, and never has, shown a magic aura."

Bella's eyebrows shot up to disappear under her thick black bangs. "If he's magic, if he did magic, he'd have an aura, Chris."

"Yeah, I know. Technically, you're right. But I'm telling you that he didn't. Yet, the energy he gave off, that he used to calm this man, couldn't be anything but magic. I'm talking the man was all the way calm, like he was completely normal, completely clear-minded in spite of the drugs the hospital had dosed him with."

"This is what you were referring to when you asked me if a spell could dampen magic powers?"

"Yes. I thought maybe there might be something weird here that was keeping me from seeing Alec's magic aura."

"But the guiller activity wouldn't cause that."

"So you said."

"Maybe it's not magic then. There are a few Ordinaries from time to time who exhibit magic-like abilities, who are able to channel the energy like we can, except to a lesser extent, and only for brief moments."

"I know. But it's more than that with Alec. And after tonight, I know it."

"What do you mean?"

"Remember when I said Alec called me when the guiller attacked?"
Bella nodded.

"I didn't mean he called out to me with his voice. He called me…in my mind."

Bella's red-lipsticked mouth opened and her eyebrows went up again. "How?"

"I don't know. I just…felt him. It was clear as crystal. I knew right away who it was, knew he was in trouble. I felt his pain." He closed his eyes briefly as the memory washed over him. "He called me. There was no doubt about it. And thank God he did, or else I wouldn't have gotten there in time to save him."

"Christian…" Her mouth closed. Opened again, then closed once more.

"I know. Only a handful of mages have the ability to communicate like that."

"It's powerful stuff," Bella added, still looking more than a little shocked.

"There are also the dreams."

"Your dreams? The ones you have sometimes?"

"Not exactly, although…" He frowned, wondering.

"Although?"

"Alec and I…have had similar dreams this week."

"What kind of dreams? More of the Mensi stuff?"

"No." And no way in bloody hell was he telling her any details about the erotic experiences they'd shared in the dreams and then in person. "No Mensi. But they were, maybe, somewhat prophetic. You're always saying my other dreams are."

"These were prophetic in what way?"

"Things that each of us dreamed about came true or turned out to be real. I mean accurate to the smallest detail." He thought again of how he had known the taste of Alec's cum before he'd ever had it, and of how he remembered every detail of the small silver medallion he wore, even though Alec always kept it tucked inside his shirts and he'd never actually seen it in person until tonight.

"We both had similar dreams. There's a connection, Bella. And I think it's got something to do with his magic ability. But the thing is, I don't think Alec's aware of it. I don't think he even realized he called out to me. When I tried to talk to him about his powers tonight, he denied it and accused me of making it all up. He acknowledges he can do the healing thing, says it's something his grandmother used to do on him when he was scared or sick when he was little, but he blows it off as just some parlor trick. I think down deep inside he knows better, but he won't admit it."

"Tell me about this grandmother."

"His parents died when he was very young and he lived with his grandmother. But she died when he was ten and he was raised in foster homes after that. So even if she was magic, she apparently didn't tell him about it."

"Why would she have kept something like that secret? If she was a mage, she had to have known there was a possibility he would develop magic abilities also and that when they surfaced he'd have to learn to deal with them."

"I don't know. I have no idea why a parent or grandparent would do such a thing. Hell, for all we know, she did tell Alec when he was young and he just refused to accept it."

"Would you…" She frowned and bit her lip as she studied him.

"What?"

"You seem to have grown close to Alec this past week."

Christian felt heat creep up his cheeks. He stood quickly and walked over to the window to look out, hoping Bella hadn't noticed. Damn, he hated this. Hated hiding his feelings about Alec. But the old fear of his friends discovering his true desires almost paralyzed him.

"We've become friends," he said, still not facing Bella.

"I can see that."

He heard her rise and walk over to him. Felt her gentle hand on his back.

"I'm glad you two are…friends. And since you are, before I start digging around, I want to know if it would be okay with you for me to do some checking up on Alec? If I researched his family and tried to find a connection to magic somewhere?"

He nodded. "Of course. I don't know much to help you get started, though." He turned back to face her. "His name's Alec Anderson. I already told you all I know about his parents and grandmother." A worried, frustrated huff escaped him. "I don't even know for sure how old he is. I think about our age. Early thirties. And I do know he's lived in this area at least since he was a teenager."

"Okay, I'll see what I can find."

Bella patted him on the cheek and for a moment, from the sympathetic look in her eyes, he wondered if she knew.

God, this would be so much easier if he could just tell her, blurt out his worries, not just about the guiller and Alec's magic abilities, but about how he was afraid he'd scared off the only man he'd ever fallen in love with.

*   *   *

"Can I help you find something, dear?" The short, middle-aged, curly-headed woman smiled at Alec and the long strands of colorful beads she wore around her neck clicked and clattered together as she reached out automatically to push a book back onto the shelf nearby. But her owl-eyes behind thick glasses were focused only on him.

"I'm looking for the astrology books."

"Ah, certainly, follow me."

She led him off through the maze of shelves in the bookstore, toward a back corner filled with squashy, comfortable-looking chairs grouped around a low, central table. "Any author in particular you're interested in?"

"Maura Wetherly?" He hoped the woman wouldn't laugh at him and tell him no such person existed. If he'd been near a computer he would have Googled the name, but he'd decided not to risk going home in case the killer came back, so he'd gone to a hotel when he left Christian last night. A hotel far away from the Englishman's.

His still-aching head throbbed and was followed by a sharp pain centered in his gut at the memory of the look on Christian's face when he'd left him, at the defeated, resigned slump of his shoulders. His stomach felt like it was turned inside out every time he thought of Christian. Which he did constantly.

The sales clerk was bobbing her head in eager excitement. "Oh, yes, Maura Wetherly!"

She led him to a floor-to-ceiling shelving unit and showed him an entire row of books with the name Wetherly on the spines. Several were face-out on the shelf, large paperbacks showing moons and stars and planets on the covers.

"Maura's one of the best on the subject. Have you read any of hers before?"

Alec shook his head.

"Well, then, you'll want to start here." She pulled a royal blue book off the shelf and handed it to him. "Oh, and here." A purple book followed. "Oh, and you have to read this one as well! She gives her interpretations of sun signs and how they relate to romance in it!" A hot pink book joined the stack.

"You've, um, read all these?"

The woman looked at him aghast. "Of course! Anyone interested in astrology has read Maura. She's a goddess." Her large eyes flitted back to the shelf and she practically squealed. "Oh, my goodness! And I almost forgot this one, though I don't know how I could have. This is a must read! In fact, read it first. It's probably her best, most comprehensive book on the subject." She piled a three-inch-thick red volume on top of the others he held.

Shit. Yeah, clearly it covered everything that could possibly be known on the subject with that many pages.

"May I ring all these up for you, dear?"

"Um, no, not just yet. I'd kind of like to browse a little first."

"All righty. Fair enough. But you give me a holler if you need me!"

"Thanks." He really just wanted her to go away so he could open the books and see if he could find anything personal about Maura Wetherly.

The clerk took two steps away, but then turned back. "Are you aware Maura's speaking in Chicago this weekend?"

That captured Alec's interest. "She is?"

"Yes. There's a small new-age bookstore in downtown Chicago called Moonlight Fantasy. They're small, but they have a wonderful PR person who puts together workshops and lectures. Maura's there today and tomorrow in the little theater connected to the shop. I'd hope to attend, but"—her face fell—"I have to work."

"What time is she speaking?"

"Let me just trot up to the register and write down the information for you!"

"That would be great. Thanks."

Chicago. He didn't know why he'd bothered to ask. Chicago was a two hour drive away. Just far enough to make him sick as hell, thanks to his affliction. An hour drive at regular highway speeds was pushing it for him—he'd be sick as a dog, but he could do it if he had to. Two hours, however... He shuddered at the thought.

He hadn't even had a chance to open one of the books before the clerk was back, waving a piece of purple note paper. "Here you are! She spoke at six on Saturday—that's this evening. I'm sorry, dear, but you've already missed that one. She's on again at two o'clock tomorrow afternoon, though. Oh, she's such a lovely, lovely person," the woman gushed. "I got to meet her last year when she did a weekend class. Oh, you'll just love her!"

"Um, thanks." His head hurt already and between the woman's chattering and the canned Christmas music playing in the background, he was wearing down fast. "I, um, I'm just going to look around now."

"Of course. Of course!"

He watched her toddle away, and his head pounded with each clink and rattle of her beads.

A wave of dizziness washed over him. He made his way to one of the well-cushioned chairs, grateful no one else occupied the seating group at the moment, and dropped into it. He closed his eyes, trying to calm the pounding in his temple. When it had eased off to a dull thud, he sorted through the books the woman had handed him. Choosing one, he turned to look at the back cover and found what he'd been hoping for. There was no picture, but definitely a bio...

Maura Wetherly is the best-selling author of Astrology for a Woman's Soul; A Layman's Guide to Astrology; Love, Sex, and How Your Chart Can Help You Become a Better Lover; Charting Your Career; and Transform the Quality of Your Life Using the Stars. *She's written the monthly horoscope for numerous major publications and has more than thirty years experience recording weekly and extended forecasts for notable political and influential figures. She lives in*

London with her husband and six cats. When not charting the stars, she's frequently found in her herb garden or teaching.

Her husband.

Alec quickly flipped to the front of the book to find the copyright date.

It was three years earlier. When, if Christian had been telling the truth, his dad would still have been alive. He quickly looked at the dates and bios on the other books. Two had the same bio and older copyright dates. The last book, however, didn't mention a husband in the bio. The copyright date: earlier this year.

Alec wanted to ignore his relief that the bios and dates seemed to back up what Christian had told him, but couldn't. He sighed and rested his head against the comfortable chair, closing his eyes again.

Damn it. Why did he so badly want to believe in the man? Everything Christian had told him was a load of BS. No sane person could possibly believe in all that stuff about magic and dark mages who wanted to take over the world and teleporting and protective shields.

You saw the proof.

No. He didn't know what he'd seen. Whoever had attacked him last night had given him a hell of a knock on the head, so he couldn't trust anything after that. He'd hallucinated the creature—probably based on Frank Sandell's tale in the hospital. And Christian showing up? Alec figured he'd probably called out for help. With his voice. And Christian had run in when Alec hadn't seen.

And the thing with his hands? The white bolts of energy that came from them?

That had probably been when Alec slipped into unconsciousness. He'd been dreaming that part.

The white-light sphere in the hotel room? Breaking the lamp on it? Did you dream that, too? And what about the teleporting?

"Jesus, stop! Just stop!" he muttered to himself, opening his eyes. "It was all a trauma-induced dream. Nothing more."

But his hand, of its own volition, slid into his jacket pocket and pulled out the DayGlo orange foam basketball Christian had given him last night. His thumb slid into the familiar gouge where the foam was missing—a casualty of a screw sticking out of the leg on his desk and the ball getting caught on it a year ago.

As he studied the ball, a conversation he'd once had with Drew

103

came back to him.

"Why do you always think you have to have proof something exists before you can believe in it?" Drew had asked when they'd gotten into a hot and heavy debate about religion one Sunday afternoon as they were folding laundry.

Drew had been raised a Catholic, and although he'd quit attending mass when he was a young adult, he still believed in what he'd been taught. Alec on the other hand hadn't been raised in any religious tradition and he'd never really understood Drew's blind faith.

"Because if something's real, then you should be able to touch it, see it, smell it, taste it."

"What about love?" Drew asked, his hazel eyes sparkling with mischief.

"What about it?"

"It's not really a tangible thing, so do you believe in it?"

"That's different."

"How?"

"Love is...I don't know. You *can* feel it—I feel it every time we touch. I see it in your eyes. I taste it and smell it, too."

"Those things you're touching and seeing and smelling aren't love. Those things are me. Love is nebulous—you can't touch it or prove it. You just have to believe in it. It comes from your heart, your gut, your mind. So how do you explain its existence, Mr. Logical?"

Alec glared at him, but there wasn't much heat behind it. Sometimes Drew just liked to provoke him. Still, the question made him think. "Love is someone giving up their life to save someone else's."

"Not always. Some people do that for complete strangers they've never met before."

"But they might do it because they love and cherish life in general."

"Then why risk their own?"

"Now you're just being difficult."

"Okay, let's pick something else. Let's pick...the universe. You know it exists, right? But you've never been off this planet, never touched it, smelled it, tasted it."

"I've seen it. Telescopes, remember?"

Drew flashed him a smile. "Yeah, there are pictures. But still...how can we trust the pictures from the telescopes? How can we even trust that when we lay out on the hammock in the backyard at night and look up at the stars that what we're really seeing are stars? How do we know we're not in the *Matrix*?"

"Oh, for crap sake!" Alec threw a balled-up pair of socks at him. "You watch too many movies."

Grinning, Drew deflected the socks with one of his big hands. But then he sobered. A rare occurrence for him.

"All I'm saying is that sometimes you just have to have a little faith. There are things in life, precious things, that you won't ever experience if you don't. You do that thing with your hands when you think I'm not looking—I've seen you do it on hurt animals, people at crime scenes who are so distraught they can barely function, and I've even felt you doing it on me when I've injured myself, when you think I'm asleep. You can't explain it, yet it works, and still you deny you're doing anything special. That's your problem, Alec. You're in denial. That's why it's so hard for you to accept there might be things in the universe that are unexplainable yet still completely real."

Back in the here and now, Alec studied the orange basketball with a lump in his throat. Christian had done his damnedest to give him proof, something tangible. Wasn't he holding it in his hand right now? And yet, even now, just like when he saw the clear results of the "thing he did with his hands" he still couldn't accept it was real.

Had Drew been right? Was there something wrong with him? Was he going to go through life missing out on precious things because he couldn't have an open mind and always needed proof?

Or maybe that was beside the point. Maybe this wasn't about proof. Maybe it was about what Drew had said…him learning to have a little faith.

Still, a lifetime of needing cut-and-dried facts and answers was hard to shake.

He picked up the piece of purple paper the clerk had given him and stared at the small, neat, curvy writing.

How badly did he want answers? How important was it to him to get the facts and tangibles he so desired?

Or maybe you should be asking yourself why believing in Christian is so important to you?

Damn. Why was it so important to him?

He rested his head against the chair cushions and let his thoughts drift.

Blue eyes alight with warmth and emotion filled his vision, and he could almost feel the gentle stroke of Christian's hands on his skin, kneading the muscles in his shoulders, his back, and moving lower, fingers teasing against the crease in his ass, stirring a longing in Alec so powerful he could barely breathe.

"Feel good, love?" One hand moved around to stroke Alec's shaft and pull him in close until his ass nestled against Christian's groin and his back pressed to Christian's warm, solid chest.

Alec rested his head on his lover's shoulder, enjoying the way Christian's hand moved over his cock with a confident knowledge of just how it felt best.

"Always. I don't think I'll ever be able to get enough of your touch, Chris. I crave it, crave you all the time. I've never needed anyone else like I need you."

"I need you, too. We belong together, Alec. This was meant to be." The words were soft puffs of breath against his ear.

"I know. I've always known. I'm so in love with you…"

Alec's head jerked up from the back of the chair and his eyes flew open. His breath came out in ragged surges and he looked down to discover the stiff line of his very erect cock pressing against the seam of his jeans.

Blinking, he glanced hastily around to see if anyone had noticed him, but he was still alone in his corner of the store.

Alone, but also lonely as hell.

I'm so in love with you…

"Oh, shit."

*   *   *

Alec sank into the empty back row of the small theater a few minutes before the talk was to begin. And he used those minutes to gather himself.

The trip up here had been hell, as predicted. He'd even tried breaking it up into parts. He'd left last night, straight from the bookstore, and driven until he could no longer stand the throb in his head and the wracking nausea in his stomach. He'd stopped, gotten a room, and slept for several hours.

By the time he woke up this morning, he'd hoped to have slept off the worst of it and be ready to drive again. He'd even managed to choke down some breakfast without it coming back up. But within minutes of being in his Jeep and returning to the highway, it had started again with a vengeance. That time he'd managed to go only twenty minutes before he had to stop. He'd parked in a truckstop parking lot and tried to doze, again hoping sleep would help. When it didn't, he'd popped a couple of motion sickness pills he bought inside and downed a bottle of Sprite. It had taken the edge off for a short while…until he'd been back on the road. By the time he'd gotten into downtown Chicago he was in bad shape. He'd had to stop twice to heave.

He'd asked himself several times over what the hell he was doing and why he was putting himself through this torture. If he just had it in him to trust, if he could just muster up some faith… But he wanted to know for sure. And this was the only place he knew to start.

He didn't have a picture of Christian and couldn't draw worth a damn. But maybe he could figure out a way to get chummy with Maura Wetherly after the talk and get *her* to show *him* a picture of her son. Or get her to tell him some more about him so he could really know for sure this was Christian's mother and really believe he'd told the truth about this. If he'd told the truth about her, then…

Then what? It might be easier to believe he told the truth about other things?

He could almost see Drew shaking his head in disgust at how Alec was completely missing the point. Alec didn't know why that made him feel so horribly guilty, but it did.

A flash of Christian's hurt, tortured expression the last time he saw him was the nail in the coffin.

"How far are you going to take this, Christian? Okay, you used me. And you concocted this elaborate story. But now you're trying to turn me into one of your fantasy characters. Is the real me not good enough for you?"

Christian sank onto the edge of the bed, and Alec could not only see the other man's shock, he felt it rippling off him.

"My God," Christian whispered, his eyes churning with hurt. "How could you even think that?"

"You tell me."

"Alec, what I feel for you doesn't hinge on whether or not you have special abilities or the fact you're in charge of the murder investigation. I fell for you because you're a good man. Because you care about people and it shows in everything you do. Because you're intelligent and strong. And because you touched me in here." He placed a hand over his heart.

The scene switched and Alec was once again in the dream he'd had at the bookstore last night.

"We belong together, Alec. It was meant to be."

"I know. I've always known. I'm so in love with you…"

"Oh, crap. What am I doing here?" Alec whispered, looking around the little theater and squeezing the foam basketball in his pocket. A wave of aching loneliness seared through him and the need to see Christian became an agonizing torment. "Oh, God, I've been such an ass."

He rose to leave, but at that exact moment, a tall, regal, older woman stepped onstage and smiled. Christian's smile.

And Alec was lost.

Without consciously realizing he was even doing it, he sank back into his seat. He couldn't take his eyes off the woman. Her long, gray-almost-white hair shone in the stage lighting, and her voice, with that now familiar soft British accent, was like a soothing balm on his stressed and stretched-thin senses.

She talked and he tried to follow, but the vast majority of what she said was lost on him since he wasn't even remotely familiar with anything astrological. Mostly he just listened to the sound of her voice and watched her graceful movements as she walked, smiled, chit-chatted with audience members, and laughed in response to things they said. For that hour, he almost forgot his pounding head and his still-churning stomach. Almost forgot how wretched he felt at the way he'd treated Christian Friday night. Maura Wetherly was like a soft spring breeze amidst the harsh winter chill. Even her clothes—soft colors and soft folds in her sweater and skirt—helped create that impression.

He could see where Christian got his gentleness, but he also saw hints of Christian's confidence as well.

The time was up and people began filing out of the theater almost before Alec realized it. They'd closed the rear doors and were having people exit through the front one, giving everyone reason to pass Maura Wetherly. Most of the attendees were taking advantage of it, stopping to thank her or shake her hand or talk for a moment. And she was generous and gracious with them all.

Finally, Alec rose from his seat, dreading the return of the nausea he knew would hit him as soon as he moved around and, sure enough, it did. Damn, he was a mess.

He was the last one in line to exit the theater, although he hadn't planned it that way. He pasted on a smile when it was his turn to pass Maura, but before he could even say a word, she took one look at him and pressed him back into a seat in the front row.

"You sit right there, love, and don't move. You look pale enough to scare even a ghost."

Alec looked up into blue eyes so startlingly like Christian's it almost hurt to see them. And the way the woman called him "love" in that soft voice was all too similar to the way Christian had called him the same thing in his dreams. He dragged in a deep breath and then another, trying to fight the surge of emotion that suddenly filled his chest.

Maura stepped back onto the low stage, but returned in seconds, holding a bottle of water. She removed the cap and put the bottle in his hand. "Small sips."

He did as she said, savoring the cool dampness in his mouth and throat.

"Better?" She sank into the seat next to him and pressed a cool, gentle palm against his cheek.

He nodded. "Thanks."

She smiled that hauntingly familiar smile again and held out a hand. "Maura Wetherly."

Alec grasped it and she squeezed it between both of hers.

"Alec Anderson."

"I hope it wasn't my talk that made you ill." Her eyes twinkled and again Alec was startled at how much like Christian's they were.

A smile escaped him in spite of how crappy he felt. "No, of course not. Not at all. I just…well, I get really car sick and the drive up here was tough."

"Hmmm." She studied him with that calm smile and thoughtful eyes. "You don't look like the type who usually attends my little talks, so I have to wonder what about me could have appealed to you enough to make you suffer like this to get here."

Alec felt heat creep up his cheeks in spite of the cold clamminess that covered the rest of him. His original purpose for coming here no longer mattered to him. He'd already made his decision before he ever saw her, so he didn't have a clue what to say to her now without looking like an idiot. And yet, sitting face to face with Christian's mother, he felt closer to Christian than he had since before the guiller attacked.

"I picked up some of your books at the bookstore and the saleswoman told me you were speaking here today."

"I see. Tell me, Alec Anderson…do you know anything at all about astrology?"

He looked at her for a moment, at the way her eyes crinkled in a smile that yearned to escape. He was so busted.

His own lips curved into a sheepish smile. "Not a thing."

She chuckled softly. "I thought not. So what took you to the bookstore to look for my books then if it wasn't a burning fascination in astrological charts?"

Confession time. "Your son told me about you. He said I could find your books in any bookstore, so…I went looking."

"Mmm. And you and my son are friends." It was a statement, not a question.

A lump lodged in Alec's throat. "I hope so," he whispered without thinking. But then remembering where he was and who he was with, he said aloud, "We've been working together. While he's…here in the States."

Her hand pressed to his cheek again and the gentle smile never wavered off her face. "Does Christian know you're in love with him?"

"What?" Alec blinked and shook his head. "I…" He remembered Christian's mother wasn't supposed to know Christian was gay.

Her eyes were twinkling again. "It's all right. He thinks I don't know, and I let him believe that. He'll tell me when he's ready. Though I suspect"—her gaze softened—"that if he feels the same way about you as you feel about him, he'll be telling me sooner rather than later."

Alec swallowed hard, the lump still clogging his throat. "How could you possibly…?"

"It's in your eyes when you speak about him. Along with great oceans of pain and sorrow." She laid a hand on top of his and squeezed. "Whatever it is, whatever you think has come between you, as long as you stay true in your heart with one another, everything will work out. There's no greater gift than love. And something tells me"—fine lines creased her forehead—"you two need each other more than you realize."

Alec stared at her, his heart thudding almost painfully in his chest. "Has Christian talked to you? How do you know so much?"

Her laughter was as soft and gentle as she was. "No, I haven't spoken to him since last week, before he left home. Let's just say I have my own gifts. Now…" She patted his hand. "Let's see what we can do to help you with this travel problem you have." She rose and stepped back onto the stage, this time rummaging through a large tapestry handbag. She pulled a brown bottle from it, then moved to the stage door. "Leslie?" she called.

When a thin young woman appeared, Maura said, "Leslie, be a love, would you, and bring us a couple of bottles of juice out of that cooler you showed me earlier?"

Alec wanted to tell her not to bother, that whatever she thought she could do wouldn't matter. Nothing worked. And he'd probably already overstayed his welcome as it was. He started to rise, but Maura caught him at it.

"Uh, uh, uh. You sit down."

Leslie reappeared, handed Maura two glass bottles of what looked like apple juice, and left.

Maura came to sit next to Alec again, who'd slid back into his seat because, in truth, it would have taken too much energy to argue with her.

She unscrewed the cap on one of the juices, the cap on the brown bottle, then dumped some of the golden powder from the bottle into the juice.

"I, like you, have difficulties traveling in vehicles as well," she said while she worked. "So I always carry some with me in case I need it. It's ginger powder mixed with a dash of a special herb I grow in my garden at home." With deft hands, she put the top back on the juice bottle and shook it, then handed it to him. "It won't cure the problem, I'm afraid." She gave him a sympathetic look. "But it can help make it a smidge easier to deal with. Drink. Slowly."

"Special herb?" The cop in him couldn't help but ask. He didn't feel any kind of internal cop sixth sense warning that he shouldn't drink the concoction, and, in fact, he twisted the top of the bottle off as he spoke. But he felt compelled to ask.

She studied him and he got the impression she was reading something about him. She held his gaze steady with hers. "Would it concern you or stop you from drinking it if I told you it had certain *magical* properties?"

A low buzz filled his head and sped through his veins at the word. He didn't know if it was a buzz of secret knowledge or excitement or what. But, he realized, with a start, it definitely wasn't concern.

"No," he said softly, keeping his eyes focused on hers. "It wouldn't concern me." And then in an ultimate act of faith, he tipped the bottle to his lips and drank.

Within seconds a tiny hint of warmth spread through him, chasing away the cold chill that had been with him since he'd begun feeling sick on the drive last night. His stomach still felt pretty awful, but after a minute or so, he had to admit he thought he might be able to stand up and walk out of here now without having to make an immediate detour to the bathroom to heave. And, oddly enough, the pounding in his head that had been a constant plague since the attack on Friday night eased up as well.

Maura rubbed his back. "Like I said, there's no real cure for the problem, but this can help a bit."

"I think it already is helping." He could hear the surprise in his voice.

"Mmm-hmm, it probably is. Take this and put it in your pocket." She held out the brown bottle with the powder. "And this." She handed him the other bottle of apple juice, which he tucked into his other jacket pocket. "Drink some more of the mixture in a couple of hours. About a teaspoon full of the powder added to the juice. It works best with juice. Do it every two hours while you're traveling. Once you're home, take it three times a day for as long as you need to until the symptoms pass. And try to get some sleep, love. It really helps."

Alec nodded and rose. He turned to her. "Thank you. For everything." A thought occurred to him and he tilted his head to the side, studying her. "How do you know my symptoms don't pass for several days like with the regular motion sickness? I never told you that."

"As I said to you earlier, I don't travel well in *vehicles* either."

He barely had time to ponder that comment and try to figure out what the hell she meant by it, before she squeezed his hands between hers and gave him a soft smile.

"You're a complicated man, Alec Anderson. But I think it's safe to say there's more to you than meets the eye."

She pressed her palm against his cheek again in a motherly fashion that almost made his eyes sting with emotion because it made him remember his grandmother.

"Give Christian a message for me, will you?"

"Of course." A tight band squeezed around his chest. If Christian hadn't already left town and if he could ever stand the thought of seeing Alec again.

"Tell him…" She smiled warmly. "Tell him that I approve."

The lump was back in Alec's throat, so full and tight he couldn't speak. He could only nod.

Maura kissed him on the cheek. "Be safe, Alec." Then her expression turned deadly serious for the first time since Alec had met her. "And promise me something?"

He nodded again, his heart pounding.

"You and Christian watch out for each other. I sense a storm is coming and you two will need each other more than you yet realize."

CHAPTER 9

Alec didn't show up at work Monday morning.

Christian was sick with fear.

It had been two, long, awful days Saturday and Sunday and although he'd wanted nothing more than to go find Alec, he hadn't, deciding the man needed time, *deserved* it after everything Christian had dumped on him Friday night.

Instead, he'd spent the weekend worried about and missing Alec like hell, and dealing with a double helping of bad news from England. Jamie had called while Bella was still with Christian Saturday morning to say that a set of scrolls had been unearthed at one of the archaeological sites, but within hours of the find, they'd been stolen. Clearly Rogan had found what he was looking for. So now the pressure was on even more to find the amulet before Rogan did.

Christian had been forced to return to England briefly on Saturday to deal with some things, but had returned Saturday night. Although the double round of teleportation—there and back again on the same day—had left him exhausted, he couldn't stand the thought of being away for any longer than necessary in case Alec tried to get in touch with him or needed him.

But now he wished with all his heart and soul that he'd gone looking for Alec sooner.

When Alec hadn't arrived at the police station by 8:00 A.M.—late for him, at least since Christian had been working with him—Christian went to his house. No Jeep Wrangler parked in front, and the house was empty and just as they'd left it Friday night. Empty beer bottles still littered the coffee table. The bed hadn't been slept in. The pillow he'd pulled to the floor to rest Alec's head on after the guiller attack still lay in the same spot. It didn't look like Alec had even been home. With one exception...the folders containing the victims' background information were missing.

Had Alec gone back to his house to get them after he'd left the hotel? But if so, then what? Had the guiller found him and killed him wherever he might have gone? Except there'd been no reports of another murder or a dead body. Christian had already checked through the records this morning at the police station when Alec first hadn't shown up.

He called the hospitals, but none of them had admitted a patient with Alec's description.

He contacted Bella and had her do a locator spell—something she was quite adept at—but it turned up nothing. She couldn't find him anywhere. It was like he'd dropped off the face of the Earth.

When Christian returned to the station, he went to Martin Shanahan. Alec had said the man was a good friend and like family to him, and right now, Christian needed someone to talk to.

"Captain, do you have a few minutes?" he asked, standing in the doorway of Shanahan's office.

"Sure, come on!" The gray-haired burly man smiled and waved him in from where he sat as his desk.

Christian entered and shut the door behind him.

"Sit. What can I do for you?"

He sank into the vinyl chair across the desk from the captain. "I'm worried about Alec."

The man's jovial expression was immediately replaced by one of concern. He leaned forward on his elbows propped on his desk and his dark eyes, behind wire-framed glasses, leveled a stare at Christian. "Why? What's happened? Is he okay?"

"I'm not sure. I hope he's okay. I haven't seen him since Friday night, and he hasn't shown up here this morning. I wondered if maybe he'd called in sick?"

"I haven't heard from him." Shanahan glanced at his watch and frowned. "It's eleven o'clock. That's not like him."

"Yeah, I know. I went to his house. He's not there either."

"Have you tried his cell phone?"

"Several times. There's no answer. It's turned off."

"Maybe he's off chasing after a lead on this murder case. He can get pretty intense sometimes when he's working a case. He has a tendency to stay focused on the job, sometimes to the extreme."

"Maybe."

Christian debated how much to share with Shanahan, but decided telling him the killer had gone after Alec on Friday night probably wasn't the best thing to do right now. Unless *he* was prepared to do some serious memory manipulation work and a lot editing and massaging of the story.

Damn. Where was Alec? He rubbed a hand against the ache in his chest.

"Is there something going on between the two of you?"

Startled, Christian looked up to find the other man's steady gaze on him. "I…I'm not sure what you mean."

Shanahan sighed and leaned his sizeable girth back in the squeaky chair. "I don't make any secret around here of the fact that I think of Alec as my own. I've known him since he was a wayward teenager and I care about him. He's been through his share of heartache in his lifetime. I don't know how much he's told you, but he lost his parents and his grandmother when he was young, was raised in foster homes, and then a year and a half ago, his partner was killed in a shooting. His male partner…who was also his lover."

Heartache ate at Christian. "He told me about all of that."

Shanahan's eyebrows rose. "Did he then? Well, that's good. It means he trusts you."

He leaned forward again, folding his hands on the desk in front of him. He studied Christian, then seemed to come to a decision about something. "I don't typically make a habit of sharing my cops' personal lives with others, but if there is something going on"—he gave Christian a pointed look—"there are some things I things I think you should know. However, what's said in this office stays in this office. Understood?"

"Of course."

"All right then. I don't think I have to tell you how tough it can be for a cop to be openly gay. Jokes, harassment, even threats…not just from the community but within the working environment as well. And even if your co-workers are decent sorts for the most part—and I like to think most of the folks in this building are—it's a sad shame, but there are always going to be a handful of people who can't or won't accept diversity of any kind. Alec's been on the force for going on nine years now and I think it's a pretty damned fine testament to his character that he's never hidden who he is. He's weathered some tough times because of it, too, let me tell you. When he and Drew, his partner, were together it was easier for them both, I think, because they had each other to lean on.

"When Drew was killed, I was worried how it would affect Alec. It was yet one more loss in a long line of losses in his life. He held up much better than I expected, though. He's a strong man. Stubborn. Sometimes to a fault. And he doesn't… What's the word I'm looking for here? He doesn't…bend easily, if you know what I mean?"

At Christian's nod, he continued. "I think losing his family young and being tossed around from foster home to foster home caused him to formulate rigid standards in his life. Because he couldn't count on people being there, he had to have something in his life that he could depend on. Facts instead of faith. Evidence instead of theory. Logic instead of emotion. Those standards are part of what make him a good cop. They also help him cope in a world that's not always been friendly to him. But at the same time they make life difficult for him because, at heart, he's an emotional man who wants to give, wants to trust, wants to love and be loved."

He shifted in his chair and studied Christian. "Now I'm sure you're wondering why I'm telling you all this, so let me set you straight. I watched the two of you together last week, saw the way you looked at each other when you thought the other wasn't noticing. But in spite of the way he was looking at you, I also saw him holding you at arm's length. Alec's the friendly type, easy to get along with for the most part, so I can't fathom him holding you off like that, unless being around you makes him feel things that he's afraid to feel. Big emotions." His gaze grew intense. "I think you know what I'm talking about."

The room seemed to close in around Christian, making it hard to breathe.

"And if that's the case," Shanahan continued, "and if he thought you felt big emotions in return, then it's possible right now he's putting distance between you two."

Christian's pulse raced. If he acknowledged Shanahan's observations it would be admitting, in public, for the first time ever that he had feelings for another man.

But then visions of Alec filled his head—Alec's eyes overflowing with emotion and longing, Alec moaning with desire as Christian brought him to climax, Alec lying pale and unconscious on the floor of his bedroom and Christian terrified he might die. And then the sad, drawn look on his face when he'd left the hotel on Friday night.

While this wasn't exactly the same as admitting his desires to his mother and friends, he realized if he ever wanted to move forward with his life and be happy, he was going to have to quit hiding in the sodding closet. And, damn it, Alec… The tight band around his chest that had been with him since Friday gave a particularly brutal squeeze. Alec was worth more than Christian's stupid fears. Worth more than anything.

He nodded at Shanahan, who nodded back.

"Give him time, Christian. You've shaken his world. I could see it in his eyes last week. Give him time to come to terms with that. And, I don't think I have to tell you this but I'm going to anyway…" His eyes narrowed. "Don't hurt him."

Christian swallowed hard. He'd shaken Alec's world in more ways than the captain could ever imagine and already had hurt him. It was hard medicine to swallow that, even with time, he might not ever earn back Alec's trust.

*   *   *

Christian sat in Alec's chair at his desk, staring at the computer screen, trying to track down more information on the guiller's victims. With the folders missing from Alec's house, and apologetic assurances from the young female sergeant who'd done the research for Alec in the first place that those were the only hard copies and she wouldn't be able to retrace the information until tomorrow due to a prior commitment, Christian had decided to do it himself.

While the Vargazian ritual could certainly be used for other things beside gaining power over the Amulet of Sulisa, Christian knew obtaining and activating the amulet was Rogan's only goal. He suspected Rogan had been looking for clues to its whereabouts for the past thirty years, but he must have come up with some pretty compelling information recently, something convincing enough to assure him he could, indeed, lay his hands on the amulet this time, for him to have gone in search of the Vargazian texts. And he'd sent the guiller after these mages here in the States for a reason. He either suspected one of them knew the amulet's location or that one of them might actually have it. And yet, what the hell was the connection between these U.S. mages? Why them specifically? Did Rogan suspect someone had had contact with Jason Ansley before he died? If so, who?

In a spur of the moment decision, he abandoned a search on the victims and took a different tack—with a bit of magic aid—and logged into Bella's files about the Ansley family. Specifically, Jason Ansley. Maybe he could make a list of people Ansley had had contact with for several weeks or months up to his death and cross reference that with the victims.

An hour later he tossed down the pen he'd been scribbling notes with. He'd been trying his damnedest, but the truth was, he couldn't concentrate because of his intense concern for Alec. Where was he? Was he okay? Could he be lying hurt somewhere and Christian wasn't out there looking for him?

He closed his eyes and fought back an almost crippling wave of guilt for letting Alec leave the hotel on Friday night and not going after him.

With a ragged sigh, he reached back and rubbed his aching neck. It was so stiff and knotted from stress he could barely turn his head from side to side. He rubbed harder and still found no relief.

Firm, cool hands brushed his out of the way and pressed against the base of his skull where the pain was the worst. An instant tingle stirred in him at the contact and heat rushed through his veins.

"Oh, God. Alec?" He tried to turn to see him, his heart pounding, but the hands held him in place in a surprisingly strong yet gentle grip.

"Shhh, be still. I'm sorry my hands are cold. They'll warm up in a few seconds."

Alec's voice sounded tired, a bit raspy as if he were coming down with a cold, but still the very best thing Christian had heard in days.

"Are you okay?"

"Christian, be quiet and let me concentrate."

The words were warm and spoken close to his ear, sending ripples of emotion and arousal through him.

He nodded and closed his eyes, giving himself up to the incredible flood of heat that began to spread out of Alec's palms and into his neck.

When he'd watched Alec work on Frank Sandell, he'd felt the healing energy swirl into and around him. But that had been him standing on the sidelines, catching just the overflow. This was something else all together. The energy flowed into his neck in what felt like surging, golden waves, then spread out into the rest of his body, skipping across his nerve endings one by one, each one shimmering brighter and more vibrantly than the last. And yet, at the same time, a slow, warm, underlying thrum gave him a sense of utter relaxation and peace. It was a strange and powerful dichotomy.

But what stirred him more than anything, what filled his heart so full it felt like it might explode in his chest, was knowing the man wielding the power was safe and standing behind him.

"There," Alec said, his voice soft. His hands gently kneaded Christian's neck, then one slid up to stroke his hair for a moment, sending a new tug of arousal and love through Christian. "How does that feel? Any better?"

Christian turned his head from side to side. "The pain's gone," he whispered in surprise. And, yet, he wasn't really surprised. "Thank you."

"You're welcome."

He swiveled the chair around and soaked up the sight of Alec, dressed in jeans, boots, and a red plaid flannel shirt buttoned over a white tee—different clothes than what he'd worn Friday night—and, of course, his ever-present gun in the shoulder holster. His light brown hair was rumpled, and he was way too pale, with dark circles under his eyes. Still, Christian almost couldn't breathe his relief was so intense to see the man standing there solid and alive.

"Hi," Alec said softly.

Christian stood. He looked into Alec's needy gaze and saw his own emotions mirrored there. Not giving a damn that they were in the middle of the public police station and the cubicle walls were barely taller than they were, he cupped Alec's cold cheek in one hand and pressed a gentle kiss to his lips. Alec responded, lingering for a moment as if he weren't willing to break the contact just yet, and neither was Christian. But then reality intruded and they stepped apart to maintain a little professionalism in the workplace.

Christian's fingers itched, though, to draw him close again. "Are you okay? You don't look okay."

Alec sank into the visitor's chair with a tired-sounding sigh. "I've been sick as hell."

Christian's sat in the desk chair and pulled it up close to Alec so their knees almost touched. "From the attack Friday night?" He kept his voice low, not wanting anyone passing near the office to hear.

"No, not from that. Well, I've had a headache from that, but no, this is from the frigging road trip to Chicago and back. I told you I don't travel well. I get sick as a dog and it hangs with me for days. Car, train, plane, whatever. It's been like this all my life."

Christian reached out to brush a lock of hair away from Alec's eyes. He suspected he knew what the problem was. "There's a thing you can take, ginger and another herb, that might help."

"Yeah, I know. Your mom gave me some and believe me, I know I don't look it, but I'm way better now than I was yesterday."

"You...saw my mother?"

Alec swallowed hard and nodded almost apologetically. "In Chicago. Long story. I'll tell you later, okay?"

Christian pushed back the burning urge to question. "Okay."

Alec reached over to the desk and for the first time Christian noticed Alec's down jacket and the pile of missing file folders on the desktop. He picked up the first folder in the stack. "I found the connection. Two, actually."

"Two?"

"Yeah. I went back and had a chat with Frank Sandell this morning. They've released him from the hospital and he's home. He said his wife was part of a group for many years. A group of friends who met once a month somewhere here in Shelton. He never went with her, but she always told him the group got together to 'make magic happen.' He didn't admit it to me, but I think he probably knew his wife was a mage and that 'making magic happen' probably wasn't just a catchy phrase. He told me about this group because the reason I went to see him was to show him pictures of the other victims, see if he recognized any of them."

"And he did?"

Alec nodded. "Two of them, in fact. Edward Seymour and the younger victim, Shelley Banks, the forty-one-year-old. Seymour was in Mary Sandell's 'group.' The younger woman was the daughter of another group member, Caroleanne Connelly, who died about five years ago."

"Damn." Christian's mind spun at this information. "So it's possible, likely even, that the rest of the victims were in this same group."

"That would be my thought."

"You said you found two connections."

"Actually, you found the other one. You were right. They've all been to England."

"All of them?"

"Yep. Some of them more than once, but here's the kicker. They were all in England for at least a few days right around the end of June thirty years ago. I was able to dig up old records from inns and hotels in the London area. They didn't stay at the same place, but they were definitely all there. The younger victim, Shelley, was only eleven years old at the time. She was there with her mother."

As the words sank in, the hair on the back of Christian's neck rose. "The end of June. That's when Jason Ansley and his family were killed."

"And when the amulet was supposedly lost," Alec added. "There's just one exception to the victims…me. I've never been to England."

His eyebrows furrowed together. "I don't think that thing was after me, Chris. I think it might have been after you. But you would have been a very small child thirty years ago, yes? And you certainly don't live here in the U.S. like the other victims. So I can't make the connection. Did your family maybe know the Ansley family?"

"Not that I'm aware of. My father was an operative for the Bureau—"

"Bureau?"

"Sorry. The Bureau of—Are you okay with hearing this?" He didn't want to put Alec into magic overload again. Didn't want to do anything to scare him off again.

Alec's fingers laced through his, and as tired and pale as he looked, his expression was open. "Yes. Tell me. I want to know."

Christian's heart fluttered. "Okay. My father was an operative for the Bureau of Dark Magic Affairs like I am now. It's possible he could have been one of the agents who investigated Rogan's attacks on the Ansleys—pretty much the entire Bureau was focused on them at the time. But I never heard my father mention that he knew any of the Ansleys personally."

He grimaced. "There is another possibility, though. The guiller attack at your house may not have been directly related to the other murders. Rogan may have realized I was here and… He and I have a history," he admitted. "We had a run-in many years ago. I almost killed him."

"Jesus," Alec whispered. "Then you're still in danger from him."

His eyes were heavy with concern and Christian realized Alec was genuinely worried about him. That was followed by a flood of guilt.

"Alec, I'm sorry. I would never have put you in danger intentionally. I knew when I came here there was a possibility Rogan might try to harm me, but I never dreamed you'd be hurt instead."

Alec curled his fingers tighter around Christian's and squeezed.

"Don't. It's not your fault. You had no way of knowing. But right now my immediate concern is making sure he doesn't get another shot at you. I don't have your abilities, so I don't know that I could do for you what you did for me on Friday night. I don't know how I could stop that thing. But I'm not going to lose you. I'll do whatever I have to make sure of that."

His expression was so full of protective determination it tore at Christian's heart.

"Nobody's losing anybody." He cupped the back of Alec's head and pulled him close until their faces were only inches apart. "I'm not losing you either. I care about you too damned much." *I love you too damned much.*

Alec's gaze burned into him with an intensity that sent ripples of heat and arousal all the way to Christian's toes. He thought he could lose himself forever in those rich, honey-colored eyes.

Alec reached up and brushed his fingertips over Christian's cheek. "I *was* a fool on Friday night," he rasped, his voice low, meant only for Christian's ears. "A fool for leaving. I know you've dreamed about it like I have. I know you feel it, too. I don't understand it and I don't need to understand it. I just know we belong together, Christian."

The words from the dream rang in the depths of Christian's soul. "I know that, too."

Alec nodded. "But right now…you have to go home, back to England."

"What?" Christian pulled away from him and stared.

"It's the only way you'll be safe. I'm sure back there you have better ways to protect yourself, more resources at your disposal, than you do here. Your Bureau can protect you."

"No—"

Alec stood. "Yes. Christian, it's the only way to be sure."

"No!" Christian rose also, his hands clenched at his sides. "Listen to me," he said, trying to keep his voice quiet so they wouldn't be overheard. "We don't know for sure Rogan wants me. There still may be a reason its you he wants dead—because you're investigating this case or because you're getting too close to something. Plus, he's got the amulet to find and he seems to think it's here. So here is exactly where I need to be and exactly where I'm staying. I'm not leaving you."

"Damn it." Alec was inches from his face again, but this time a frustrated anger radiated off him. "This is no time for you to be stubborn. I told you I'm not losing you. I'd rather be away from you and be sure you're alive than have you here and dead."

"Who's being stubborn? Don't be a sodding git. I'm not going."

The gravelly sound of a throat clearing at the entrance to the cubicle silenced them.

"Gentlemen."

They turned to find Martin Shanahan waiting for their attention. He gave no obvious reaction to what he'd walked in on aside from one elevated gray eyebrow.

"We just received an anonymous call saying a body's been found. A man walking his dog saw it in one of those old warehouses over off Chestnut Street."

"Could it be a mugging victim, or a druggie who got on the wrong side of his supplier?" Alec asked, instantly in work mode. "Those warehouses are notorious locations for drug buys. A body doesn't necessarily mean it's one of our killer's victims."

"Ordinarily I'd agree with you. But the dog walker...saw a strange floating light."

"Shit," Alec muttered under his breath. He and Christian exchanged a knowing glance.

"How long ago did the call come in?" Christian asked.

"Less than five minutes."

"We're on it."

"Fine. I want you two to report in to me as soon as you know anything," Shanahan said. His gaze lingered on Alec. "You don't look well."

Alec took the jacket Christian handed him. "It's that car sick thing I get. You know what it does to me."

Shanahan shook his head, his worry apparent. "Where the hell'd you go? You know better than that. The last time you took a road trip you were in bed for a week." He turned to Christian. "You look after him, you hear? And as soon as you've confirmed there's a body over there, I want you take him home. He doesn't need to be out wandering around in this cold weather investigating murders when he looks like he's about to fall on his ass."

"Oh, for God sake, Martin. You make it sound like I'm ten."

Shanahan shook a stubby finger at them both. "Just do it. A quick look, call in forensics, then you get him home."

Christian smiled, more at Alec's grumpy expression than the captain's tirade. "You have my word."

"Good." Shanahan huffed out of the cube.

"Do I *look* like I'm ten?" Alec asked, rolling his eyes, but Christian noticed he was hanging onto the desk to steady himself and all the standing had made him appear even more green around the gills than he'd been before.

"No. You look like you're sick. He's concerned because he cares about you."

"I know," Alec sighed.

Christian shut down the computer to keep anyone else from seeing Bella's files he'd tapped into, slid his arms into his leather jacket, and turned back to Alec.

"I care about you, too. And I'm not leaving, Alec. Don't bring it up again." The words were spoken quietly, but edged with steel. At Alec's surprised look, he softened his tone. "Whatever happens, whatever we have to face, we're going to do it together. Okay?"

Worry lines marred Alec's forehead. "Damn your stubbornness."

Christian saw him struggle with himself and he understood. He'd lost Drew in an act of violence and was running scared the same thing could happen to Christian. Which it could—life was never predictable. But they couldn't spend their days tiptoeing around and not living because of fear.

Finally Alec sighed and looked at him. "All right. But I'm telling you right now, nothing damn well better happen to you."

"It won't. I'll have you watching my back. Just like I'll be watching yours." He brushed the back of his hand against Christian's jaw. "Are you sure you're okay to go do this right now? Do you want sit this one out?"

Alec arched an eyebrow. "How can I possibly watch your back if I'm sitting it out?"

"And you think I'm stubborn?" He sighed, hating that Alec was feeling so awful. "I wish I could do the healing thing for you and make you feel better."

Alec smiled weakly. "I wouldn't say no if you could. But I'll be okay. Come on. Let's go do this. Suddenly the thought of going to bed"—he gave Christian a heated look—"is sounding better and better."

A jolt of need centered in Christian's groin, but he had no intention of acting on it until Alec was feeling better. "To sleep, love. You need to go to bed and sleep."

As they left the cubicle a tired but undoubtedly sexy grin teased at Alec's lips. "Yeah, but nobody said I had to sleep alone."

*   *   *

"Are you parked out front or on the side?" Christian asked, as they got off the elevator.

"Side."

It felt better even than Alec had thought to have Christian next to him again, feel the heat of his body nearby and the brush of their fingers as they walked. They weren't openly holding hands for work reasons, but with each step, they were so close together their hands made contact. And each time they did, their fingers would link for just a moment, or Christian would rub his fingertips against Alec's palm. It filled Alec with an almost giddy contentment, but was also causing little jolts of desire to spread through him in spite of how tired and crappy he felt.

He hadn't been kidding about bed sounding better and better. The thought of sliding between the sheets in a nice soft bed, skin to skin with Christian's warm, muscular body pressed to his and falling asleep in the man's arms was pretty much sounding like heaven right now. And then, when he was rested up and feeling better... A tremor spread through him, making his balls tighten. Jesus, he'd never felt like this about anyone. Never had such a powerful need to be with someone in every way.

Alec had the sudden urge to tug Christian to a stop right here, look into his eyes, and tell him how damn in love with him he was.

But duty called and the middle of the police station wasn't the ideal location. So he kept his mouth shut.

When they exited the glass door and emerged onto the sidewalk, Christian immediately halted. Alec felt thick waves of tension rippling off him.

"Chris?"

"Stay back." Christian's voice was threaded with that same steely tone he'd used inside, but there was also an underlying unease to it.

"What's going on?" He moved up to stand next to Christian in spite of the man's warning, earning a sidelong glare from him. But Christian's gaze quickly returned to a strikingly handsome man standing only a few feet away.

The stranger was several inches taller than he and Christian— probably six-four, Alec's cop eye assessed—with light brown hair graying at the temples, a neatly clipped beard, also graying, and a large nose that didn't detract from the man's looks but rather added interest to his face. His lean build and broad shoulders were those of a man who kept in shape and took care of himself. He wore an expensive-looking gray wool suit covered by a black, cashmere overcoat, exuding a sense of wealth and power.

But if Christian's heated stare at the man was indicative, this wasn't a friend.

"Christian Wetherly. At last we meet again." The stranger's voice was accented, but different from Christian's. Alec wasn't familiar with all the various accents in the UK, but he thought it sounded Irish.

"Rogan."

Alec's eyes widened. So this was Rogan.

"Get out of here, Alec," Christian said quietly through gritted teeth, his gaze never leaving the newcomer. His voice was stretched thin and tight. "This doesn't concern you."

"You already know I'm not leaving." Alec could have a steely voice, too, if the situation required it.

Rogan laughed and little lines crinkled at the edges of his eyes, making him even more handsome. But on closer look, Alec could see a cold chill in the eyes themselves.

"There's no body on Chestnut Street, is there? This is your doing. What do you want, Rogan?" Christian took a step backward and to his right. Alec recognized that he was angling for position. His hands stayed at his sides, but they were now turned palm out, and a surging energy built around him.

Alec glanced at Rogan to see if he was doing the same—and noticed one of Rogan's hands was black and shriveled into almost a claw. He didn't appear to be building any magic energy himself as Christian was. In fact, he seemed extremely calm and unconcerned Christian might cut him down. But Alec realized he knew next to nothing about magic and suspected either Rogan was protecting himself in some way other than an obvious energy shield like Christian had shown him, or he was simply so cocky and sure of himself he didn't consider Christian a threat. Either way, Alec's fear for Christian cranked up a notch.

"Ah, Wetherly, do I really need to explain? I thought for sure you'd be expecting me. After all, men like us don't hide in shadows if we have something we need to say." He gestured up and down the street with his good hand. "We keep our fights out in the open."

The narrow side street was eerily empty and silent in the cold, gray, sunless afternoon. Only a few vehicles, including Alec's Jeep, were parked at the curb. Most of them belonged to cops who used the side door to enter and exit the police station. The ten-story empty brick building across the street—formerly a bank that had closed its doors two years ago—loomed over the area like an abandoned, hulking giant.

"Fine," Christian was saying. "But this is between you and me. Let Alec walk out of here, then you and I can talk."

"Christian!" Alec growled under his breath.

But Rogan only laughed. "Oh, I have no interest in him. My pet tells me he has no useful information. He was merely to be an appetizer before the main course last week. But I do find your need to protect him amusing, which makes me think I'd rather keep him here. It makes it more"—he smiled and shrugged—"more personal."

Alec got the distinct impression that if he did try to leave, Rogan would stop him using some magical means. He slid his right hand inside his jacket and curled it around the butt of his gun so he'd be ready to use it if the need arose, hoping Rogan's focus would stay on Christian and not notice what he was doing.

The man tsk-tsked. "Still trying to save innocents, Wetherly. I expected that from the green youngster you were back then, but I would have thought life experience, and your inability to save people the last time we met, would have hardened you. Made you aware such righteous humanitarianism is useless."

What exactly had happened between Christian and Rogan in the past? Alec glanced again at Rogan's withered, blackened hand...and wondered.

"What are you doing here in the States, Rogan? What do you need with all these people your guiller's been killing? The Amulet of Sulisa was lost thirty years ago. How can innocent American mages possibly help you?"

"Mmm." Rogan smiled. "Interesting thing that. A few weeks ago my pet was helping me with another job, unrelated, and happened upon a fascinating story in someone's mind. About a group of American mages who thought, many years ago, they could work together and secretly destroy me. How well do you remember your history, Wetherly? Are you aware Jason Ansleys' mother-in-law was an American?"

"I am. She died not long after you murdered her daughter, grandchild, and son-in-law."

"Ah, yes. Tragic. Expired from grief, some said, and laid to rest at a secluded, private locale. But being the practical type I am, I had other thoughts on the matter and made a point of chatting with her parents and brother all those long years ago. Unfortunately, they chose not to answer my questions."

"So you killed them. Why not just say it?"

The man chuckled. "Very well. They chose not to tell me what I wanted to know, so I found no reason to let them live."

"But after thirty years, and ignoring the fact you screwed yourself over by destroying the woman's entire family, thereby ending any chance you might have of getting what you really wanted, you've suddenly, conveniently discovered you have a…what? A story told to you by a creature who has no loyalty toward you or anyone but itself and would just as soon murder you in your sleep if it gets hungry? I must say, you have fascinating, trustworthy allies."

"Charming. You're just very charming, Wetherly. You know, of course, that I'm not going to let you live?"

He was smiling again and a chill crept up Alec's spine at just how much malignancy churned below the surface of the man's good looks and magnetism. He wondered briefly why Christian didn't try to do that energy thing to Rogan like he'd done to the guiller. But the cop in him understood why not. Christian wouldn't use his powers against Rogan unless Rogan either used or made a direct threat to use his first. It was too risky otherwise.

"I'm running scared." Christian's tone was dry.

Rogan laughed. "Still a young, idealistic fool."

"What are you doing here today? What do you want, Rogan? You're risking a lot showing your face in public like this. You know what the Council will do if they get their hands on you."

"The old bastards wouldn't know what to do with their very own pricks if they had them in hand," Rogan scoffed. "You truly haven't grown any wiser over the years if you think I give a bloody goddamn about them. No, I think you know very well what I want, Christian, my boy. I'm *this* close"—he measured a minute distance between his thumb and forefinger—"to getting my amulet, and I already have the means to use it."

"The Vargazian texts are written in Mensi. It's a dead language. No one can read it. So how do you expect to use the ritual?"

Rogan's eyes gleamed. "I have my ways. Now…let's get back to your question about what I want. Clearly the amulet, which I'll soon have. But, really, discovering you were here was just, as they say, icing on the cake. I decided it might be amusing to see if your hero skills have improved at all since the Gathering." He glanced up at the police station behind them. "How many souls in there this time of day, do you suppose? I figure fifty or sixty."

Christian blanched, every bit of color fading from his cheeks. Cold fear radiated from him, startling Alec with its intensity. Christian shook his head. "No."

"Oh, yes."

"Alec, run!"

Rogan's smile turned icy with glee. "Too late. Goodbye, Wetherly."

Before Alec could pull his gun free and fire, Rogan vanished into thin air.

"Run, damn it!" Christian ordered again, shoving Alec toward the narrow street. Then he turned liked he was about to re-enter the station.

Alec didn't know what exactly what going on, but the air surrounding them was beginning to crackle with what felt like static electricity, and everything in his gut screamed that Christian could *not* go back into the building.

"No way." He grabbed Christian by the arm and pulled him away from the door.

"I have to, Alec. I have to get them out."

The hair on Alec's arms stood on end and his skin practically sizzled. A sense of awful foreboding filled him, and although everything in him urged that he run into the building also, warn Martin and the rest of his colleagues, he knew the terrible truth. "It's too late," he shouted, grabbing Christian by the arm and jerking him toward the street.

With a horrible roar, the building behind them exploded. Alec felt himself jerked away from Christian and thrown through the air in a blast of heat and debris. And then everything went dark.

CHAPTER 10

"Alec!"

The voice was faint. Faraway. It sounded as if it were muffled, coming from inside a box. Alec wondered if he was dreaming it. His head felt muzzy and he couldn't seem to open his eyes. Yes, definitely dreaming. He let himself slip back into sleep.

But the voice gave him no peace.

"Damn it, Alec, answer me! Please! Answer me so I know you're okay." The voice sounded ragged, almost desperate, and the raw emotion in it made Alec mentally scramble to pull himself up through the fog and haze of darkness and open his eyes…to more darkness.

The warmth of sleep disappeared and he was instantly assailed by the cold…and a world of hurt. It felt like everything in his body ached. Why was it so dark? And where the hell was he? He tried to move, but his body didn't cooperate. God, he didn't want to think about what that might mean. The best he could do was bring a hand up to his face. He rubbed his eyes, which were gritty and stinging, but the dark still surrounded him.

A wracking cough assailed him, sending sharp pain ripping through his chest. It was hard to drag in air, and what little he could was dusty and dry.

"Alec? Is that you?"

"I…" He coughed again, harder this time, and with each movement his chest grew heavier. "Yeah," he finally managed.

For some reason the events on the street outside the police station chose that moment to return to his memory. Rogan. His threats. Christian's pale face and panicked expression, his attempt to go back in the building. Alec pulling him away, telling him there was no time. And then…

Oh, Jesus.

"Christian?" His voice barely came out as a croak, so he tried again. "Christian!"

"Alec! Thank God. Talk again so I can find you."

"Are you okay?" Alec asked.

"I'm…I'll be all right."

But Alec heard pain in his voice and wondered just how badly hurt Christian was, wondered how bad off he himself was.

"You're a terrible liar," Alec said. The words triggered another round of coughing. Not quite as violent as the last, but still making him hurt like hell.

He saw a small white light moving toward him, slowly, erratically. As it drew closer and offered faint illumination of the few feet around it, Alec got his first view of where they were.

Steel beams, crushed and broken concrete, sheet rock from what had once probably been walls, filled the space they were in. It looked like a child's erector set gone mad and then squashed under a giant's heel.

He heard scraping and grunting. The flickering, erratic light came close enough to touch, but he couldn't figure out what it was. Had Christian found a flashlight somewhere? Then he felt a hand on his leg.

"Alec…" The relief in Christian's voice was palpable. And Alec felt it right back.

"Hey." He tried to turn toward Christian, but couldn't. Any kind of movement sent agonizing fingers of pain through his chest. He hissed and tried to breathe past it, but breathing was hard. Damned hard.

Christian dragged himself up next to Alec and lay on his side facing him. Beams and debris rested only a few feet above them, so it would have been impossible for him to sit up. It was then Alec noticed the faint, odd white light was coming from something in Christian's palm. It looked like a tiny star.

What the hell?

But the sight of Christian's face, covered with grit and streaks of blood, instantly squashed his curiosity about the light.

"Jesus, you're not okay." He reached up and pressed his palm against Christian's cheek. "You're bleeding. From where?" It looked like Christian had a cut along his hairline. That was probably the source. But he knew instinctively something else was wrong, something bigger and more important than a cut on his forehead. "What else is hurt? There's something you're not telling me. I see it in your eyes."

"Alec, I'll live. Tell me how you are." Using the light in his left palm to see by, Christian's gentle right hand smoothed over Alec's face, then down his arms and legs. When it settled on Alec's chest, it triggered another fit of coughing. When the coughing eased and Alec had wiped the dampness from his eyes, it was to find Christian's lips drawn into a thin line and his expression grim. He wiped his thumb against Alec's lower lip and when he pulled it away, Alec saw blood on it.

"Oh, God," Christian murmured. "Can you breathe okay?"

"It's hard," Alec admitted. It took a lot more energy than it should have to talk, and he felt like he couldn't drag in a deep enough breath. "And it hurts like hell to move. I think I probably have some broken ribs."

Christian's hand rested lightly against Alec's chest. "I think it's more than that. I think you might have a punctured lung. What else hurts?"

Alec tried to laugh, but it came out as a gasp. "It would probably be easier to list what doesn't." He didn't want to worry Christian by mentioning that other parts of his insides felt somehow wrong, too.

"I think we're in the building across the street from the station. The blast was big enough it probably threw us over here and damaged this building also. There's no way out of here that I could see. We're trapped."

"You can teleport," Alec reminded him.

"Yeah, but that would involve leaving you here while I got help. And I don't know how stable this place is…"

His words were drowned out when the wreckage around them groaned and trembled for several seconds, shaking loose new billowing waves of dust and small debris. It rained down on them, making it even more miserable for Alec to breathe.

"Shit. Not liking the sound of that," Alec rasped when it cleared.

"Neither am I." The tiny light in Christian's hand disappeared. He scooted in closer to Alec and slid one of his arms under Alec's head, cushioning it, but also bringing them even closer together.

The white shimmering sphere of a magic protection shield emerged from Christian's palm, but this one wasn't just around Christian. Alec found himself inside it as well, probably a result of Christian wrapping Alec in his embrace. And he knew why the man had put them both in it. Christian was using it to keep any more debris from falling on them.

It gave off a wavering light of its own. Enough he could see Christian's tense, worried expression.

"You need to get out of here, Chris. Before this whole thing collapses."

The other man shook his head. Emotion churned in his eyes. "No. It's too risky. You heard this place. If I leave, I…"

His voice caught, but Alec knew what he'd been about to say. If he left, he might not make it back in time before the rest of the building collapsed and killed Alec. But if Christian stayed, it would just kill them both. He couldn't hold up the protection shield forever, and while it would no doubt protect them from minor debris, Alec suspected Christian probably wouldn't be able to keep it up under the pressure of thousands of tons of concrete and steel.

Alec winced as another stab of pain shot through his chest. And damn he was cold. So cold. It ate through his clothes and he felt it deep in his bones. He began to shiver.

Christian moved closer to him. "Better?"

He nodded, grateful for even the tiny bit of extra body heat the man offered. Then he cupped Christian's cheek in his hand and turned his face until he was looking at Alec. "You have to go. You know…" Damn, it was getting harder to talk. His breath came out in ragged wheezes. "You know it's the only way. I'll be fine…until you get back."

"No."

Another minor tremor shook around them and the sickening groan of steel filled Alec's ears.

"Christian—" Another wave of coughing hit Alec. This time he didn't need to see the look on Christian's face. He felt the coppery taste of blood in his mouth. "Listen to this place," he gasped. "Go. Now."

"I'm not leaving you."

"You have to." A wave of pain in Alec's chest was so intense it stole his words. He fought to drag in air.

"Alec!" Christian wrapped his hand around Alec's.

"Just…go, damn you," Alec huffed. "Save yourself, you stupid fool." Tears welled in his eyes. He didn't want Christian to die here with him out of some idiotic sense of honor or loyalty.

Christian pressed a kiss against Alec's lips. His were soft and his breath was warm against Alec's mouth. "We're going to get out of here, Alec. Together."

"You know we can't."

"Yes, we can." Christian's jaw tightened in what looked like resolve. "We're going to teleport together."

"No! Christian!" A fit of coughing wracked Alec's body again, and with each convulsion he could feel himself growing weaker.

"Even if I do have some kind of…magic ability, I don't know…how to use it that way. And you said…" It hurt to drag in air. Hurt to talk. Hurt even worse to think of never seeing Christian again. "You said teleporting us both might kill you."

"No one's going to die. No way in hell I'm losing you, Alec."

"But you said…"

"Fuck what I said. We're going to do this. You and I. Together."

The building rumbled again and another rain of rocks fell onto the glimmering protection shield. Alec, even with his fading sight, could tell it was taking all Christian's strength to hold the shield in place. "You…you need to conserve your energy," he whispered. "You'll need it to get yourself out of here."

"I'll have enough. Now listen to me. I'm going to tell you what to do."

The groaning around them had escalated to a deep thrum, and a horrible screeching noise joined it.

"Too…late…" Alec whispered. His vision was growing dim. Darkness was falling around him in spite of the shimmer of white light. "Too…late…for me."

"No, it's not! Damn it, Alec! You stay with me!"

Alec used the last of his strength to press his fingers against Christian's lips. "Love you…"

Seconds later, with a sickly boom and an explosion of concrete, dust, and sheetrock, the building collapsed.

CHAPTER 11

The damp chill of water droplets pinging on his face woke Christian.

He opened his eyes, only to squint and close them again to keep the rain out of them. Disoriented, he raised a hand to his face for protection and eased them open once more, trying to place where he was and what had happened. It was dark—nighttime. He was lying on his back in a cold puddle in the mud. The wet, earthy scent of home washed over him. What the—?

In a split second he remembered.

Alec!

Christian sat up, then groaned as his mangled leg protested the sudden movement.

Holding out his hand, palm up, he created the small, twinkling, star-like light he'd used earlier.

He found Alec lying only a few feet away, also on his back, the cold rain falling on him, beading up, then sliding down the unnaturally pale skin of his face.

"Alec! Oh, God, Alec! Alec!" Christian dragged himself over to him.

Please don't let him be dead.

He was so still. Too still.

Oh, God, had he made the wrong decision, bringing them all the way here, instead of getting them straight to a hospital in the US? But he still felt like if there was any way at all to save Alec it was better to be here. Magic healing had a better chance of saving his life.

As long as it's not already too late.

His heart pounding and tears stinging his eyes, one of Christian's cold, wet hands burrowed into the hollow of Alec's neck under his jacket. His fingers were so icy he couldn't feel anything at first against Alec's equally cold skin.

"Damn it, Alec. Give me a sign here. Please!"

He lightly rested his other hand on Alec's chest, hoping to feel movement.

At last he discerned a faint, slow flutter of pulse against his fingers. Much too faint and slow to be healthy, but it was there at least.

"Thank, God."

Christian glanced around and realized the teleport had deposited them in the driveway of the house he shared with Bella and Jamie. They were only about twenty feet from the front door. They couldn't materialize in the house because of protective anti-teleportation spells woven around it. He glanced up and saw lights in the third floor windows where Jamie and Bella lived.

Shouting to get someone's attention would be useless with the rain pounding down. And in any case, the enormous amount of magic energy he'd had to channel to get the steel beam off his leg in the building and then the long teleport with him and Alec had sapped nearly all his remaining strength. It was better to put what little he had left to better use.

He put out the light and levered himself up onto his knee on his good left leg, trying to be cautious of his right. But something about the movement twisted it, sending shooting pain up through it all the way into his hip. "Unnnh, God!" he cried out, closing his eyes for a moment against the agony. But there was no time to coddle himself.

"Hang on, Alec. This isn't going to be graceful." And he hoped to God he wasn't going to do any more damage to Alec. With his muscles shuddering and a ragged groan, he dragged Alec into a sitting position, then with another groan and another god-awful surge of pain in his leg, he draped Alec over his shoulder and somehow managed to stagger to a standing position.

Normally he would have been able to use a hovering spell that would lift Alec in the air and float him to the house. But the star light, with its tiny energy requirement, was about all he had strength for. He knew he was close to collapse and channeling any more energy would drain him to the point of unconsciousness again.

"Stay with me, Alec," he mumbled. "Stay with me and, God, please don't die."

Every step toward the house was slow and torturous. His leg quivered in agony, but Christian shut off his mind to how bad the pain was. Alec was more important.

By the time he stood in front of the door, he barely had the energy left to bang on it.

"Alec, please hang on. Don't leave me."

The door was thrown open and warm light enveloped him.

"Christian! Oh, God! Jamieeee! Evaaaan!"

Bella's shriek barely registered. Christian's head grew light and even his good leg trembled from strain.

Jamie appeared, and Evan's red head right behind him. "Bloody hell!" Strong hands eased Alec off Christian's shoulder.

"Don't let him die," Christian gasped as Alec's weight shifted off him.

"Christian, my God, what's happened?" Bella's arm went around his waist, but it was too late. His legs crumpled beneath him and he sank to the floor in the doorway. Blood pounded in his head and a sick dizziness swept over him.

"Christian!" Bella sank to her knees next to him.

"Bella, you can't let him die." He found her hand. "Save his life. Swear to me…"

The darkness and peace of unconsciousness tugged at him, promising no more pain or worry.

He succumbed.

*   *   *

Christian came around to the sound of whispered voices. His eyes fluttered open to see that he was in his own room, in his bed. The warm flicker of flames in the fireplace was the only light. His leg still ached—a dull, miserable throb now, but better than the sharp agony of before.

He tried to sit up, but suddenly Jamie was standing next to the bed. He pressed Christian back down onto it, his freckled face tight with concern. "Don't move, mate. The healers had a hell of a time with your leg and you shouldn't be moving around or you'll just mess up everything they did."

"How's Alec?" Christian asked. His voice was dry and hoarse.

"He's a fighter." Jamie poured a cup of water from a pitcher next to the bed and held up Christian's head so he could take a sip.

He swallowed, grateful for the moisture in his parched mouth. "He's alive then? He's going to be okay?"

"He's alive. They think he'll pull through, but it's still too soon to tell."

"I need to see him." Christian threw off the covers, but once again Jamie's big hands restrained him.

"No, you need to stay right here and let the healers do their jobs." He tugged the sheet and blanket back up over Christian. "Here, drink some more." He held the cup up to Christian's lips again and encouraged him to drain it.

"We need to get some people to the States. Find out if there were any survivors."

"We're already on it. We've got agents over there right now."

"I…couldn't stop him…Rogan…"

"Don't even think about blaming yourself, Chris. You know how Rogan works. It's not your fault."

Christian grimaced. A knot of guilt had formed in his stomach the moment he'd realized what Rogan was going to do, and it remained, its heavy weight eating into him.

"He did it…to taunt me." His mind seemed to be getting fuzzy and his body was growing more relaxed with each passing second. And then it hit him. "Bloody hell. What was in the water?"

Jamie had the grace to blush. "Sorry. But you have to rest, Chris. You were in bad shape when you got here. Probably worse than you realize."

"Damn it. Need…to see…Alec."

"You can see him when you wake up. We'll look out for him."

It was the last thing Christian remembered.

*   *   *

The next time he opened his eyes, he was alone. A fire still burned in the fireplace, but the heavy, dark green drapes had been pulled open a few inches and he could see the gray sky and falling shadows of afternoon through them. A glance at the clock next to the bed showed it was 2:00 P.M. His sense of time was completely messed up, his internal clock not sure if he was in Illinois or Wiltshire. He wondered how long he'd been out and what day it was.

With no one here to stop him this time, he pushed back the covers. He discovered his right leg was in a black, padded brace that covered him from mid-thigh to mid-calf. It allowed him only limited movement, but enough he decided he could get around. He eased his legs off the bed and stood, initially putting all his weight on his left leg, then slowly testing how much his right could take. A dull throbbing ache pulsed from it already, but the added weight didn't seem to make it much worse.

Someone had left his blue terry cloth robe at the foot of the bed. He pulled it on and tied the belt.

He still felt drained and weak, and suspected he could probably do no more than the simplest magic yet, but at least he was up and functioning. And he had only one goal—to find Alec.

It didn't take long. He was in the guest room just down the hall.

Bella sat next to the bed in a gold damask-covered wing chair, reading, with a huge ball of gray fur on her lap. When she heard Christian, she turned and smiled. "I thought you might be waking up soon."

She laid her book aside, waited for the cat to stretch and jump down, then stood. After pulling up another chair next to hers, she took his arm to help him to it.

Christian didn't sit in it right away, though. He couldn't. The sight of Alec sleeping in the bed, his hair tousled, his face still much too pale, but not as bad as it had been the last time he'd seen him, and the sight of the easy rise and fall of his chest beneath the burgundy comforter caused an ache in Christian he could barely breathe past. He moved to stand next to him and, without thinking, picked up one of Alec's hands and squeezed it gently.

But then he realized Bella was watching him curiously. He set Alec's hand back on the comforter, but didn't rush to do so, and gave it one more squeeze before he released it. He was tired of this. He didn't want to hide his feelings about Alec. It was time to tell his friends.

Soon, he decided. *Very soon.*

"How's he doing?"

Bella helped him into the chair. "He's doing very well, all things considered. If you'd gotten him here even five minutes later…" She winced and shook her head as she sank back into her own chair. "The healers said he probably wouldn't have made it. He had so many internal injuries. He might not have survived if you'd taken him to an Ordinary hospital."

So he'd done the right thing, bringing Alec here.

"Has he been awake?"

"No. Not yet. But he's resting comfortably. Has been for hours now. He's out of danger."

Bella's hand covered one of his and he realized it was shaking.

"It was so dangerous, Christian. What you did, bringing him here."

He looked at her, really looked at her, and saw the worry in her dark eyes, noticed how drawn her face was, and how tired she appeared. She had her legs tucked up underneath her in the chair, and her skin was nearly the color of the pale gray sweater she wore. "You both could have died," she breathed.

"But we didn't."

"Teleporting with him like that…by all rights you should have died. You shouldn't be here, either one of you. To go that far with someone who's non-magic…"

"I told you, Bella, Alec does have magic ability. We couldn't have gotten here if he didn't and you know it. Without his added power, there's no way. There's something blocking him or holding him back, but he is magic."

"Still, it was a terrible risk."

"One worth taking." He looked at Alec and knew he'd do the same thing all over again if it meant having Alec alive.

"You shouldn't be up and around on your leg. The healers did everything they could, but it was so messed up. They're…"

She hesitated, bringing Christian's gaze back to her.

"They're what?"

"They're not totally positive it'll ever heal properly. You may have a limp and have to wear a brace the rest of your life." She looked ready to cry.

He hugged her and kissed the top of her head. "I'll deal, Bella. I'm alive. Alec's alive. That's what matters."

She sniffled. "I know. I just… I hate Rogan!" She pulled away, swiped at her eyes and glared. Not at him, just in general. "I hate the bloody bastard for everything he's done over the years. I don't even care if the Council catches him and tries him anymore. I just want him dead. He deserves to burn long and slow for all he's done. I know that sounds completely wicked of me, but I don't care."

"I hear you. Do we know anything yet about survivors at the police station?"

"Jamie's gone over there to help. The place was demolished, as was the building across the street."

"I think that's where Alec and I were trapped—across the street."

"I talked to Jamie last night and he said it looks bad. The debris is so awful, even using magic it's going to take a while."

The guilty knot in Christian's stomach gave a painful twist. "Rogan did it because of me. To taunt me. Alec and I saw him right before it happened."

"What?" Bella's eyebrows had disappeared up under her thick bangs.

"Yeah. He said he was close to having the amulet and already had means to use it once he got it."

"The texts. But he doesn't have any way to read them."

"He claims he does. He also said he'd found out there was a group of American mages who'd conspired against him around the same time as the Ansley family died thirty years ago. He indicated Jason Ansley's mother-in-law was one of them. She was an American."

"Yes, I know. She died not too long after her daughter and family did."

"Rogan apparently believes someone in the group knows where the amulet is. He also implied he wasn't convinced the mother-in-law did die. I think he thinks she either had the amulet herself or gave it to one of the people in her group of friends. Alec discovered all of the victims were in London around the time of the Ansleys' death. We know for certain three of them were in this group Rogan referred to, but it's highly likely they all were."

"Then we need to find out who else was in that group and try to protect them from Rogan. If he hasn't yet found what he wants, he'll probably continue to send the guiller after people."

"Agreed."

"I'll look into it." Her expression grew concerned. "You said Rogan destroyed the police station because of you, to taunt you? Why would you think that?"

"He told me. He said discovering I was in the States was like icing on the cake and he wanted to test my hero skills, see if I was any better at saving people than I was at the Gathering thirteen years ago." The words tasted bitter in Christian's mouth and guilt nearly crushed him.

"Bastard. First of all, you weren't even an agent when the Gathering thing happened, and none of the experienced agents or Council members who were there could stop him either. And second, Christian, you know you have no control over Rogan's actions. He wanted you to believe it was your fault because that's the way he is. He gets off on taunting. He wanted to send you to your grave feeling responsible for a whole lot of deaths, when in truth it probably wasn't about you at all. I suspect he did what he did to send a message to the Council. To show them he was back, still as powerful as before, and still capable of thumbing his nose at their laws."

"Maybe."

"You can't let his mind games get to you. He and he alone is responsible for any deaths that result from this. He likes big, showy displays of his power and the more people who die, the bigger it inflates his ego. He has a history of this kind of behavior, a history that began long before you or I were even born." Bella gave him a fierce look and shook her finger at him. "So don't you dare, for one second, let him work you like this."

"I'll try not to."

"You do better than try."

Christian nodded, but couldn't banish the ache in his gut. Alec had almost died and a lot of other people probably had died because Rogan wanted to hurt Christian. Logically he knew Bella was right, but emotionally, it was something he feared he was going to live with the rest of his life.

"You want some tea?" Bella asked, her face softening.

"Sure. That would be really nice."

"I'll be back in a few minutes."

The moment she was gone, Christian scooted his chair closer to the bed and picked up Alec's hand again, wrapping his fingers through the other man's, savoring their warmth and the slow, steady beat of pulse he felt from Alec's wrist against his thumb. He remembered the last words Alec had said to him in that final tense moment before he passed out and they teleported. *"Love you..."*

"I love you, too," he whispered. He pulled Alec's hand up and pressed a kiss against his knuckles.

Alec's dark eyelashes fluttered and his eyes slowly opened. Christian's heart pounded as the man's sleepy, golden gaze settled on him.

"Chris." The soft, raspy whisper rippled through Christian.

"Hey. How are you feeling?"

Alec's tired smile was the most beautiful thing Christian had ever seen.

"Alive. You okay?"

Christian nodded.

"That's twice you've saved my life now." Alec's voice was still barely above a whisper. "Thank you."

"Don't thank me."

"Don't tell me what to do." He reached up and pulled Christian's face close to his. Their lips met in a soft, gentle brush. "Thank you," he whispered again. "I was supposed to be watching your back…"

A lump formed in Christian's throat. "We were watching each others'."

"I'm so tired."

He looked like it. His eyelids were drooping again.

"Sleep's the best thing for you right now. It's the best way to heal."

Alec nodded, his eyes already closed. But then he opened them again and his gaze locked with Christian's. "Will you stay with me?"

"I'll be here when you wake up," he promised. *I'll always be here for you.*

Alec gave him a half smile and dropped back off to sleep.

Christian held his hand until he heard Bella coming up the hall, cups and dishes clinking on the large tea tray he knew she'd be using.

He and Bella shared a pot of tea and ate toast with blackberry jam as they talked quietly. They were just finishing when Bella's cell phone beeped. She went out in the hall to answer it and Christian heard her speaking softly.

When she came back in the room, she looked as pale as Alec did.

"What is it?" Christian's heart pounded, dreading Bella's news.

Her eyes welled up.

Christian pulled her down next to him. "Bella, tell me."

"They finished the body recovery."

"And…"

"Thirty-nine people dead. There were only two survivors. Four, if you include you and Alec."

"Oh, God." The ball of guilt in Christian's gut churned with a vengeance and for several seconds he was afraid he was going lose everything he'd just eaten.

"Jamie said it was lucky more people didn't die. Apparently lots of cops were on patrol or out on cases, so there weren't as many people in the building as there could have been."

Christian nodded, remembering how quiet the homicide division had been that afternoon. But it was small comfort. Thirty-nine people gone forever. "The survivors…did Jamie know who they were?"

He knew the possibility of one of them being Martin Shanahan was slim to none, but for Alec's sake, he had to ask. Had to hope.

"Both women. One's a sergeant. I think Jamie said her name was Maria Koslowski. The other was a dispatcher, Betty Wilde."

Christian closed his eyes and rubbed his face in his hands. Maria Koslowski was the young blonde woman who'd helped Alec research the murder victims, the one Christian had spoken with the day of the explosion. He was grateful she'd pulled through. But his gut surged again at the thought of Martin Shanahan being dead. The one steadfast constant in Alec's life.

Bella seemed to know what he was thinking, at least in part. "How's Alec going to take this news?"

"How do you think he's going to take it?"

"I know. Stupid question."

"Fuck." Christian pushed himself to a standing position, then swore again when his leg throbbed in a vicious ache of protest.

"Sit down." Bella had stood, too, and wrapped an arm around his waist.

"I can't." He stared at the painted Victorian mural on the wall, breathing hard and fighting back waves of self loathing.

"Stop it right now." Bella jerked on his arm until he turned to face her. Her voice was low in deference to Alec sleeping, but her eyes flashed with anger. "I mean it, Christian. Stop wallowing in guilt right this instant. This was not your fault, and every second that you beat yourself up and blame yourself, you're giving Rogan exactly what he wants. So snap out of it. You can't afford to do this right now. You have to be the strong one. Alec's going to need your friendship and support and you have to be there for him."

Was Alec ever going to be able to forgive him for getting Shanahan and all the rest of the people killed?

"Christian!"

He nodded slowly. "I hear you."

"Are you sure?"

"Yes. I'm sure. Who's with Jamie in the States?"

"John Donnelly and Cayleigh."

"How are they doing on containment?"

"They've had to do moderate modification charms. It was the only way to cover things up. The police and fire investigators now officially believe the explosion resulted from a faulty gas main under the station and the street."

He scrubbed a hand over his face. "We need to report this to the Council, if it hasn't been done already."

"I did, right after you and Alec got here. They've called a special session. It begins in the morning."

Christian nodded and sighed. "What time?"

"Seven. But you're not going. I am."

"It was my assignment, not yours. I need to go and take responsibility for what happened on my watch."

"Damn it, I'm going to tell you this one more time and then we're not going to discuss it any more, do you hear me? This isn't about you, Chris. This about Rogan. About his blatant disregard for human life and everything that the people in this world—mage and Ordinary—consider sacred. You did nothing wrong. The Council knows you did nothing wrong. The session isn't about you. It's about how the hell to capture and contain Rogan once and for all."

He winced. "I should still be there."

"No. You need to be here. I don't think you realize just how bad a shape you were in when you got here night before last. You almost died. And as your second in command, I'm telling you that I'm going to handle the Council this time around and you're going to stay here. Where you're needed." She glanced over at Alec. When she turned her gaze back to Christian he saw sadness in it. "In truth, Christian, you've got the hardest job of all. He's going to wake up in a strange place, a strange country, and find out…" Her eyes welled up again and she sniffled. She'd always been tender-hearted.

"I know." Christian's heart felt like lead in his chest.

"The Council's meeting in Athens this time. Will you be okay if I leave this afternoon? I'd rather go early and get some sleep there than be dead tired from the teleport tomorrow morning. Especially since you know how long these Council sessions can drag on. Sometimes for days."

He sighed and nodded, then forced a smile on his face. "Of course. Are you sure you want to do this, Bell?"

"I'm sure." She looked at him fondly and, standing on tiptoe, kissed his cheek. "You just promise me you'll take it easy over the next couple of days."

"No marathon runs, I promise."

"I don't just mean physically. I mean take it easy on yourself in here, too." She tapped his temple, then his chest.

He nodded, acknowledging her. But he suspected, as she left the room and gave him another glance over her shoulder, that she wasn't buying his act.

145

Christian looked at Alec, sleeping and unaware, and wondered again how Alec could ever forgive him if he couldn't even forgive himself?

CHAPTER 12

Alec opened his eyes, feeling much more alert than he had the last time he'd been awake. And grateful to an infinite degree that he was alive and able to open his eyes at all.

He wondered how long he'd slept and what time it was, but when he looked at his wrist to check his watch, he discovered his watch was gone. He had a vague memory of seeing it smashed after the explosion.

However, he was lying on his side and discovered a small digital clock on the bedside table. It was nearly eleven-thirty at night. A small, red beaded lamp sat next to the clock, giving off the only light in the room. And next to the bedside table, in a gold armchair, sat Christian, fast asleep, his cheek balanced on his hand, his legs stretched out in front of him on a small tapestry ottoman. He wore a red sweatshirt and navy blue sweatpants and, as Alec studied him, he realized Christian's right leg, under the sweats, looked bulkier than his left.

A twinge of memory shot through Alec. Of how Christian had been badly hurt in the collapsed building and hadn't wanted to tell Alec about it.

But before he could think it through, Christian's eyes opened and a smile curved his sexy lips. For a brief moment. And then it faded and sadness replaced the joy in his eyes.

Alec's heart stalled. What was that all about?

"How are you feeling?" Christian asked, dropping his left foot to the floor but keeping his right leg, Alec noted, still stretched out. He leaned close and pressed a hand against Alec's forehead.

"Better. How are you?"

"I'm okay."

"Want to tell me about your leg?"

Christian's eyes widened. "What?"

Alec propped himself up on his elbow and pointed. "Your leg. What happened to it?"

"How can you…?" But then he looked at it and must have decided the way he was keeping it up on the footstool made it rather obvious. "In the building, a beam fell on it. I'll be okay. Nothing to worry about."

Alec nodded, but sensed Christian wasn't telling him everything. There'd been a little too much "really, it's fine" in his voice to convince Alec. But he didn't push.

There was a strange awkwardness between them that Alec had never felt before. Not even the last time he was awake for those few brief minutes. His recall was hazy, but he thought he remembered Christian holding his hand, remembered them kissing and Christian promising he'd stay while Alec slept. And he clearly had stayed. Still…something didn't feel right.

Alec looked around the room again. "Where are we?"

"My house in England. We teleported here. I brought you here because I was afraid taking you to an Ordinary hospital wouldn't be enough. You needed magic healing."

England. Alec wasn't sure what to think about that. How could they possibly have teleported all the way to England? Christian had made it clear teleportation took huge amounts of stamina, and the longer the distance, the more of a drain. Yet Christian had managed to bring them both here? And hadn't died?

"Jesus," he whispered, "that was risky."

Christian looked apologetic. "I wasn't trying to hurt you more than you already were."

"I'm not concerned about me. I mean it was risky for you. That's a long way. You could have died, Christian." The thought made Alec almost sick to his stomach.

Christian's dark brows drew together and he looked surprised for a moment. Then his expression grew soft and more like the Christian Alec knew. "I just wanted to do whatever I could to save you."

Alec reached out and captured his hand. "I know I already told you this, but I'm going to say it again. Thank you."

The other man swallowed hard, and as he had before, he shook his head and mumbled, "Don't thank me."

"You're a stubborn man."

He huffed out a soft laugh, but it didn't quite reach his eyes and push away the sadness that lurked there. "Can I get you anything? Something to drink? Are you hungry?"

"Yeah, I am kind of hungry now that you mention it. But, you know, what I'd really love is a shower."

Christian did smile at that. "I know what you mean. I felt the same way when I woke up. You can use my bathroom. Are you okay to get up?"

Alec pushed the covers away, noticing he'd been stripped down to his blue boxer briefs, and sat up, gingerly testing his body and discovering that aside from a slight ache around his ribs, he felt pretty good. A little weak and shaky, but that was probably from being out of it for so long.

"How long have we been here?" he asked.

Christian stood and Alec noticed just how cautious he was about not putting too much weight on his right leg. "We got here night before last."

"Two days only? Damn, those magic healing people of yours work fast, don't they?"

"Yeah, it's definitely accelerated healing from what someone might find at an Ordinary hospital."

Christian held out a hand and Alec grasped it, letting the other man help pull him to his feet. He was a bit dizzy for a few seconds, but it passed and he was able to walk without Christian's help. Although he wouldn't have complained at having Christian touch him. He longed to feel the other man's gentle hands on him. But Christian didn't seem to be aware of his craving.

Alec paused in the doorway. He remembered Christian saying he lived with his friends. "Um…I'm not exactly dressed to be wandering around."

"It's okay. No one's here but us."

"Ah. Okay then"

Christian led the way, with a pronounced limp that made Alec's heart ache, down the hall to the next doorway.

When they entered the large room, Alec stopped again, this time to stare, as erotic memories swept through him. "This room," he whispered.

Christian paused and turned to look at him. "What about it?"

"I remember it. It was in one of the dreams I had. We…"

His gaze focused on the stone fireplace, dark now, but definitely the same one from the dream. He turned to look at the huge panel bed draped in moss green covers and pillows and remembered how soft the mattress had been under his body, remembered how Christian's hands had felt on him, how Christian had entered him from behind and their bodies had been a perfect fit together.

"Damn," he whispered under his breath. His cock stirred as he faced Christian. The other man's breathing had definitely become erratic, and Alec wondered if he'd experienced the same dream and was remembering also.

For a moment, from the longing in his eyes, Alec thought Christian was going to kiss him.

But he didn't. Instead, in an abrupt movement, he turned his back on Alec and entered the bathroom.

Confused at Christian's actions and reactions, he followed him into the bathroom, where Christian pointed out clean towels, found him a new toothbrush, razor, and brought him some clothes to wear. Then, without lingering or talking or touching him in any way, he left Alec alone to take his shower.

Alec watched him go, his body thrumming with unfulfilled need, and a vise squeezing his heart.

Why was Christian suddenly shutting him out?

*   *   *

Alec felt better after his shower, though he was confused and hurt at Christian's withdrawal. Still, they'd both been through a lot the past few days, so he decided Christian had a right to draw inward. Maybe he just needed time to deal with everything.

Alec had his own concerns and knew he was going to have to ask, although he dreaded the response. He kept remembering the explosion at the police station. He could hear the sound repeating in his mind over and over. He and Christian had survived. Barely. But they *had* survived. So he had to hope others did as well. Martin's face came to mind. Was he alive?

Christian had started a fire in the fireplace by the time Alec came out of the bathroom, and had made thick roast beef sandwiches, toast, sliced apples and oranges, tea for himself, and Alec's heart caught in his throat when he saw Christian had even made him hot chocolate. He'd spread the food out on a low table in front of the fire between two comfortable-looking armchairs.

"I wasn't sure what might sound good to you, so I brought an assortment," he said.

They sat and fixed themselves plates without talking. Christian seemed lost in his own thoughts, and God knows Alec was, too. The more he replayed the scene on the street outside the police station and the sound of the explosion, the more knotted his stomach became, until the thought of trying to choke down even a small bite of food was too much to bear.

He gave up and put his plate on the table. Christian had already set his down and was turning to him at the same time.

"Chris, I need to know—"

"Alec, I have to tell you some—"

They both paused.

"Go ahead," Christian said.

"Do we know if anyone else made it?" Alec asked, his throat so tight it hurt to get the words out. Unable to look at Christian for fear he'd see the answer he didn't want on his expressive face, instead he studied the elaborate carving on the table legs.

Christian's voice, when he spoke, was slow and raspy with pain. "There were only two other survivors besides us."

Alec nodded, expecting the news, but still shocked at the grim reality of it. "And Martin?" he whispered.

He finally looked up to see grief welling in Christian's eyes.

Christian shook his head. "I'm so sorry."

Alec stood, needing to move, but not having a clue where to move to. He made it as far as the fireplace, where he stopped and stared into the flames. It was hard to breathe. Not like it had been in the collapsed building with his ribs and lungs a mess, but because…it just….was.

He felt Christian move up to stand behind him and waited for him to pull him close or offer some kind of comfort. But Christian didn't touch him. And that hurt almost as much as anything else. What the hell was going on? Why was everything suddenly falling apart?

"The two other survivors…who were they?" he mumbled.

"The young woman sergeant who helped you do research."

"Maria Koslowski?"

"Yes. And a dispatcher. Betty—"

"Betty Wilde. I know them both."

"Does Martin have family? Someone we should contact?" Christian's voice was quiet. Too quiet.

"No. There's no one. He was raised in foster homes like I was. His wife left him about ten years ago. They never had kids." Alec shook his head and grimaced as he remembered his friend. "He never stopped loving her, never stopped wearing his wedding ring, and wouldn't even look at another woman. He was such a good man." He fought the wave of emotion that threatened to drown him. "Just like he was my only family, I think I was his only family, too."

"Alec... God, I'm sorry."

The raw whisper was the final straw that put Alec's barely restrained emotions over the edge. Jesus, he needed....he didn't know what he needed.

Move. He needed to move.

Numb, he managed to get one foot in front of the other, headed toward the bedroom door.

"Alec..."

He didn't look at Christian. Couldn't. He held up a hand to stop him from talking, following. "Can't. I can't do this."

Somehow his feet managed to get him out of the room and into the hallway, but he didn't get far. Grief tore at him and suddenly, instead of moving, all he wanted to do was stop. Sleep. Forget.

The door of the guest room where he'd spent the past two days beckoned. He went in, shut off the lamp, and crawled between the cold sheets, lying on his side with his back to the door.

God-awful waves of pain tried to swallow him and he tried hard to breathe past them. In...out. In...out. But his chest ached like hell, and so did his throat. His eyes burned, but he refused to give into the emotion, afraid if he let it go and broke down, he wouldn't be able to stop.

He heard the soft squeak of the door open and shut, and froze. His heart beat a ragged, painful tattoo in his chest as he listened to slow footsteps approach the bed.

The covers were pulled back, the bed sagged, and then Christian was there, wrapping his arms around Alec and pulling Alec's back against his chest. He didn't say a word. Didn't have to. His heat and the knowledge that he was there was all it took.

The storm broke. All the pain and grief and loneliness poured out of Alec in ragged sobs he couldn't have stopped if he'd tried. Christian murmured soft sounds of comfort and held him through it all, almost fiercely, as if he felt every bit of Alec's hurt.

When the storm had passed and Alec lay emotionally drained and exhausted, somewhere in that hazy state between waking and sleep, he realized the one thing he'd wanted more than anything was to hear Christian tell him he loved him and that everything would be okay.

But it never came.

At some point later, he felt the bed shift and Christian's warmth desert him. He roused enough to see him leaving the bed.

"Chris?"

The man turned, smiled sadly down at him, and pressed his palm against Alec's cheek. "Shhh. Go back to sleep."

Alec watched him leave the room. He returned a few short minutes later. But rather than get back into bed with Alec, he sank into the chair next to the bed.

In the dark, his heart so full and tight it ached, Alec's watched him and wondered what had gone wrong between them.

CHAPTER 13

Alec awoke and stretched, then rolled to his side.

Daylight sliced through the partially open drapes, indicating he'd slept several hours. But when he saw Christian asleep in the chair—not in bed with him—it was like a sword piercing straight through his heart.

Why, he asked himself again for the hundredth time since last night, had Christian shut him out?

Needing to get out of here for a while and get some air, he slid from the bed as quietly as possible so he didn't wake the other man. His chest ached as he looked at him, his body twisted in what had to be an uncomfortable position, his legs propped on the ottoman. Alec had the urge to brush the hair off his forehead and cover him with a blanket. But he didn't. Instead, he forced down the tenderness, afraid it would be rebuffed anyway, and with his heart in his throat, stuffed his feet into his hiking boots near the door and went downstairs.

He found the back door and made his escape from the beautiful old house.

It was a cold, hazy day. Probably mid to late morning, Alec decided, looking at the sky. He hadn't thought to check the clock on his way out.

His breath misted as he walked, and the chilly air seared into his lungs. But it felt better than the quiet agony that clogged his chest each time he looked at Christian. The sun peeked out occasionally from behind thick, billowing clouds, and its warmth, faint and wintry as it was, felt good. Especially since he hadn't bothered to find a jacket and wore only a T-shirt and the flannel pajama pants he'd put on last night after his shower. It was the first time he'd seen the sun in days, he realized.

But it did little to lighten the weight pressing on him.

He didn't know what the hell to do now. There was something seriously wrong between Christian and him. They needed to talk about it, whatever it was, and get it out in the open. But with Christian holding him at a distance, completely shut down, he didn't know how that was going to happen.

God, he couldn't bear to stay here like this, with the way things were between them. It was too hard. Hurt too much. Yet he couldn't leave either.

He stopped walking and stared out across the fields, soaking up the haunting beauty of the countryside, but also experiencing the full reality of just how isolated they were out here. Christian had told him days ago, back in Illinois, that he lived in an old house in the country, and he hadn't been kidding. The house sat at the top of a hill that looked out over rolling smaller hills. But there wasn't another house in sight.

"Alec?"

He hadn't heard Christian come out of the house. The other man came up behind him and offered a navy wool pea coat, which Alec shrugged into. It smelled like Christian, clean and spicy, with a hint of musk, and the scent caused a deep quiver of longing, and sadness, in Alec.

"What is it?" Christian asked softly.

Alec ached for his touch but, once again, Christian didn't offer it.

He drew in a slow, ragged breath. "I'm trapped here."

"What?"

"You brought me here and now I'm trapped here, whether I like it or not. I can't go home. I feel almost like a prisoner in a way."

"My, God. Alec." Christian sounded shocked. "What do you mean?"

"There's no way for me to leave. I already told you I can't travel. It makes me horribly ill. What for anyone else would have been an easy two-hour car ride from Shelton to Chicago took me two days and I was still sick as hell and wanted to die. Put me on a plane from England to the US and I would die. And I'm not just saying that. It would, quite literally, kill me."

He felt Christian place a hand on his back, but then jerk it away, as if touching Alec burned him. Alec sighed and his heart sank a little lower.

"No, Alec. I know why you get sick. It's called Forten's Syndrome. It's exclusive to mages. Some mages' central nervous systems are so finely tuned for magic that they can't handle conventional travel. My mother has it. It's like your body isn't built for riding in cars or planes or other vehicles. It's built to teleport, so when you do travel conventionally, it sends mixed messages to your nervous system and you get terrible motion sickness."

"Except I'm still stuck here because I can't teleport either."

"Yes, you can. How do you think you and I made it here? I couldn't have done it alone. I directed where we were going and focused the energy, but you helped channel the energy itself."

"Okay. Fine." He swung around to face Christian. "Then tell me how to make it work again so I can get the hell out of here."

Christian took a small step backward as if he'd been struck and all the color drained from his face. Alec felt a twinge of guilt for so obviously hurting the man, but he was hurting, too, and so much crap and confusion swirled in him that he felt turned inside out and upside down.

"You...you don't want to be here." It was a statement, not a question, and was said with a pain so vibrant it hurt Alec to hear it.

Alec bent over, picked up a small, flat stone, and threw it, trying to work out some of his frustration, but it didn't help.

"I don't know where I'm supposed to be. I don't know where the hell I belong anymore. This place is so different. This world you live in is so different. You keep telling me I have magic abilities, and yet I don't feel it. I feel like a regular guy, a police detective from Illinois. Except my life in Illinois is..."

He fought to hold back the misery that threatened to bring him to another breakdown like he'd had last night. "My life in Illinois, everything I knew there, my job, my colleagues...Martin...they're all gone now. So I don't know who I am anymore. Or where I'm supposed to be." He dragged in a deep breath. "But I think I don't belong here with you either."

"Why do you think that?" Christian's voice was hoarse with barely restrained emotion.

"You can't even touch me. You barely look at me. Last night, in your room, I know you felt something when we were talking about the dreams, but then you turned your back and walked away from me. And later, as soon as you thought I was asleep, you got up and left, and when you came back into the room, instead of getting back into bed, you slept in the damn chair. All I can figure is that you don't feel comfortable being with me here. It was okay in the States where you didn't know anybody, but here, it's your home."

He ran a hand through his hair. "I understand how hard it is to be open about being gay, Christian. I understand it's scary to think of your friends finding out. I really do. But…I *am* out. And I just…" He swallowed past the enormous lump that filled his throat. "I can't stay here and be satisfied with an occasional touch and secretive glances. I can't stay here and live a half-life. Hell, I don't even know if you feel the same things for me that I feel for you."

He turned away, not wanting Christian to see how utterly miserable he was.

"Alec… You think I haven't been touching you or being close to you because I'm afraid of being out around my friends? Because I don't care about you enough to take that risk?"

"I just said that's what I think, didn't I?"

"Oh, God, I've so fucked this up. That's not it at all. I know I did a sodding awful job of comforting you last night, and I hate that. I hated it then and I hate it now. I just …I was trying to give you space because I thought that once you found out, you'd probably hate me, blame me for…for what happened."

Drawn by the total desolation in Christian's voice, Alec faced him again. His heart thudded so hard in his chest it made him hurt all over. "Blame you? For Martin's death? For what happened at the police station?"

At Christian's nod, anger flared in Alec. But not at Christian. At this whole damn mess. "Why in hell would I blame you, Chris? You have no control over that psychopath. I met him only the one time and even I know he's the type who gets off on hurting people. He wanted you to blame yourself, but that doesn't make it your fault!" He shoved his hands in the pockets of the borrowed coat and kicked another small stone with the toe of his boot. "You stupid ass. You shut me out because you made an idiotic, wrong assumption."

He started to walk away, but Christian put a hand on his shoulder, stopping him and turning him back around until they were face to face. Warmth from Christian's hand seeped through the coat and into Alec's skin. But it was the look in Christian's eyes that sent a flood of scalding heat through his veins.

"You made a wrong assumption, too. No, I haven't told my friends yet that I'm gay. We've been a little busy, almost getting killed. And in case you haven't noticed, they're not here right now to tell. But if you think for one millisecond that my fear of them finding out would ever keep me away from you, would ever be more important than spending my life with you, then you're a daft prick."

The lump in Alec's throat almost choked him.

"Because you see…" He cradled Alec's face between his hands. "I'm in love with you, Alec. The kind of love that not only makes my balls ache, but that makes my chest so tight sometimes I think I can't breathe. The kind that makes my skin tingle and my heart pound and my knees weak whenever I'm around you. I'm deeply…powerfully… unequivocally in love with you."

The words and the passion behind them stole Alec's breath. All he could do for several seconds was simply stare at Christian, his pulse racing at what he'd just heard.

"If you want to go back to the States, fine," Christian said. "But—"

"Christian?"

"What?"

Alec burrowed his hands into Christian's soft, thick dark hair and pulled his face close. "Shut up and kiss me."

It was no gentle peck or sweet caress. It was filled with raw hunger, surging love, and a lifetime's worth of pent-up passion. Their bodies melted together, their lips tasted and roamed, and their tongues dueled in an erotic dance that sent fire licking through Alec's veins. That made him crave the feel of hot, bare skin next to his, and the give and thrust of slow, sweaty lovemaking.

"I need you so much."

"I need you, too, damn it." Christian's gaze was filled with emotion and a hot intensity that promised everything Alec longed for.

"We never made it to bed the last time." Alec's voice was almost hoarse with longing. "I don't plan to make that mistake again."

"You read my mind."

By the time they made it to Christian's bedroom, Alec could barely stand for the raw desire coursing through him, leaving him shaking. Christian didn't seem to be any better off. Their coats and boots off, they faced each other, standing in front of the fire, and in spite of the urgent haste that had brought them here, time seemed to slow.

Alec slid his hands underneath Christian's sweatshirt, loving the heat of sleek skin against his palms. Inch by inch, he pushed the sweatshirt up, pausing to lick circles around Christian's flat nipples, drawing a soft hiss of breath from him. Christian's hands moved up to bury themselves in Alec's hair, and his softly murmured, "Alec...Christ," filled Alec with more pleasure than he ever could have imagined.

Smiling, he nudged Christian's arms up and slid the sweatshirt off completely. Christian didn't waste any time doing the same for the T-shirt Alec wore.

Their gazes fused, blue eyes locked with golden-brown, they began to slowly divest each other of remaining clothes, both pausing to fondle swollen cocks until their breathing came out in sharp rasps and soft words of lust were exchanged. But as Alec knelt and pushed the blue sweats down over Christian's lean hips and thighs, his gaze dropped to the brace Christian wore and his heart squeezed. He eased the soft fabric of the pants over it and waited while Christian stepped out of them.

"Lie on the bed," he said, moving over to it and pulling down the covers.

Christian didn't question, just limped to the bed and lay on his back. The relief on his face at being off his leg was clear. It was hurting him more than he'd let on.

Alec slid onto the bed next to him and sat facing him. He smoothed a hand over Christian's upper thigh, above the brace, loving the feel of the crisp dark hair against his palm, and the sight of Christian's cock responding to his simple touch.

Damn, the man was beautiful clothed, but breathtaking nude.

"Stubborn man. Why didn't you tell me sooner how much it was bothering you?"

"You had other, more important things on your mind. And it doesn't bother me that much."

Alec shook his head. "Have I mentioned before what a terrible liar you are?"

Christian sighed and a small, pained half-smile curved his sensuous lips. "Yeah, you have."

Alec searched out and found the Velcro closures that held on the brace and began to work at unfastening them. "Tell me what the healers said. About your leg."

"They told Bella it was so messed up they weren't sure it would ever heal properly and that I might have to wear a brace the rest of my life."

Alec nodded. When he had all the Velcro undone he very carefully slid off the brace. Apparently magic healers didn't do surgery like regular doctors did because there were no obvious scars or stitches. He had none on his own body either—he'd noticed when he was in the shower last night. But Christian's leg was still a mix of angry reds and mottled purples and blues, and the area around his knee was swollen.

He smoothed his palms gently over the entire length of his leg, drawing a tremble from Christian that, he suspected, had more to do with the state of his erect cock than the pain in his leg. Alec smiled and looked up at him. "Hold that thought."

"I'd rather be holding something else."

A soft chuckle slid from Alec, and it felt good. "I know. But first, let me help you, okay?"

Christian nodded. "Do you think you can?"

Alec looked into those warm, love-filled blue eyes and was pretty sure as long as he was with Christian he could do almost anything. "Yeah, I think I can. But before I do, there's something you should know."

"What's that?"

"I love you, too. More than I've ever loved anyone. And even if I do learn how to teleport, unless you plan to kick me out, you're pretty much stuck with me. Because the only place I want to be…is with you."

Christian's sculpted chest heaved as he drew in and let out a ragged breath. His eyes filled with emotion, he sat up, grasped the back of Alec's head with one of his hands, and pulled him into a kiss.

"We belong together, Alec." His breath was warm and minty against Alec's lips.

"I know. I'm so in love with you, Chris."

"God, I'm so in love with you."

They kissed again and it was as slow and sensuous as the one outside had been hard and urgent. Alec's cock ached and that same fire of earlier licked through his veins. But first things first. He didn't want Christian to hurt any more, and that was something he could help with.

He held him away, hands on Christian's shoulders, and pressed him back on the bed. "Let me help you," he said again. "Close your eyes and relax."

Christian nodded and closed his eyes, but he was far from relaxed as evidenced by his rapid breathing and his beautiful cock pulsing with need. It took all Alec's self control not to wrap his hand around the base of it and lower his mouth to have a taste.

Jesus. He didn't think he'd ever be able to get enough of this man.

Refocusing back on the task at hand, he closed his own eyes and let his mind empty of all thoughts except what he intended to do. Normally, the warm energy he associated with healing would begin to flow through him, and it did this time as well. He'd never really understood where it came from, hadn't known how to control it. But remembering all the things Christian had told him, this time he made a concentrated effort to feel where it came from, and damned if he didn't sense it, rippling all around him. He tried drawing more of it into him—channeling, Christian had called it—and was pleasantly surprised to discover he could pull in extra. To a certain extent. But then it got harder. He could sense plenty of energy outside himself, but when he tried to pull it toward him, it was almost like a barrier was in the way, a wall or screen that made it tough to get through. He fought against it and was able to draw in a bit more, but finally decided it was something he'd have to work on later. He had enough for now to do what he needed.

He rested his hands lightly on Christian's leg and felt the energy flow naturally from him into Christian—a steady surge of golden heat that made his palms tingle. He could sense where the healers had done their work, could feel little twinges of their lingering energy, and he added to what they'd done. But there were areas they hadn't been able to get to, dark spots, as he thought of them, and those were the places he concentrated on the most, flooding them with energy, feeling the tendons, ligaments, and tissues flicker back to life and begin to heal.

He didn't know how long he worked, had no sense of time passing, just stayed at it until, when he ran his hands up and down Christian's leg, he felt no more dark areas, only warm, healthy life.

When he opened his eyes and looked, even the discoloration on Christian's skin had begun to fade, and the swelling had gone down completely.

He felt a little drained, but pleased with what he'd accomplished. "How does that feel?" he asked, looking up at Christian.

Christian's eyes fluttered open and his gaze zeroed in on Alec. "It doesn't ache anymore."

"Move it. Gently. And see how it feels then."

Grimacing as if he were expecting pain, he moved it slowly, but the grimace turned into an expression of shock. He slid his foot up on the bed until his knee was bent. He stared at Alec. "It doesn't hurt. I can move it…and it doesn't hurt."

Alec smiled. "Good, that's what I was shooting for."

"I thought…" Christian shook his head. "I thought maybe you could help ease the pain, but I never dreamed…" He sat up so he and Alec were face to face. "Do you have any idea how powerful you are?"

Alec shrugged. "So you've said, but I keep telling you, I'm just me."

"I don't even know how to thank you." Christian's voice was quiet.

Alec reached between them and captured Christian's cock in his hand. "Oh, I think you do."

CHAPTER 14

At the scorching invitation in Alec's eyes and the feel of his hand on Christian's cock, squeezing in a slow pulsing motion that was already making his balls tingle, Christian pulled Alec's face close, taking his time, exploring and savoring every millimeter of his hot, sexy mouth. Their tongues began a slow screw and Alec's hand on his shaft mimicked it, until stars danced behind Christian's closed eyes.

"Okay, that's it," he growled, pulling his mouth free. "Lie down and roll onto your stomach."

Alec flashed him a mischievous smile and did as he was told, stretching out on the bed in a relaxed pose, his head resting on his arms, his legs slightly spread. The firelight played over his broad shoulders and athletic body, accentuating how damned masculine and handsome he was. Which only made Christian want him more.

He straddled Alec's legs and let his hands roam over the man's back, his sides, hips, down his thighs and calves. Then he worked his way to Alec's ass, where he took his time, massaging his gluts, enjoying the hell out of seeing Alec tremble whenever one of his thumbs or fingers slid along the tantalizing crease between his cheeks.

"Feel good?"

"God, yes."

Christian continued to tease, eventually letting his thumbs burrow generously into the warm cleft on each pass. And each time they did, Alec's fingers would dig into the mattress and his hips would lift slightly off the bed until, eventually, tremors shook his entire body and

Christian had to chuckle at his desperation.

"Is there something you want, love?"

Alec gave him a frazzled yet completely x-rated glare over his shoulder. "Yes, damn it. Touch me."

"I am touching you," he said calmly.

"Shit."

Another chuckle escaped Christian. He couldn't help it. He smoothed his hands over Alec's butt yet again, appreciating the feel of hot skin against his palm, and the way Alec's firm ass rounded off into strong, muscular legs. He eased a hand between them and brushed the tight, wrinkled skin of his sac.

"Please…" Alec moaned. "You're torturing me." His hips rose from the bed and he pulled himself up to his hands and knees in silent invitation.

An invitation Christian couldn't pass up. The sight of that beautiful, pale ass raised and ready for pleasure almost undid him. His cock was hard and eager to be buried in Alec's warm, willing body. But he was enjoying Alec's responses too much not to prolong it. Besides, he could think of many ways he yearned to touch the other man, to explore him.

He spread Alec's cheeks open and a new surge of gut-deep desire filled him at the sight of his tight opening. *Damn.* He bent and licked the soft skin around the quivering hole.

Alec's body jerked and shuddered.

"How about this? Is this what you want?" Chris asked softly before blowing warm air over the sensitive opening, then burrowing his tongue into it.

"Yes…God, yes…" Alec panted.

His body opened willingly and pulsed around Christian's probing tongue. With each slow thrust, Alec pressed back against him, making guttural noises of lust and need that filled Christian with a primal hunger he'd never felt before. He probed faster, harder and Alec writhed at his assault.

Pausing, leaving Alec breathing hard and protesting, he pulled open the drawer of the bedside table and found the tube of lubrication he kept there. He generously coated his fingers and pressed two of them deep into Alec.

"Shit! Unnh…Chris…"

Christian closed his eyes and fought back the burning in his cock. Watching Alec respond like this was almost too much, too hot. But he couldn't not look for long. The allure was just too powerful. Damn, the man was incredible, and his love for him welled up like a live thing.

He alternated between tonguing Alec and using his fingers until even he was turned on to the point of agony. Alec practically vibrated against him.

"I want you inside me," Alec demanded. His eyes were squeezed closed. "Fuck me. Fill me."

Aching to do just that, Christian reached again to the drawer, this time for a condom, but Alec stopped him and looked back over his shoulder. "We've both been tested. We don't have to."

Christian had never been inside a man without protection and the thought of being able to really feel Alec with no barrier between them was a gift he'd never expected.

"I trust you," Alec said, his eyes golden seas of love and barely restrained desire.

Christian put the box away and shut the drawer. "And I trust you. Always." Damn, he loved this man.

Alec's smile quickly turned into a shudder as his body reminded them both what they craved. His eyes closed again. "Jesus…need you, Chris."

Christian squeezed lube into his palm, slicked his shaft, pressed the tip of his slippery cockhead against Alec's opening, and pushed.

Bloody hell. He'd never seen anything so erotic in his life as watching his swollen cock disappear into Alec's firm, perfect ass. Alec's body was throbbing and eager, and so damned hot.

They both groaned when Christian buried himself to the hilt. And when Alec pressed himself back, seating Christian even deeper still, they groaned again.

"God, you feel good," Christian growled.

"So do you."

The hot, tight pressure of Alec's muscles squeezed Christian so hard he was almost dizzy. He grasped Alec's hips and held him against him, not moving, just savoring how damn perfect they were together, letting the scorching heat of Alec's body seep into him.

But when they were both shaking and almost beyond reason, Christian couldn't have stopped his body from surging into motion if he'd tried. Holding Alec's hips in his hands, he thrust hard and deep, then pulled out slowly, only to thrust in deep again.

"Yes, yes," Alec panted.

With his right hand, Christian reached around and grasped Alec's cock.

All the sensations—tight, hot channel, soft skin, the throb of hard prick in his hand, his and Alec's soft grunts, the scent of their lovemaking—swirled in his head, driving him to even greater need. He couldn't get enough of Alec, couldn't bury himself deep enough or feel enough of their skin pressed together. His hand on Alec's hip splayed over the slick flesh, wanting him closer, wanting to lose himself forever in this man.

"Christian, I've never…unnh! I've never let anyone come in me before…without protection. Do it…. I want you to do it. I want you to explode inside me."

The words filled Christian's heart so full he thought it might burst. The thought that Alec had never shared this experience even with Drew, his lover of three years, made him realize just what a gift it truly was.

Alec's ass thrust back against him harder, harder, and then his muscles clamped down on Christian's cock and he gave a shuddering cry. The warm gush of thick cream covered Christian's hand as Alec came. Seconds later, he found his own release. He pounded into Alec as liquid heat jetted from him deep into Alec's core.

Gasping for air, Christian slid free from him and they collapsed onto the bed, snuggling together, Alec's back and ass to Christian's chest and groin.

It was several minutes before they managed to catch their breath and relax.

"I love you so damn much, Alec."

Alec turned his head to look at Christian with a hot gaze, and his arm curled back around Christian's head, pulling him into a still-hungry, open-mouthed kiss. "I love you, too. How's your leg?"

Christian smiled. "How do you think it is? I doubt I could have been doing the things I've been doing if it wasn't okay."

Alec gave him a fairly wicked smile. "Nothing like taking it for an all-out test run." He rolled toward Christian. "And I have to say, for someone who's only just coming out, you are not inexperienced in any way."

Christian smiled. "No, I'm not."

"So let's hear it."

"Yeah?"

Alec gave him a pointed look, along with an I-dare-you smile.

He chuckled. "All right. My last two years of university I dated a girl who had a kinky streak. There were a few times when she suggested we get together with a gay guy friend of hers and get it on, the three of us together. The first time she suggested it, I was kind of taken aback. But the idea didn't shock me as much as I might have thought, so I figured what the hell. It turned out not just to be two guys on one girl, it was also guy on guy. What did surprise the sodding hell out of me, though, was…"

"Was that you liked it better with him than with your girlfriend," Alec said knowingly.

Christian nodded. "Yeah. I wasn't about to tell her that, though. It happened a few more times, and then, when she and I eventually broke up, the guy and I got together a couple of times—no sex, just to hang out. But I wasn't ready to take the plunge completely at that point. It seemed somehow okay for a straight guy to have an occasional threesome that included another man. In my mind I could chalk that up to having a kinky girlfriend and being adventurous. It was different, though, to admit that I wanted one-on-one without the girl. So I decided I was going to put it to the back of my mind. I convinced myself it was just a wild streak I had while I was younger and it didn't have any bearing on who I was as a man."

"But?"

"But even though I didn't want to think about it, I did sometimes. And when I finally broke up with Bella's sister Kate, I couldn't stop thinking about it. Wondering. Then on a trip to Paris summer before last, I ran into the guy from college. There was no one around I knew, and he was currently unattached, as was I, so we spent a long weekend together. We both knew it was just the weekend, nothing more. But I learned a lot about myself those three days. I knew there was no point in trying to pretend with myself anymore, although I wasn't ready to announce it to my friends or the world either."

Alec stroked Christian's cheek. "Are you sure you're going to be okay with your friends…about us?"

A surge of possessiveness shot through Christian and he pressed a fierce kiss against Alec's mouth. "You're part of my life now, the most important part, and I'm not about to hide it."

"Your mom already knows."

"What?" Christian felt his eyebrows rocket up and his heart pound.

"I'm sorry," Alec said quickly. "I didn't mean to spring it on you like that. It just kind of came out. You okay?"

Christian dragged in a deep breath. "Yeah. I'm okay… I'm sort of over it now. The shock. Can you give me some details here?"

"I went to Chicago to see her, your mom, to find out more information about you. I'm really sorry, I should have just believed in you and, for what it's worth, I realized that as soon as I got there."

"Alec, it's okay. You don't have to apologize. I understand why you'd want to know more about me. I told you some pretty strange stuff that weekend. You had every right to go looking for information."

"Well, I felt awful about it and once I was there, decided I'd been an ass and I trusted you and I didn't need to hear it from anyone else. But her lecture had already started by that point, so I figured I'd stay to be polite. Then I was so sick and, as I was leaving, she saw me and made me sit down. We talked. I didn't tell her about you. She already knew."

"How?" Again, Christian's pulse throbbed.

Alec shrugged. "I don't know, but she apparently has for a while. Here's how the conversation went. We'd barely started talking. I'd only said maybe a half-dozen sentences to her, told her I'd found out about her through her son and that we'd been working together while you were in the States. I swear, that's all I said. And then out of the blue she looks right at me and with this knowing smile on her face says, "Does Christian know you're in love with him?""

"Bloody hell! She said that?"

"Yeah. Took me by surprise, too, believe me. So there I am thinking, oh, shit, what am I going to say? But before I could respond, she says, 'It's all right, he thinks I don't know and I let him believe that. He'll tell me when he's ready. And if he feels about you the way I can see you feel about him, I suspect it'll be sooner rather than later.'"

Christian sank back into the bed, suddenly drained of energy. "How did she seem about it?"

Alec propped himself on his elbow and rubbed a hand over Christian's heart. "Totally cool with it. Smiling. Real smiling, not fake. She…asked me to give you a message."

"She did?"

"She asked me to tell you that she approves."

"Of my being gay or of you?"

"I think both."

Christian brushed a lock of hair out of Alec's eyes and studied this man he'd fallen so hard for. "You're a hell of a man, Alec."

Alec's eyebrows drew together and his smile was curious. "What do you mean by that?"

"You're a hell of a cop, a hell of a human being, increasingly I'm realizing you're a hell of a mage...I'm not surprised my mum fell in love with you."

"I didn't say that."

"You don't have to. I know my mum. She's a damn fine judge of character."

Alec chuckled. "And what about you?"

"I'm a damn fine judge of character, too."

"So why don't you kiss me and refresh your memory?"

"You think it needs refreshing?" he asked, turning back onto his side facing Alec.

"I do," Alec breathed against his lips. "Maybe several times over."

They kissed for a long time, savoring each other, until Christian was shocked to realize he was getting hard again.

"Damn. Look what you do to me," he said, bringing Alec's hand down to feel the stiff length of him wedged between his groin and Alec's thigh.

Alec smiled, draping a leg over Christian's hip. He took one of Christian's hands and brought it down to his own bulging erection. "Look what you do to me."

Christian grinned. He cupped Alec's ass in one hand and pulled him closer until their cocks nestled together. He slipped a finger between Alec's ass cheeks and teased it over his opening, still slippery with lube and cum, then pushed it inside just a few centimeters.

Alec's eyes glazed over. "Jesus. You realize, of course, that if you keep that up...unnnh!" Christian slipped another finger in next to the first. "Oh...crap." He brought Christian's mouth back to his and kissed him deeply. "I really love you," he rasped, his eyes filling all over again with that hot, mischievous invitation that set Christian's insides on fire.

"How much?" He began to plunge his fingers in and out of Alec, loving the way Alec shuddered in response and ground his groin against Christian's.

"Shit! I love you enough I'm going to make you pay for this."

"Promises, promises."

With a heated looked and little other warning, Alec suddenly rolled Christian onto his back with him straddling Christian's hips.

Christian still had his fingers inside Alec, although it was harder to reach now—he propped pillows behind his head, raising himself up enough he could keep them there.

Alec gave him another devilish look that promised paybacks would probably be hell. He found the lube somewhere in the covers and, with a smirk, squeezed a generous amount into his hand.

"I'm not taking mine out," Christian told him, curving his own fingers deeper inside Alec and rubbing gently against his prostate.

A ragged huff of breath escaped Alec, but the sexy smirk never left his face. "Fine."

He turned around until he sat astride Christian facing backward, with full access to everything Christian had to offer in front of him.

Christian's cock pulsed in excitement at this new turn of events.

Alec looked at him over his shoulder and shot him a grin. Then he spread Christian's legs apart, slid his lube-coated hand beneath Christian's balls, found his opening, and pushed a finger inside.

Christian gasped.

Alec stroked his finger in and out few times, then slowly moved it in circles inside him, stretching him wider.

Christian slid his knees up and opened his legs farther, giving Alec better access.

Alec pushed another finger up to join the first and then, with Christian writhing beneath him, slowly added a third.

"Damn! Oh, God…"

"Feel good?" Alec asked, looking at him again over his shoulder. But this time the smirk was gone and raw desire etched his face.

"Christ. You know it does," Christian gasped. He probed his own fingers deeper into Alec, setting up a counterpoint between Alec's thrusts into him and his in Alec.

But what almost drove him to the brink of madness was when Alec slid his well-lubed hand around Christian's prick and began pumping it hard.

"Oh…sodding…hell," he moaned, closing his eyes and drowning in the incredible sensations of his cock being worked in Alec's hot, slick hand, and the insistent, slippery fingers filling him. His hips bucked of their own volition and he knew he wasn't going to last long. But, good God, he wanted to. He wanted to so badly.

The combination of sensations was too much, though, and with Alec giving him no quarter, his hand and fingers tirelessly working their sensual magic on him, he came in an orgasm so hard he could feel it pulsing in his skull. And came and came and came, shocking himself at how much he had in him after already having had a powerful orgasm earlier.

Finally, his body sagged into the mattress, completely spent.

Alec eased himself off Christian's fingers and turned to face him. The moment he did, Christian could see from the look in his eyes that Alec wasn't done with him yet. *Holy mother of God.* The man was insatiable. And, yet, he didn't know how it was possible, but a spark still burned deep in him and he suddenly knew that whatever Alec wanted, he'd give him.

He rose to his knees between Christian's parted legs. His gaze grew hot and heavy once again. His thick shaft jutted from dark curls, eager and at attention, glistening with drops of Christian's cum that had splashed on it. The sight made Christian's mouth water.

"What do you want?" he asked Alec, smiling up at him. "You know whatever it is, I'm going to say yes."

"I want to be inside you." Alec's voice was low and filled with hunger.

Christian's pulse raced at the thought. "God, yes. Do it."

He thought he saw a flicker of surprise in Alec's eyes.

"Why does that surprise you?" he asked.

"Drew...always liked to be the top. Always."

"I like both."

Alec's eyebrows knitted together. "Are you just saying that to be nice, or do you mean it?"

"I think we're kind of past saying things just to be nice to each other, aren't we? I love being inside you, I love the way it feels when your body swallows me. I love how hot and tight you are. I loved coming inside you. Those things are all a huge turn-on. But as much as I love all that, I also love the thought of you doing those things to me. As far as I'm concerned, this is an equal partnership, Alec. I wouldn't want it any other way. Would you?"

A slow smile spread across Alec's face and the heat in his eyes intensified. "No, I wouldn't. It's one of the things I love about you."

Christian let his arms fall out to his sides and grinned. "So have your way with me."

"I intend to."

Oh, he loved that daring grin.

Finding the lube again, Alec spread it over his cock until it gleamed in the firelight. He pushed Christian's legs up and rubbed himself against Christian's balls, eliciting a hiss from him. And then the tip of his rigid shaft found Christian's hole, pressing, pressing with a slow insistence that had Christian gasping.

He felt Alec's bulbous cockhead push past the opening and stretch the tight rings of muscle inside him. He heard his own fast, heavy breathing in his ears, and wondered if his own gaze was as clouded with love and lust as Alec's was.

"Fuck…Alec…" Oh, bugger it was good. So good.

Alec bent to kiss him, his tongue moving in slow, languid thrusts, then his mouth slid lower, nipping at Christian's neck, his collarbone, sucking in one of his nipples and biting down on it with just enough pressure the pleasure/pain of it nearly shot Christian off the bed.

And always Alec's stiff, prodding shaft was pushing slowly inward until Christian was nearly insane with need and the desire to have Alec buried balls-deep inside him. He lifted his hips and ground his groin against Alec's, moving in rhythm to the sucking and biting on his nipple.

Finally, at long last, he felt Alec's heavy balls press against him. The man's thick cock stretched his opening, making it sting, but only in a good way, not unlike the tingling pulse in his nipples, which Alec continued to play.

Alec raised his head and gave him a smile that promised all manner of delights, and once again Christian knew he'd never, ever tire of being with this man.

"How do you want it?" Alec asked. "Deep and slow…?" He stroked slowly in and out of Christian, pulling nearly out to the tip, then driving back in so deep Christian thought he could feel the tip of Alec's cock in his heart. "Or hard and fast?" He grasped Christian's hips and pounded into him until Christian couldn't breathe and his own cock and balls ached.

Christian gripped his head and pulled it down into a kiss. "Deep and slow," he said, his eyes burning into Alec's. "I want to feel every inch of you for as long as possible."

Alec's eyes flickered with emotion and his smile this time shone with love. "A man of my own heart," he said quietly.

They moved together in slow, soul-searing passion, and Christian had never felt closer to anyone in his life.

Working together, they brought Christian to yet another orgasm, surprising him, spilling his seed over their hands and his abs only moments before Alec stiffened and spilled his own deep inside Christian.

Exhausted, utterly sated, they fell asleep wrapped in each other's arms.

CHAPTER 15

It was evening before they stirred, and late evening before they made it out of bed and into the shower….and a while still before they made it out of the shower.

But hunger—for actual food—finally forced them to leave the bedroom.

"Does this require putting on clothing?" Alec asked, gazing with much un-longing at the pile of clothes on the floor.

"Not if you don't want to." Christian's smile was daring. "I'm not putting on any. I told you, no one's here but us."

"Where are these housemates of yours?"

"Jamie's in the States right now. Bella's in Athens."

"Athens, Greece?"

"Yeah."

"You guys get around don't you?"

"Sometimes." Christian shrugged as he led the way downstairs to the kitchen.

Alec meant to ask next why that was and what kind of jobs Bella and Jamie did, but his train of thought completely fled at the sight of Christian's nude backside a few steps ahead of him. Damn. They'd spent the day in bed, and yet the man still had the ability to send heat scudding through his veins. But what pleased him most was that Christian wasn't limping at all.

"Are you ogling my ass?" Christian asked, looking back over his shoulder as he entered the big kitchen. He pointed a finger at the fireplace, did some kind of small movement with it, and a fire whooshed to life.

Alec chuckled. "I am. Got a problem with that?"

"Yeah, I do, since I'm not getting to ogle yours, too."

Alec shrugged. "Next time don't be Mr. Macho Leader and rush off to be the first in line. Sometimes it pays to hang back. The view's better."

"Oh, I don't know." Christian stopped and turned to face him. "I'm not really complaining about the view from here."

Even with the flickering flames the only light in the big room, Alec could see every contour of Christian's nude body, including his hardening shaft.

He padded up to Christian and kissed him. "You keep looking at me like that and there's going to be less eating of food and more testing uses for kitchen utensils."

Christian's blue eyes grew heavy-lidded and dark with desire. "Keep talking like that and I'm thinking I'll gladly wait for the food."

"Food. Hmmm. That could be interesting, too," Alec said with a grin. He opened the freezer side of the huge, stainless steel refrigerator and pulled out a large plastic container full of ice produced by the icemaker. He picked up one elongated cube and, giving Christian a come-hither teasing look, sucked on it.

Christian's gaze grew even more passionately intense.

Alec chuckled, knowing he shouldn't tease, but it was so worth it to see that expression on Christian's face.

"Where are the glasses?" he asked, looking in the first cupboard he came to.

He was suddenly spun around and bent over, face down, against the granite-topped island. "They can wait," Christian said hoarsely.

Shit. Alec's heart pounded as Christian spread his legs apart with warm, insistent hands. His body tingled in anticipation, wondering what Chris was up to.

But he quickly found out. He heard the rattle of ice in the container and then Christian was kneeling behind him, spreading his ass cheeks apart. His tongue—his *cold* tongue—flicked out to prod at Alec's hole, eliciting a moan from Alec. Christian's tongue probed in and out a few times, quickly bringing Alec's cock to an eager ache. And then, suddenly, he felt a piece of ice slide past his opening and up into him.

He jerked in surprise, but Christian held him place, not letting him move.

Christian tongued him a few more times, and then another cube slid into place.

"Shit...shit!" Alec panted, his blood boiling in spite of the slow freeze that was beginning to tingle in his ass.

Christian kept at it until he done it twice more. Alec was trembling at this point, so fucking turned on, his cock so hard it felt like it was going to explode, and his ass burning from the ice inside it.

Christian stood, still keeping Alec bent over and pressed against the counter, but Alec heard him doing something. Not the ice bucket this time. He couldn't tell what. He felt motion behind him and then Christian's cock was pressing against his entrance. It was slippery and hot in contrast to the wet freeze inside him.

Holding Alec's hip steady in his left hand, and his thick cockhead slowly easing past the tight trembling rings of muscle in his ass, Christian's right hand came around and grasped Alec's cock. It was warm and slippery as hell. And it had a faint scent to it. Olive oil.

With a groan and a deep thrust, Christian's cock slid home.

"Oh, fuck," Alec gasped feeling the ice inside him move deeper to make room for Christian's long shaft. He'd never felt so full. So cold. So hot. All at the same time.

"Bloody hell," Christian groaned behind him, apparently experiencing something of the same thing.

Alec was completely out of his mind with desire at this point and began to rock his ass back against Christian's groin. Christian responded in kind, plowing deeply into him, holding them together for a few seconds, pulling almost out, then plowing in again. That rhythm—thrust, hold, out—became a mantra in Alec's mind, and it was copied in the motion Christian's slippery fist was making with Alec's cock.

"God...oh...my...God!" Alec panted over and over. His balls burned, his ass ached, and his cock throbbed steadily in Christian's hand. He was close. He felt Christian's cock growing stiffer inside him and knew he was close, too.

"Now, Alec!" Christian's body tightened, and at the same time, Alec's cock erupted in one of the most powerful orgasms he'd ever had, shooting thick, ropy streams of cum all over Christian's hand, the floor, and God knew what else. Christian cried out and Alec felt his release as well, pouring into him, coating his passage thoroughly with slick, hot cream.

They stayed locked together for several long seconds after their orgasms had faded, breathing hard, trembling.

When Christian's cock slipped free, he helped Alec stand and turn around, then they simply stared at one another. Alec had never in his life experienced anything so purely erotic before. Had never completely lost control like that either. And he could tell Christian was as shaken by what had just happened as he was.

"Jesus," Alec whispered at last, unable to vocalize it any better.

"I know." Christian's voice was low and raspy. His eyebrows drew together. "I don't know what got into me."

"Have I told you tonight just how much I love you?" Alec asked, hearing his voice tremble.

Christian shook his head, his eyes alight with emotion.

"I do. Completely."

Christian's tongue flicked out to moisten his lips. "Alec…God…I'd be so lost without you."

The kiss they shared, so tender and filled with love, made Alec's heart ache.

*   *   *

They cleaned up the kitchen in quiet solidarity, took another shower filled with gentle caresses and kisses rather than steamy sex, then fixed and ate sandwiches.

Two hours later, they were back in bed, full from their late dinner, freshly-shaven, and emotionally and physically sated. There was a closeness between them, something about the incident in the kitchen, that had ripped away any lingering inhibitions or fears, leaving them both exposed and laid bare for each other. And every time Alec looked into Christian's eyes, he felt loved and cherished in a way he'd never known before, and knew Christian felt the same. It was like they'd somehow become one whole.

They lay on their sides facing one another, talking quietly.

"It was the strangest thing that I saw this in one of the dreams I had last week," Christian said, rubbing a finger against the small silver medallion Alec wore. "Every detail in the dream was perfect. It looks a bit Celtic. Where'd you get it?"

"You know, I've had it and been wearing it since I was really little. I remember my grandmother telling me my dad had given it to me and that it had his love and protection woven into it." He smiled. "I guess that's what's kept me wearing it over the years. I just liked the way that sounded. Made me feel like I still had some family."

Christian leaned up on his elbow. "She said that specifically...that it had love and protection woven into it?"

"Yeah."

"Do you always wear it? Do you ever take it off?"

"Yeah, I guess I pretty much do always wear it. I don't take it off very often." Alec gave him a curious look. "Why?"

Christian studied him for a moment, his head tilted. A little half-smile curved one side of his lips. "Can we...try something?"

Alec grinned. "Is it kinky?"

Christian's laugh send new spikes of heat through him. "No. Not this time."

"Oh. Damn. Well, yeah, what do you want to try?"

"Will you take it off? The medallion?"

"Sure." As he unfastened the clasp he gave Christian another little grin. "Are you sure you're not planning something kinky?"

"I'm sure. At least not with this."

As he laid the necklace on the bedside table, Christian's smile, already a thing of beauty, seemed to grow even more dazzling.

"What?" he asked, wondering what about him taking off his old necklace could possibly have put that smile on his lover's face. But then he suddenly saw something about Christian he'd never noticed before. "What the...?" He blinked as he stared at the man. "There's a...you have a..."

"Yeah? A what?"

Damn, could the man smile any bigger?

"There's a...um...well, I don't quite know how to say this without sounding crazy, but there's this glowing bluish light thing around you." It surrounded Christian like a full-body halo with a flush of gold and sparkling bits of white mixed in with it. "Damn. Damn. It's really beautiful."

"You should see yours."

"Mine? What do you mean? Do I have one, too?"

Christian laughed softly. "Ohhhhhh, yeah. Oh...definitely....yeah."

"What the hell is it? Are they?"

Christian's warm palm smoothed along his cheek and then drew his face close for a lingering kiss. His eyes danced with love and heat and pleasure. "What you're seeing, and what I'm seeing around you, is a magic aura."

"A what?"

"Remember I told you that I couldn't understand your abilities because they had to be magic but I couldn't see a magic aura on you?"

"Yeah, I vaguely remember that."

"Everyone has an aura, a field of energy surrounding them. It's made up in part of the vibrational energy that surrounds us all and in part by the energy that sustains that body in particular. The colors can change depending on people's health or even their moods. Not everyone can see the regular human aura—usually just folks who have a natural talent for it or who've taught themselves to see it or feel it. But a mage's aura is a bit different. It's usually brighter with a blue cast to it—it can still have other colors mixed in, but blue tends to be the dominant one. And unlike the regular human aura, virtually all mages can see magic auras on other mages. It's one of the ways we can identify each other if we're in a large group of people and want to know if there are any other magic folk present."

"So what are you saying? And why I can I suddenly see yours?"

"I've been telling you that you have magic gifts, Alec. The healing, the ability to call me with your mind, sharing dreams with me, and then your ability to help teleport us here when the building collapsed. I couldn't see your magic aura, though, and I didn't think you could see mine either or else I figured you'd have said something. It just occurred to me as you were talking about your medallion, when you said your grandmother told you it was woven with your father's love and protection, that maybe the medallion was what was hiding your aura and suppressing your powers."

"Because my grandmother said it was for protection?"

"Partly. But also because of the wording. She told you it was 'woven' with love and protection. When a mage does a spell on something, we say we 'weave' the spell."

"And you think my dad did this to the medallion? Why would he do that?"

"To keep you safe, I suppose. It's kind of like a protective shield. Stuff can bang on it from the outside and not get in, but remember I told you that while a mage is holding a protective shield he also can't use his magic on anything outside of it?"

Alec nodded.

"Well, the medallion and the protection it gives off has probably been preventing you from accessing your full power."

"You know, I had a thing happen earlier today, when I was working on your leg. I'd never really paid attention before to where the healing energy came from, but I was thinking about what you'd told me, so I noticed. And it was odd because it almost felt like there was something blocking me. Like I couldn't quite access as much energy as I was sure I should be able to."

Christian nodded. "Yeah, that sounds about right. Like there was an actual barrier of some kind you couldn't bring the energy past?"

"Yeah. Well, I mean I could access some energy—I've always been able to—but it's like I knew there was much more and I couldn't get at it."

"If you think about it, the stuff you've been able to do has all happened during moments of big emotion—your sympathy and caring for people that allowed you to access enough of your powers to heal, or the moment the guiller attacked and you were able to call out to me, or I don't know about you but I was scared as hell that building was going to collapse on us. I've no doubt that fear is what allowed enough of your power to bubble over the edge of the protection spell for you to be able to teleport. But at the same time, while a protection spell like that would restrain your own powers, it would also keep other mages from seeing them. So if your dad were concerned about you..." He shrugged.

"Is that normal?" For a magic parent to do that? To want to hide their children's power?"

"No, not really. But maybe he was just overprotective, or maybe there was a specific event he wanted to keep you safe from. And since he died when you were so little, I'm sure he probably never meant for you to wear the medallion all your life."

Alec frowned. "If what you're saying is the case, that means my parents, or at least my dad was a mage?"

"Almost certain. Magic tends to run in families. It's rare to see it pop up in someone from an Ordinary family, and when it does, it's usually because an Ordinary woman has had sex with a mage without realizing he's a mage, then they part ways and she has a baby. Or maybe a baby from a mage family ends up adopted by an Ordinary family, although that's pretty rare because magic folks tend to look out after their own and a mage family would always try to be found for a mage baby. Magic's pretty much hereditary."

"What about my grandmother? Was she one, too, since she could do the healing with her hands?"

"Probably."

"Why wouldn't she have told me what she was?"

"I don't know, Alec. We may never know." He lay down and pulled Alec into his arms again. They rested like that for a few seconds, but

179

then Alec propped himself up on his elbow and gazed down at Christian. "So you're telling me that if I'm not wearing that medallion I'll be able to see this glowing aura on anyone who can do magic?"

A smile quirked Christian's lips. "Yes."

"All the time? I'll be able to see it all the time? And they'll be able to see mine?"

"Yes."

"Okay, that's just…bizarre. I mean, how do you get used to something like that? I look at you and it's just so…there. And so bright. And are you saying your mom has one of these, too?"

Christian chuckled. "Yes. Don't worry. You'll get used to it and pretty soon it'll just become a natural part of your vision and you won't think twice about it or find it a distraction. And you know…" His hand slowly stroked down Alec's back and then teased leisurely circles over his ass, while at the same time, the fingers of his other hand plucked at one of Alec's nipples. "It can also come in handy because just like a regular human aura, the colors in it can change depending on the person's mood or, say, their current emotions and"—his fingers plucked harder, making Alec gasp—"state of arousal."

Christian's aura, still a deep, bright blue with gold was beginning to glimmer a clear red closest to his body and Alec wondered if his was doing the same thing.

"I don't really think I need to see your aura to know that," he whispered, letting his own hands roam and eliciting a few gasps of his own from Christian.

*   *   *

Christian swam up from a deep sleep to what sounded like a soft bang somewhere in the house. He listened for it again, but nothing else happened.

He raised up enough to look over Alec's shoulder at the clock next to the bed. A little after seven in the morning. The first fingers of gray light crept through the drapes, and the fire on the hearth had died down to only glowing coals.

Too early to get up just yet, he decided. Especially when he had a warm bed and even warmer lover to stay in bed for.

He snuggled in closer to Alec's back and draped his arm around Alec's waist. In his sleep, Alec pulled it up against his chest and wound their fingers together, bringing a smile to Christian's face. He already couldn't imagine ever sleeping alone again, without Alec's heat-producing body stretched out next to him. It was so heat producing, in fact, Alec had kicked off the covers around his legs and only had a sheet tangled around his groin.

Christian pressed a kiss against the back of Alec's neck, then closed his eyes and let himself drift off again.

Until the squeak of the bedroom door jolted him wide awake in an instant.

He raised up in time to see the outline of Bella standing in the doorway, hear her gasp, and, he wasn't sure, but he thought he heard her give a soft squeal.

"Bella!" he hissed in a loud whisper. "Sod off!" He threw one of the spare pillows from the bed at the doorway, but she'd already shut it and left.

Alec stirred and shifted, turning to his back, but didn't wake up.

His heart beating double-time in his chest, Christian stared at the dark doorway. *Bugger.* He'd been planning to talk to Jamie and Bella when they returned anyway, but it was supposed to be at time of his choosing. Not like this.

Damn, damn, damn.

Knowing he'd never be able to go back to sleep now, not with his pulse still tripping like mad and the dull knot gnawing in his gut, he quietly slid out of bed and found a pair of pants to pull on.

But before he left the room, he gave Alec one last glance in the early morning light. He was sound asleep, one hand on his chest, the other arm stretched above his head.

A sense of calm fell over Christian as he looked at him, this man he was so damned in love with. Alec gave him a strength he'd never had before. The strength to stand up for who he was and what he wanted. And, quite simply, he wanted Alec.

With that in mind, he went in search of his best friends, hoping they'd accept his revelation and his and Alec's relationship, but knowing if they didn't, he'd already made his choice.

He found them in the kitchen.

They were talking quietly, making tea when Christian entered. Both turned when they saw him, and Bella started to speak, but Christian held up his hand and stopped her.

"Don't say a word. I'm going to do the talking."

She and Jamie shared a look—Christian couldn't tell what it meant—then they both nodded.

Christian stalked around the huge, trestle dining table to the fireplace, where Bella and Jamie must have started a new fire when they got in this morning. He stared at the flames for a few seconds to gather his thoughts, then took a deep breath. He turned to face his friends and wondered if it had been subconsciously intentional for him to have placed the big table between them and himself. Deciding he didn't like that, he moved back into the kitchen proper.

"Here's the thing. I'm gay. I've know for, well, really a long time now, but just wasn't ready to do anything about it until recently. And Alec…is important to me." He pushed on ahead before he lost his momentum. "I'm in love with him. Like, forever in love with him. He's a part of my life now. I don't know how you guys are going to feel about all this, but…well…there you go. Now you know."

He swallowed hard. His instinct was to turn away and not look at them so he didn't have to see any anger or disgust in their eyes. But they were his best friends and, as hard as it was for him, he felt like he owed them the respect of keeping eye contact and giving them a chance to speak.

"Can we talk now?" Jamie asked, keeping his gaze even.

"Yeah. You can talk now."

Bella responded with a squeal. She launched herself at him and hugged him close, then stepped away and grinned.

Jamie was smiling, too.

"What?" Christian asked, wondering if they'd even heard anything he'd said.

"We already knew, Christian," Bella said, still grinning from ear to ear.

Jamie nodded.

Christian shook his head, so taken aback at this turn of events he didn't even know what to say. This wasn't any of the possible reactions he'd imagined. "But…what?" he said again, still reeling.

"Did you think you were the only one who experimented in school, mate?" Jamie asked with a grin.

"School? You mean university? How in bloody hell do you know about that?"

Bella shrugged. "Your girlfriend at the time, Angie Watson, was a friend of mine. We had Western Civ classes together. She told me."

That bit of information barely registered before the other part of Jamie's question sank in.

"Experimented?" Christian looked at the lanky blond man in shock. "Are you saying what I think you're saying?"

Jamie rolled his eyes and laughed. "Do you really need me to draw you a picture? Good fecking God's bollocks, I hope not! Anyway, once Bella and I got together she won my heart and I didn't feel the urge to be with anyone else." He gave his wife a warm, heated stare, then looked back at Christian. "But you'd have to be pretty daft to think either of us would look down on you for...well...any reason. We're family. Unconditionally."

Christian stared at his friends, not sure whether to be pissed or throw up in hands in frustration. "Does everybody know? I just found out from Alec that Mum knows, too.

"Really?" Bella's shock was obvious. "I didn't know that. Did you know that?" she asked Jamie."

"Nooo."

"Why didn't you guys say something to me? Let me know you knew?"

"Because you would have denied it," Bella said, patting him on the arm. "Your dad's negative and vocal views on the subject did a number on you, Christian. You kept your thoughts and feelings to yourself out of necessity. But we knew eventually you'd find the right man and when you did"—she smiled—"when you really fell in love, you wouldn't be able to hide it from yourself or anyone else. You're too honest to live a lie."

"Why didn't you say something when I was with Kate all that time?"

Bella sighed. "Because you and Kate really enjoyed each other's company and there's nothing wrong with that. And don't beat yourself up over what happened with her. She was young and stupid and thought getting married was the be all end all of life. I knew you two wouldn't make it to the altar, that one of you would break it off before that happened. And, selfishly, I didn't say anything because as long as she was with you it was that much longer she wouldn't be with some dick-fuck who'd use her. And it worked...it delayed the inevitable for a while. I was hoping she'd grow out of it and start thinking she wanted to make something of herself besides being some man's arm piece." Her voice rang with disgust.

"Didn't work," Jamie muttered. "She ended up married to Decker the Pecker."

Christian knew Bella's family had been furious when, only four months after she broke up with Christian, she married a smarmy young salesman from Bexley named Decker Peckingham. She'd left him two or three times, but always ended up getting back together with him.

"Anyway," Bella said loudly in an attempt to draw the conversation back in line, "my dimwit little sister isn't the point here. Christian, what's important is that you've found someone. And we're tickled pink about it."

"I'm not tickled *pink*," Jamie said with a groan. He turned to Christian with an expression of mock horror. "Do I look pink, I ask you?"

Christian chuckled.

Bella elbowed her husband lightly in the stomach. "Fine be tickled green or black or something else, you arse."

Then she suddenly squealed again.

"What now?" Christian asked, looking at Jamie to see if he knew.

The other man shrugged. "Not a clue."

"Christian!" She was gesturing frantically with her hands at something. "Your leg! I just now realized when you came in here you weren't limping!"

"Oh." A slow smile spread over his face. "No, I'm not. It's fine."

"But...no, no the healers said it wouldn't be, and in any case, that would be long term, so right now you should still be wearing the brace."

"Bella. It's fine. Remember I told you Alec's a healer? Well..." He bent his knee several times and moved his leg around. "See? Healed."

"But...that's..." Her gaze came up to clash with his. "That's impossible. The three best healers in England were here working on you."

"None of them were Alec. He's really powerful, and I don't think he's even really tapped into his full strength yet."

"Bloody hell..." Bella leaned back against the counter looking astounded.

"I think you've just done the unthinkable, mate," Jamie said, smiling at Christian and patting his wife's shoulder. "You've just left her speechless. That's doesn't happen...well...ever."

"It's really healed? All the way?" she asked, staring up at Christian.

"All the way."

"You have got to hang onto this man, Christian."

Christian smiled again. "Believe me, I plan to."

CHAPTER 16

Alec entered the kitchen dressed in a pair of Christian's sweat pants and a red Manchester United T-shirt. The stone floor was surprisingly warm against his bare feet. He was just in time to hear Christian's pronouncement.

"You plan to what?" he asked.

Christian's smile was immediate, and sent a surge of desire straight to Alec's balls. He looked good enough to…well…do things to it wasn't polite to talk about in public. He was barefoot also and wore navy blue sweats not unlike the gray ones Alec had on. But unlike Alec, Christian was shirtless, and the sight of all that sleek skin and lean muscle was enough to give him wet dreams for weeks.

Alec moved across the large room to stand next to him. He wanted to touch him, kiss him, but held back, not certain how comfortable Christian would be in front of his friends.

Needless to say it shocked him and filled him with a heady warmth when Christian cupped a hand at the back of his head and pulled him close for a kiss.

"Morning," he said softly, his blue eyes filled with love.

"Morning yourself. And you plan to what?" he asked again.

"He's planning to do his damnedest to quit hiding things from his friends and realize that we want him to be happy," the tall, rangy blond man said. He smiled and held out his hand. "Welcome to the family, Alec. I'm Jamie."

Alec was struck by how truly welcoming the man's voice and

demeanor were. He met Jamie's hand with his own and the other man's fingers closed around his with no hesitation. Then, adding another shock to the mix, Jamie pulled him into a bear hug.

"We're dysfunctional as hell, but we love each other and don't hesitate to kick arses as needed to keep everyone in line." The man smiled broadly.

"I'll keep that in mind," Alec said with a chuckle.

"Yes, and the first arse to get kicked today is going to be yours, James Hughes," the petite woman with short black hair said. Her smile and eyes were also welcoming and she didn't even bother with a hand, just dragged Alec down into hug that was damned strong for such a little woman. "Don't mind him," she said after she'd planted a kiss on his cheek and released him. "We try not to let him out in public too often. Keeps the embarrassment level down."

"Hey, watch your tongue, wench!" But Jamie grinned.

"That is my husband, though I'm not always eager to admit to it unless he's behaving himself." She shot Jamie a fond look. "And I'm Bella. And you"—she patted his cheek—"are looking much better than you did the last time I saw you. How are you feeling, Alec? Did you sleep well…or maybe I should ask if you slept much?" A mischievous, knowing gleam sparkled in her dark eyes.

"Bella!" Christian groaned and scuffed a hand over his face, and Jamie just leaned against the counter and chuckled between bites of what looked like a huge blueberry muffin.

Alec grinned at her, liking her instantly. "Yes. And no." He gave Christian a side-long glance and they shared a heated moment remembering what had happened in this very kitchen last night.

Then Alec grimaced. "I woke up to the dulcet tones of a purr as loud as a freight train and to find a huge gray beast lying across my neck so I couldn't breathe."

"Xavier," Christian and Bella said at the same time.

"Oooh, but he was lying on you, you say? That's a good sign, Alec. He's particular about who he likes."

The beast in question chose that moment to wander into the kitchen. He rubbed up against Alec's legs like they were the oldest and best of friends, then moved on to look up at Bella and meow with definite displeasure in his tone.

"Yes, yes, baby." Bella picked up the huge gray tabby and rubbed her face in his fur. "I'll feed you. Did big bad Christian forget to give you your nibblies while I was away?"

Christian looked at Alec and rolled his eyes behind Bella's back, but they were twinkling. "No, big bad Christian did not. The king of the house was fed on schedule, thank you very much. Like he would have let me forget even if I wanted to."

"Muffin?" Jamie asked, passing a basket to Alec. "Better eat 'em now or she'll be wanting to give those to the cat."

Bella swatted him on the butt. "Move your arse, Jamie. Take the muffins and your jokes to the table, then get me down the big frying pan so I can start some sausages."

Alec looked up to where she'd pointed to see a huge cast iron pan, along with a half-dozen other pots and pans, hanging from a hook on the ceiling over the gas stove. "I'll get it for you." He reached up and easily unhooked it. "Would you like me to start them?"

"Oooh, I love a man who knows his way around the kitchen! Yes, please!"

"Teacher's pet," Jamie mumbled, giving him another grin as he passed by, headed to the table.

Christian opened the refrigerator and brought over a package of thick, smoked sausages and a large bowl of brown eggs. One of his hands snaked under Alec's T-shirt and stroked his back. He pressed a kiss to the side of Alec's neck. "You cook?"

Alec grinned. "You probably wouldn't have guessed it from the state of my refrigerator last week and the fact I fed you delivery pizza for dinner, huh? But, yeah, actually I do like to cook. You?"

"Only when Bella makes me. But I wash a mean dish."

"Oh, I love a man who knows how to use his hands in soapy water."

Christian chuckled softly and nipped at Alec's neck. "I'll see what I can do about arranging a private demonstration for you."

*   *   *

Twenty minutes later, the four of them sat down to a huge breakfast. A cold, gray sleet fell outside the big windows on either side of the fireplace, but in direct contrast to it, between the roaring blaze on the hearth and the open camaraderie Alec hadn't ever felt with another group of people of which he'd been a part, the room was filled with warmth.

"Yellow," he said, resting his chin on his hand and staring at Bella.

"Excuse me?" she said, scraping up egg with the side of her fork.

"It's blue with yellow. And yours"—he turned to look at Jamie—"has orange in it and maybe"—he cocked his head to the side—"some yellow also."

"Has he gone mad?" Jamie asked around a bite of sausage. "I should have warned him about that, about how being around the three of us could do that to a person."

Christian laughed. "He hasn't gone mad. He's just seeing auras for the first time." He'd pulled on a white long-sleeved T-shirt before they ate and the white only made his eyes bluer than ever, Alec thought.

"What do you mean for the first time?" Bella asked. "And now that you mention it, I can see yours, too, Alec—it's a beautiful emerald green along with some turquoise and purple mixed in with the blue— and I couldn't see it before when you and Christian got here the other night." She turned to look at Christian. "In fact, I remember you saying you couldn't see his aura at all."

"I couldn't before. Not until last night."

"Did some kinky sex thing happen that turned it on?" Jamie asked, mischief dancing in his eyes.

Bella slapped him in the arm at the same time Christian groaned again.

"Bloody hell," Jamie groused, rubbing his arm. "That hurt, Bella." He grinned at Alec who was laughing softly.

"Be glad I didn't hit you harder, you git. Now, seriously, what happened?"

"It was my medallion," Alec told her. "Apparently it's been blocking me or something."

Bella set down her fork and leaned forward with interest. "What medallion?"

"It was something that was my dad's. I've been wearing it most of my life. Last night Christian got an idea about it and had me take it off and, poof, instant aura vision."

"It apparently has a protective spell woven into it," Christian said. "A pretty damn strong one, too, I suspect."

"Can I see it? This medallion?"

"Sure."

"I'll go get it, Christian said, getting up from the table and heading across the big kitchen.

"How come he's walking? Can't he just do that pop in, pop out thing?"

"Can't teleport in the house," Jamie said before forking another sausage up from his plate. "Anti-teleport spell around it. Most mages use 'em on their homes to keep out uninvited guests."

"Not using one would be like having an open door all the time," Bella explained. "Anyone who wanted to could pop in while you're using the loo or in the middle of a private conversation—"

"Or having sex."

"Jamie!" He got another slug in the arm for the comment.

"Anyway," she said, giving her husband a glare that was one part disgust and one part bedroom eyes, "if you have up a spell like that to keep people out, it also means you can't teleport within the house either. Small price to pay, though, for privacy."

Christian returned and handed the necklace to Alec, who passed it across the table to Bella.

"She's really good with charms and spells. She has a gift for it," Christian told him, settling back into the chair next to him.

She studied the small silver disk, turning it back and forth in her hands. "If you'd like, I can try to de-charm it for you so you can still wear it but it won't be blocking you."

Alec thought for a moment, wondering if not being blocked might make him feel exposed. He'd been wearing the medallion most of his life and it felt a little strange to be sitting here without it right now, and even stranger to look at the three people sitting with him and see the shimmering auras around them and realize they could see the same with him. Would it feel odd to be out in public and notice things like that now?

"You don't have to," Christian said, wrapping his fingers through Alec's in a supportive grip.

"No, of course not," Bella added. "It's your call, Alec."

Apparently the medallion had been, in a way, insulating him from many strange, unexplainable things. Things that in his old life he hadn't wanted to accept or believe in. And there was a bit of comfort in that, like a security blanket. Maybe he'd want to put it back on sometimes and let it hide him again.

But then he looked into Christian's warm, love-filled eyes, and breathed in the closeness and friendship that resonated in this house, and, in a moment of clarity, realized he could never go back to his old life again. Didn't want to. Christian had opened his eyes and his heart to so many amazing things in the short time he'd known him. And instead of wanting to hide and explain and ignore, instead he realized he wanted to find out what else he'd been missing, to explore and trust and love.

"Yeah. Go ahead," he told Bella.

"Are you sure?" Christian asked, his eyes saying he totally understood what Alec had been thinking. He squeezed Alec's hand and rubbed his thumb over his knuckles.

Alec smiled and squeezed back. "I am."

"Okay, I'll look at it after breakfast.," Bella said. "Oh, and Christian, we also need to see if we can find out who else might have been in that American mage group you told me about. Before Rogan goes after any more of them."

"Yeah, for sure." He looked at Alec. "I told Bella what you'd discovered about the victims and what Rogan said."

"And Bella filled me in," Jamie said, his mouth full of toast.

"How'd the Council session go?" Christian asked Bella.

She made a face over her tea cup.

"That well, huh?"

"I'd tell you what she told me about the Council, but then she'd probably just slug me again on account of you're the Council's golden boy and you might tell them that she thinks they need to get their heads out from up their stodgy old arses and…ooops, I just told, didn't I?" Jamie smiled at his wife and gave her a squeeze.

She barely seemed to notice. She was too busying slamming her cup down on the table. "Urrrrrrgh! Christian, I don't know you deal with those people! They're the most thick-headed, old-fashioned, conservative dinosaurs I've ever had the misfortune of having to spend time with. And did I mention how slooooow they are? It took the entire sodding morning for them to get through all their formal greetings and such. I could bloody well have stayed home and watched my favorite shows on the telly, had a nosh at that restaurant I like in Athens, and then showed up and they probably still wouldn't have been done. They didn't get down to the business that counted until afternoon! Now I know why some of those sessions you attend drag on for days!"

Alec listened to the whole outburst with fascination, but the part that kept ringing in his mind was the bit about Christian being the Council's golden boy.

"I know. It can be tedious," Christian said. "But the Council has thousands of years of tradition to uphold and they take it seriously."

"Well, next time I get all generous and tell you I'll gladly attend in your stead, one of you whack me upside the head, will you?"

"You've attended sessions before when Chris couldn't make it, sweet," Jamie reminded her. "And you always say when you get home that you're never going again."

"Oh, I know. I'm sorry, Christian, you know I will whenever I'm needed. I just forget how bad it really is until I'm there sitting through it." She sighed loudly. But then she smirked and elbowed her husband. "Maybe next time we should send Jamie. That'd stir things up a bit."

"Now there's a thought," Christian said with a grin, before taking a sip of tea.

"Oh, no!" Jamie protested, his hands in the air. "No, no, no. I'm perfectly happy being a grunt, thank you. I'll leave you two to your boss man and assistant boss woman jobs."

"You three all work together?" Alec asked.

"We do," Bella said.

"For the Bureau of Dark Magic Affairs?"

"Bureau of Dreadfully Mad Agents. Yep, that's us," Jamie said with a grin.

"And who's the boss?"

"He is," Bella and Jamie said together, pointing at Christian.

Alec turned to look at Christian, his eyebrows raised.

"Oh, for pity sake, you didn't tell him?" Jamie asked Christian.

Christian looked sheepish. "Well, it just hadn't really come up."

"He told me he was an agent," Alec said.

"Oh, he is. But apparently he neglected to tell you he's *the* agent."

"*The* agent?"

"The Director of the Bureau of Dark Magic Affairs," Jamie said.

"The *youngest* director of the Bureau of Dark Magic Affairs in history," Bella added.

"Hand-picked by the Council and given free rein to run the organization in any fashion he chooses since the last director was a first class fuck-up they had to sack."

"The one time the old dinosaurs got something right!" Bella said with a grin.

Christian shook his head and rolled his eyes. "Oh, for God's sake, stop."

"No, don't stop," Alec said, a smile creeping onto his face. "I'm learning all sorts of fascinating things from you guys that Mr. Director here hadn't bothered to share with me."

"He's the modest type," Bella said. "Which is probably good because otherwise we might not be able to stand to live with him." She rose from the table and, smiling, pressed a kiss against the top of Christian's head as she passed, carrying dishes to the sink.

Alec gazed at Christian, feeling what could only be a surge of pride in his heart. "Youngest in history, huh?" he said quietly when Jamie had gone to help Bella.

Christian gave an unassuming shrug. "It's not the big deal they make it out to be."

"Why do I not quite believe you?"

"I told you, he goes all modest whenever anyone mentions it," Bella said, leaning a hip against the table. "But it is a big deal. Especially coming from the Council because, like I said, they aren't usually real big on being progressive and bringing in new blood."

"So where is this Bureau of Dark Magic Affairs?" Alec asked.

Bella held out an arm. "You're sitting in it."

"Here? This house?"

Jamie joined them and wrapped an arm around Bella. "Yep, one of the first things our progressive new director did was yank the Bureau out of its fetid and much too public abode in the heart of London and move it to an undisclosed location known only to the handful of trusted agents he employs."

"There were security issues at the other place," Christian said.

"Yeah, as in there was none and every Tom, Dick and Hairy-balled dark mage wannabe in the world knew exactly where to find any of us at any given time and take us out if they chose."

"Speaking of mages, I'm going to go see what I can find about that group you two discovered," Bella said. "And, Alec, I'll spend some time on your medallion also." She picked up it off the table. "Jamie, be a love and come with me. I have a research job for you."

"Oh, joy." As he followed her out, he grimaced at Christian and Alec, but his eyes were twinkling.

"The Director of the Bureau of Dark Magic Affairs," Alec said slowly, smiling at Christian. "Do I get any perks for being the director's lover?"

Christian's soft chuckle spread heat through Alec's veins. "You can have all the perks you want." He dragged Alec's face close for a bone-melting kiss that led to more than a little petting.

"I'm thinking maybe we should get a room," Alec said, breathing hard, his body tingling.

"I'm thinking…oh, yeah." The heated look in Christian's eyes said it couldn't be soon enough.

CHAPTER 17

Mid-morning found them showered again and dressing. As Alec pulled on a pair of Christian's jeans and yet another borrowed shirt, grateful they were about the same size and could so easily share clothes, he still had a longing for some of his own things. His gun and wallet, tucked into the top drawer of Christian's dresser, and his boots had been the only surviving remnants of his clothes and possessions from the day of the explosion. Everything else had been ripped, broken, and tattered beyond saving.

"Is there any way we can get some of my stuff from my house?"

Christian looked up from putting on socks and smiled. "Yeah, of course."

"That'd be cool. Then I wouldn't have to keep borrowing your clothes all the time." He smiled. "Not that I mind wearing your clothes. It's kind of…"

"Sexy? Because it is for me, seeing you in my shirts and pants and underwear." He stood and wrapped his arms around Alec from behind. "There are definitely some items that, from here on out, whenever I wear them all I'll be able to think about is how intimately they've been in contact with you," he said against Alec's ear.

Alec chuckled. "You do have washing machines here in England don't you?"

"Yes, but that's *not* the point." Christian pressed a kiss against his neck "Still, I completely understand about you wanting to have your own things."

"I can't go get them, though, since even though you say I can teleport I don't really know how."

Christian turned him around and kissed him lightly. "You'll learn. Trust me, before you know it, it'll be second nature to you. In the meantime, make a list and I'll go for you sometime over the next couple of days."

"Okay. Thanks. And, hey, do I get to see the offices of the official Bureau headquarters?"

"Absolutely. Come on."

They went downstairs holding hands and Alec was struck at how comfortable he felt here, in this house, with Chris, and even with Bella and Jamie, though he barely knew them. It was like he'd lived here for years, not just a few days. Odd…he already felt more at home here than he did in his own house back in Illinois, and his life there already seemed like part of a different world.

Christian took him across the foyer and into a set of arched wood and stained glass French doors that led to another part of the house. There were no locks or security features on the doors, which surprised Alec. He'd figured to find the "headquarters" part of the house sealed off and somehow secured. And said as much to Christian.

"There's not really any need. The house and grounds are secured from the outside with a number of protective spells and charms. If anyone besides the four of us or the half-dozen additional agents who work for the Bureau try to enter the house, the sensors kick in and they'll find themselves unpleasantly zapped and unable to enter, and an alarm will go off here in the house."

"How does this protection system know whether it's someone who's supposed to be here and someone who's not?"

"Aura scan." Christian smiled. We're going to do one on you right now and get yours listed as one of the 'good guys.' Bella did a temporary override charm the night we arrived that allowed you to come and go from the house. But we're going to make it permanent."

He took Alec to a small room lined with cabinets, had him stand still, then, using a gold rod about eighteen inches long, passed it over him from head to foot. It shimmered as Christian used it, emitting small gold sparks. When he reached Alec's feet it turned a deep bronze color, then went dark.

"Okay, that's it."

"That's just really…odd."

Christian chuckled. "No, it's magic. Come on."

He showed Alec Jamie's office, but Jamie wasn't in it. When they entered Bella's with its floor-to-ceiling book-lined walls, she was deeply immersed working on her computer. She looked up, though, and smiled when she realized they were in the doorway. "Hey, guys."

"Where'd Jamie get off to?" Christian asked.

"Cayleigh called from the States. Rather than bother you about it since you were otherwise occupied"—she gave them a knowing look and smile—"he went to find out what was up. I'm sure he'll call and report in in a bit. Oh, Alec! Here." She rose and handed him his silver necklace.

He took it in his hand. It didn't feel any different than usual.

"That was one hell of a protective charm, let me tell you," she told them. "I've never seen anything quite like it, or quite as elaborately woven. It took me a while to figure it out and reverse it. The medallion itself isn't totally silver. It's almost like an alloy of some sort, which is why, I think, the spell stuck to it so well."

"So if I wear it now it shouldn't block me any longer?"

"It shouldn't. Try it on and see."

He unfastened the clasp and put the chain around his neck, then looked at Christian and Bella. Their auras still pulsed around them in plain sight—Bella's a bright yellow beneath the blue, and Chris's blue with shimmering gold and more than just a hint of red closest to his body. Alec grinned and gave him a heated look. "I can still see your auras," he told them.

"I can still see yours, too," Christian said, his eyes flickering with an eager hunger. The red band in his aura grew wider and more pronounced.

Bella chuckled softly. "And I can see both of yours. Either go in Christian's office and shut the door or go back to bed, boys." She waved them out of her office with a good-natured grin.

When they were in the hallway, Alec commented, "It's kind of tough to be subtle, isn't it? With everyone else able to see."

Christian pulled him into a large, brightly-lit office and shut the door, then pushed him up against the door and kissed him until they were both shuddering with need.

"Do you honestly think they wouldn't see anyway?" he asked, yanking down the zipper of Alec's jeans and wasting no time wrapping his big, warm hand around Alec's shaft.

"You think the continual hard-on is the giveaway?"

Alec was barely able to muffle a groan as Christian's thumb

brushed over his slit, rubbing in the slippery drops of pre-cum that clung to the tip.

Christian dropped to his knees and shoved Alec's jeans and briefs down over his hips, allowing his cock to spring free, hard and ready. "I need to suck you. Right now."

"Shit, yeah." Alec clutched Christian's head and let his own fall back against the door as wet, hot mouth and exquisite pleasure took him over. Christian's tongue stroked over every inch of his cock, taking special time and care on his swollen crown, dipping into the ridge surrounding it, and fluttering against the ultra-sensitive underside until Alec's hips bucked and he thought he'd go completely ape-shit crazy if the man didn't swallow his whole shaft soon.

Christian seemed to read his mind because that's exactly what he did, lowering his mouth inch by incredible, mind-boggling inch until Alec was buried in the hot depths of his throat. "Oh, God." He arched toward Christian, somehow managing to shove his cock in farther, and then, unable to stop, his hips surged into the most natural, primitive motion in the world and he pumped in and out of Christian's mouth.

He opened his eyes to find Christian's hot blue gaze looking up at him, heavy with passion as Alec's cock slid in and out of his mouth. His tongue was doing something to Alec on each out-stroke that was making him even more insane with need.

"Have I told you how hot it is to watch you doing this?" he gasped.

Christian smiled around his cock and began stroking his balls.

Pressure built inside Alec. His balls drew up tight. His cock practically sizzled, growing harder and harder. And then, with a guttural growl, he was coming, waves of liquid fire bursting from him and being gobbled up by the greedy mouth that knew so well exactly how to pleasure him.

"Jesus, you're good," he said, when it was over and Christian was licking the last drops from his lips. "Stand up and pull your pants down," Alec ordered.

One of Christian's dark eyebrows rose in sexy question, but he didn't balk. His hands immediately popped open the button and slid down the zipper. He wiggled his lean hips and pushed them and his briefs down. The sight of his long, stiff cock jutting from his groin, the thick head already proudly emerged from sexy foreskin, caused Alec to suck in his breath.

Christian let his jeans fall around his ankles, then looked back up at Alec, heat flaring in his eyes.

Alec pulled his own jeans up so he could walk without tripping, but didn't bother to fasten them. He took a slow, appreciative tour around Christian, admiring his long, muscular legs, the curve of his firm ass, and once again coming back to the front to soak up some more of the mouth-watering sight of his beautiful, twitching cock.

"Enjoying yourself?" Christian asked, his voice low and throaty, a smile playing at the corners of his mouth.

"I am. And I'm about to enjoy myself even more. Masturbate. I want to watch."

He could almost see Christian stop breathing for several seconds. His nostrils flared. And his eyes turned a dark, dark blue.

Oh, yeah, he'd just turned him on big time. Shit, he'd turned himself on, too.

Christian's hand moved to his cock. He gripped it firmly, his fingers on the underside, thumb on top, and began to slide his foreskin slowly up and down, never taking his gaze off Alec.

Alec couldn't watch his face, though. His eyes fell to the erotic sight unfolding at Christian's groin. Shit, the man was beautiful. That cock was the stuff dreams were made off, and the sight of Christian's graceful hands working over it with such mastery, seeing the thick purple crown nearly disappear into the foreskin, then appear again...well, if Alec hadn't just come, he'd probably be spurting already. As it was, he was getting hard again.

Christian's hand picked up rhythm and his movements grew firmer. Alec let his gaze slide upward to find Chris had closed his eyes and his head had fallen back. His breathing was growing ragged, lustful.

Holy crap. The man was sensuality personified. He'd never seen anyone so sexy in his life.

Christian's cock had stiffened to almost impossible proportions and his hand moved faster. Alec knew the man was close, and suddenly knew he couldn't let all that cum go to waste.

He sank to his knees on the thick carpet in front of Christian. "Fuck my mouth. Come in it," he told him. "I want to taste every drop."

With a growl, Christian held his cock in one hand and grasped the back of Alec's head with his other, pulling his face into his groin. Alec opened and Chris thrust so deeply Alec almost gagged...but didn't. He relaxed his throat, latched his fingers against Christian's flexing butt, and gladly let Christian have his way with him. And he did, pumping hard and fast and deep, the head of his cock banging against the back of Alec's throat mercilessly. And all the while Alec's own cock was growing so hard again he feared he might lose his own load when Christian came.

With another low growl and a powerful shudder, Christian exploded, his salty-sweet semen coating Alec's mouth and sliding down his throat in thick bursts. Alec took it all, swallowing until his throat ached, but never tiring of the essence that was purely Chris.

With a final surge and groan, he pulled his cock free and sank to his knees, facing Alec, then they both collapsed onto the carpet in a sated heap.

"Want a job?" Christian asked, still panting.

Alec raised up on his elbow and gazed down at him with a mischievous smile. "Sucking your cock?"

"You've already got that job," he said with a lascivious sparkle in his eyes. "I mean a job here at the Bureau. As an agent."

Alec sat up all the way, his knees drawn to his chest, and stared. "Are you serious?"

"Completely. If you meant it when you said last night you wanted to stay."

Alec's heart thudded. "I meant it. But...I hardly know anything about magic yet, Chris. I think I pretty much suck as a mage at this point."

Christian's smile was so genuine and sexy he almost forgot to breathe. "I told you, you'll learn how to use your powers. And once you do, you're going to far surpass anyone in this house. You're going to surpass most any mage anywhere.

Alec felt heat slide up his face.

"Anyway, if you're interested, the job's yours. You already have the investigative skills. The pay is...well, quite good actually. The dress code is casual. The working environment is"—he looked around and shrugged—"homey. The commute's easy. Plenty of time for extra curricular activities and long lunches as needed. The boss is fairly easy going, especially when you share a bed with him and he wants to keep you happy and keep it that way."

Alec chuckled. "You make this a really tough decision."

Christian grew serious and touched his palm against Alec's cheek. "The work can be dangerous, Alec. I can't lie to you about that. People do die in this job sometimes."

Alec sobered, too, and thought of Drew. And how badly it had hurt when he was killed. He looked at Christian and his heart twisted in a knot. He was already so deeply in love with Christian that he knew if he lost him, what he'd felt at Drew's death wouldn't even compare. Being with Christian had brought him to a whole new level of love and caring, and for the first time in his life, he'd held nothing back. He'd opened himself completely to this man. Which would only magnify the hurt to excruciating proportions should something happen to Chris.

But he also realized he couldn't spend the rest of his life being afraid of shadows. And he couldn't hold Chris back either because, in the end, it would just breed resentment.

It all came back to that conversation he'd had with Drew…about him needing to have a little faith. And for this man, he was willing to do pretty much anything. When he looked in Christian's eyes, he knew he'd not only fallen hard, he'd fallen forever.

"Okay. If you're serious, yeah, I'll do it."

Christian sat up and tugged him close for a kiss. "I really love you."

"I know. And I really love you."

"Welcome to the Bureau of Dark Magic Affairs."

"Or as Jamie calls it, the Bureau of Dreadfully Mad Agents?"

Christian's chuckle was contagious. "Yeah, that, too."

*   *   *

"Hey, Alec."

Alec, sitting at the kitchen table in front of the fireplace, looked up from the thick volume of history the Council kept about Rogan and smiled at Bella. "Hey."

But his smile faded when he realized she looked odd…kind of in shock, like she'd just found out she won the billion dollar lottery and it hadn't sunk in yet. She clutched a folder against her chest.

"You okay?"

"Yeah. Yeah, I'm okay. Where's Christian?"

"He left a little while ago to go to my house in the States and get a few things."

"Oh. Okay." She dropped into the chair at the table next to him. Her dark eyes were focused hard on him. "I could wait until he gets back, but I don't think I'm going to. I think I need to share this with you now."

"All right…" He turned toward her. "What's up?"

She set the file folder on the table, but didn't open it. "I've been researching two projects kind of simultaneously—one being trying to find more information about the group of American mages Rogan has been killing, the other being, well, you."

"Me?" The admission caught him by surprise.

Bella looked a bit apologetic. "I actually started it before you came here and it's not for bad reasons. Christian was really worried about you and trying to figure out how you could do magic and yet not have an aura. So I asked him if he'd mind if I did some looking into your background, tried to find out more about your family to see if we could discover where the magic came from."

Alec nodded. He'd gone looking for more information about Christian, so it was only fair Christian had done the same about him. "It's okay," he told her. "It doesn't bother me that you were looking. To be honest, I wouldn't mind knowing more. I never really knew my parents, only my grandmother, and she died when I was ten."

Bella nodded. "Your grandmother, her name was Sarah?"

"Sarah Smith."

"What do you know about her?"

"Not a ton, I guess. She didn't really talk much about her family or where she grew up. Mostly we just lived in the here and now. We moved quite often. Not far, though, usually staying in the same regional area in Illinois. She knew how sick riding in the car for long distances made me."

"Ah, you have Forten's Syndrome, don't you?" She looked sympathetic.

"Yeah. Except I only found out that's what it was when Chris told me yesterday."

"According to your birth certificate, you were born in Illinois and your parents' names were Eve and J.P. Anderson. Sarah Smith was your mother's mother. Records indicate your father died in an accident—the information is non-specific about what kind—and your mother died when you were two from complications due to pneumonia."

"My grandmother always said she died of a broken heart because she loved my dad so much and missed him."

"And then your grandmother?"

"She died when I was ten from an aneurysm. I went into foster care after that because we had no other family."

Bella opened the file folder and pulled out a small photograph. She laid it front of Alec. "Is this your grandmother?"

He stared down at the image of his grandmother's beloved face he hadn't seen in over twenty years. "Oh, my God," he whispered, fingering the edge of the photo. "She would never let anyone photograph her, always said she hated pictures because they made her look too old. Even as a kid I never could understand that because I always thought she was beautiful. She was. Beautiful and gentle and soft-spoken. When she died, I didn't even have a picture to remember her by. We never had any pictures of my parents in the house either." He looked up at Bella. "Where'd you get this?"

Bella laid a gentle hand on his forearm. "Turn it over."

He did. And written on the back in small, neat, faded printing saw the words: *Sarah Carlton Stephens.*

"I don't understand. Her name was Sarah Smith. Did she remarry?"

"No. The woman in this picture, Sarah Stephens, was only married once. She had only one child, a daughter. Her name was Evangeline. Evangeline married Jason Patrick Ansley. And they had one child. A son. Alexander."

He stared at her, his pulse doing an odd, arrhythmic thrum. "My name is Alexander...Alec is a nickname."

Bella nodded slowly.

"What are you saying?" he whispered. But somewhere deep inside him, he already knew.

"For thirty years, everyone in the magic community believed Jason Ansley, his wife Evangeline, and their baby were killed in a fire in London. They believed Rogan was responsible, although it was never proven. When I looked into your background and saw so many similarities, I knew it couldn't be a coincidence. I dug out the old records—the investigations that were done by both the Ordinary police and the Council—and discovered only a few charred remains were found in the house for a man, woman, and baby. The fire burned so hot there was almost nothing left. But in a note in fine print at the bottom of one of the pages on the Ordinary police report it said the infant was six months old."

Her dark gaze anchored him.

"But that didn't ring true. Because according to every record we have about the Ansley family, the baby, Alexander Ansley, would have been only two months old. His birthday, you see, was April the twenty-eighth."

"The same as mine," Alec breathed.

"I know. Alexander Ansley would be thirty-one this coming April, just as you will be. Alec..." She pushed the folder over to him. "You are Alexander Ansley. Your grandmother who raised you was Sarah Stephens. She was well known in her own American mage circle as being a healer. Your father, Jason Ansley, was an extremely powerful mage, as all members of the Ansley family have been for hundreds of years."

Alec stood, but couldn't seem to move. It was hard to breathe again. "Rogan said, when Christian and I saw him, that he didn't believe Jason Ansley's mother-in-law had died after her family was killed."

"She didn't. She was your grandmother and she raised you until she died from natural causes."

Bella rose and rested a small, comforting hand on his back. "Here's what I think. I think your father, wanting to protect you and your mother, sent you away, into hiding with your grandmother. And then, when Rogan came to confront him, I think it wasn't Rogan who set the fire that burned the house. I think your father did it."

"Killed himself?" The words came out of Alec's chest sounding strangled. "My God. But…what about the other bodies? The woman and baby?"

"I discovered a mother and six-month old child had recently been killed in a village nearby in an auto accident only a few days before the fire. As awful as it sounds, I suspect your father used those bodies. He wanted you and your mother to be safe, to live. He probably knew Rogan would try to hurt you both or use you to get him to tell where the amulet was. And it was his sacred responsibility to guard that amulet and keep it out of Rogan's hands.

"I've no doubt he also felt it was his sacred duty out of pure love to keep his wife and child alive. So he sent you into hiding, gave you the medallion you've been wearing as a powerful protective shield to keep anyone, especially Rogan, from ever being able to find you and see you were magic, and told your mother and grandmother to live as Ordinaries. Then he set up the fire. When all was said and done, he wanted Rogan to believe you'd all died and there'd be no one left to give up the location of the amulet. And then you and your mother would be free to live without fear of Rogan."

"Oh, God." He grasped the back of the chair to steady himself as waves of shock rippled through him. It explained so much…so many things he'd never understood. Like having no pictures in the house, the way his grandmother had been so protective of him, never letting him go off by himself, the way they'd moved frequently, and how his grandmother had kept to herself so much. It also explained his grandmother telling him, when she did the healing on him when he was sick or injured, that he shouldn't ever tell anyone about it. All his life he'd thought she'd said that because she didn't want anyone to think they were freaks.

His gaze flew to Bella's. "My grandmother hardly ever left home, except for once a month when she'd go into Shelton to get together with friends. Do you think she was part of the mage group Rogan talked about?"

"Yes. Undoubtedly. Christian said you'd discovered several members of the group were in England around the time the Ansleys… well, Jason Ansley, your father, died. It's possible they came here to try to stop Rogan. Or maybe they came here specifically to bring you and your mother back with them."

"But if the people in the group knew, then wouldn't Rogan have already discovered from some of the murder victims that my grandmother brought my mother and me back to the States?"

"It's possible."

"No," Alec said, shaking his head. "No, he doesn't know, or didn't when he talked to Christian and me that day, because he specifically said the guiller had found no useful information in my mind. At two months old, I suppose I wouldn't have any memories of my family enough for the guiller to find. Or…considering all the other people the guiller messed with died, maybe the guiller just wasn't in my mind long enough to find everything. In any case, Rogan didn't know or care who I was that day, except that I was with Chris and Chris was trying to convince him to let me walk away."

"So maybe the group members didn't know you were alive and your grandmother brought you home." Bella frowned. "Did you ever meet any of your grandmother's friends? Anyone from this group?"

"Not that I recall. When she went out once a month, she always left me at home, usually with a local teenage babysitter wherever we were living at the time. We really were pretty isolated most of the time. She worked from home always, didn't leave the house to go to a job. Although, you know what…?"

His mind backtracked to an incident when he would have been about ten. Not too long before his grandmother had died in fact.

"I think maybe once I might have seen one of her friends. The friend, I think her name was Janice…or Janet. No, I'm pretty sure it was Janice. She came by unexpectedly one evening. No one ever came to our house anywhere we lived. And I remember my grandmother being very frazzled that this woman had come by. She sent me to my room and told me to go to bed and not make a sound. I did.

"But then I remember waking up from a bad dream. I didn't know how long I'd been asleep and had kind of forgotten there was anyone else there with my grandmother. I came out of my room and went into the living room. My grandmother was very upset and told Janice I was a friend's son she was looking after, then she hustled me back to my room. It was never mentioned after that, but I always wondered why she would have said that. It hurt my feelings. And my grandmother had never hurt my feelings before. She died shortly thereafter so I never got a chance to ask her about it."

"Janice. Do you remember her last name?"

"No. I'm not sure I ever knew it."

"Okay, we've got to find this woman if she's still alive, because if the guiller delves into her mind and sees that incident…"

"Wait. How could the guiller possibly know or suspect it might be me even if it did see it in Janice's mind? I was a kid. For all we know, Janice really believed I was someone my grandmother was babysitting."

"Let me show you something."

Bella opened the file folder and sifted through a stack of papers. She pulled out more photographs and handed them to him. "Your mother and father."

He looked at them, not sure what he expected to find since he'd never in his life seen pictures of them. But suddenly he understood. "Oh."

"Yeah. Oh. You look like your parents, Alec. Your father's face, your mother's hair and eyes. I suspect even as a boy of ten you had enough family resemblance that if Rogan is able to see what the guiller sees…he's going to put two and two together. A boy at exactly the right age, in the house with your grandmother, with the right coloring…"

"Rogan stood right next to me a few days ago, looked right at me. Why didn't he notice then?"

"He wasn't looking for you, Alec. At that point, and hopefully still, he didn't have a clue the Ansley child—you—had survived. He was totally focused on finding your grandmother because he thinks she's the one who has the amulet. It wouldn't have occurred to him then to notice your resemblance to your parents. And you said he had little interest in you that day."

"No, he didn't. He barely looked at me. He was completely focused on Christian the entire time. I was just some extra baggage that wasn't worthy of his notice. He even said as much."

"See!"

"But…Bella? There's one very big problem here. At least Rogan will see it that way."

"What's that?"

"Even if Rogan makes the connection and decides to find me, I don't have a clue where the Amulet of Sulisa is. I'd never heard of it until last week. I wouldn't even know what the hell it looked like."

"Come with me."

Bella led him back through the house to her office, then through that to a large room attached to it. Like her office, bookshelves lined every wall in here as well, and row and after row of shelves filled the center of the room, too.

"Damn. Quite the library you guys have here."

"Oh, this isn't the actual reference library for the Bureau. That's down the hall by Christian's office. This is my personal collection."

She walked to a shelf on the left wall, pulled a thick, dusty, green volume down, and set it with a thunk on the small table nearby. With the ease of someone who'd been through this particular book many times, she flipped to a page halfway through and pointed.

Alec leaned over her shoulder to see a photograph of a large stone plaque carved with many symbols and pictures on the upper half and some type of ancient writing on the bottom.

"The writing is cuneiform," Bella said. "This plaque is Sumerian. It's dated to approximately 2500 BCE. And this right here is the Amulet of Sulisa. Or a picture of it anyway as depicted by the Sumerians." She pointed to a large egg-shaped object carved into the plaque. It had elaborate designs on it, and lines radiated out from it as if the ancient artisan wanted to show it giving off light or energy. It was definitely the central focus of the piece, and there was no mistaking the other symbols were secondary to it.

"I don't know how much Christian's told you about the amulet, but it was legendary, used by kings and rulers for thousands of years for good and bad. It gave the wearer incredible power legends say—power over earth and sky, fire and water, life and death. It was so powerful many who had it feared to use it. It was said to be a large stone shaped as it's depicted here. Once it was given to the first Ansley ancestor to protect, it was never seen again. Except, presumably, by other members of the Ansley family. Or maybe not even then. Maybe its location was passed on from generation to generation, but it was sealed away from view. It is known, however, that over the generations the Ansleys themselves became incredibly powerful mages, their strengths and abilities surpassing virtually all their peers."

She looked up at Alec and patted his cheek. "I know this has all been a shock to you, Alec. But it's not all bad. You were born into one of the noblest and, in their own right, most powerful families in the magic world. From the moment the amulet was placed in the protective hands of your family, not a single Ansley has ever let it get into dark mage hands, nor have any of them ever used the amulet for harm."

Alec dragged in a deep breath, still reeling from everything he'd learned. "Let's just hope my father hid it well so it can never be found."

"Amen to that."

Bella's cell phone rang and she fished it out the pocket of her jeans. "Jamie, love? How're things?"

Alec returned to studying the picture in the book, but seconds later, realizing Bella hadn't said another word, looked up to find her pale and growing paler by the second from whatever she was hearing on the phone.

"Oh, bloody hell," she whispered. "Okay. Love you, too."

She clicked off the connection and Alec held her arm to steady her. "What is it, Bella?"

"There's been another murder in the States. Guiller. The victim's name was…Janice Feinstein."

"Damn. Possibly my grandmother's friend."

"There's more, Alec." Her eyes welled with fear. "They found a note on the body. It said, 'I know the secret now. I'm coming for you, Wetherly.'"

"Oh, fuck." Alec barely heard the words escape his mouth as terror swept through him, raw and blinding.

"How long has Christian been gone?"

Alec lifted his wrist to look at his watch, only to realize it wasn't there. "I don't know. Maybe a couple of hours." His eyes widened. "He said it probably wouldn't take him longer than an hour. Oh, God, we've got to warn him."

But then he realized he was powerless. He couldn't go after Christian because he didn't know how to teleport.

Bella seemed to read his thoughts. "Jamie and I will go." She opened her phone again and placed a call, pacing as she waited for Jamie to answer. "Meet me at Alec's house, Jamie. That's where Christian's supposed to be." She snapped the phone closed again.

"Fuck. Fuck." Alec ran a shaking hand through his hair.

"Alec, we'll find him."

"Why does Rogan want him? I don't understand…if he knows, if he realizes I'm alive, why does he want Christian?"

"God knows. The man, as Jamie has so frequently said, is a psychopath."

"It could be a trap of some sort, Bella."

Her dark eyebrows pulled together under her bangs and she nodded. "For what though?"

"I don't know. Damn it, I don't know. Go. God, please go and find him."

Bella kissed his cheek and took off at a run through the house. Alec wondered what the hell she was doing, then remembered. She couldn't teleport from inside the house.

He followed her and was just in time as he crossed the threshold of the front door to see her disappear. Sinking to a crouch on the porch, he stared into the empty space where Bella had just been. The sleet of earlier in the day had tapered off, but fog had settled in across the countryside this afternoon, thick and damp and cold as ice.

He'd never felt so completely useless in his life. Unable to go. Unable to help. Once again powerless to save someone he loved.

Oh, God, Christian. Please be okay. I can't lose you.

CHAPTER 18

"Shit!"

A thought suddenly hit Alec with the intensity of a tidal wave. When the guiller had attacked him at his house, he'd called out to Christian in his mind. Was it possible he could reach Christian that way now?

He didn't have any idea how he'd done it before. He'd been scared as hell when the creature attacked him and the first thing that had popped into his mind was Christian. And somehow that thought had managed to get translated to Christian and he'd come to help.

Taking a deep breath, Alec tried to clear his mind as he did when he was preparing to heal someone. But it was hard, his worries and fears roiling in a dark ball inside his head. He did the best he could though, and pictured Christian in his mind.

::Christian.::

Nothing. He felt like he might as well be speaking into the wind. He needed more focus.

Trying to be even more specific, he thought about how beautiful the man's smile was, how his blue eyes, the color of rich sapphires, sparkled with love and light. How he smelled—lightly spicy with a hint of musk—the tone of his voice, the warmth of his skin when they touched.

::Christian?::

He felt something that time. A tremor of energy, of connection with…something.

::Chris? Chris, can you hear me? God, Christian, please hear me.::.

Pain suddenly shot through him. And confusion. And fear. Christian's fear, but not for himself. For Alec.

::Christian! Where are you? Jamie and Bella are coming to find you.::

::No! Alec...:: The thoughts were slow. Labored. Again, pain swept through Alec and he knew it was Christian's.

::Oh, God, what's happened? If you can't tell me, then try to show me where you are.::

A vision filled his head. Gray. Cold mist. No...it was fog. Fog and rolling countryside, and...

"What the hell?" Alec opened his eyes and realized what he was seeing in his mind was the same thing he was seeing with his eyes.

::Chris, I don't understand.::

::Alec...run. It's a...::

In a rush of air, two people appeared directly in front of Alec.

"...trap," Christian gasped and fell to the wet grass only ten feet from Alec.

"Jesus! Chris!" Alec ran to him, but felt himself being lifted until just the tips of his shoes dragged the ground.

"Rogan!"

Alec was pushed backward by an invisible force of energy that left him sprawling on his backside in the mud near the porch steps. He scrambled to his feet and ran toward Christian again, only to be pushed back yet again.

"You, fuck, let me get to him! He needs help." Christian lay sprawled face down, his eyes closed. It looked like he was breathing, but slowly.

Rogan chuckled. "You should be thanking me. I didn't let my pet kill him, just play with him for a bit. I decided I'd save the grand finale so you could watch..." His eyes turned cold and speared into Alec with icy precision. "...Ansley."

Alec pushed himself back to his feet. He struggled to think of options, but there were none. He was trapped. He couldn't teleport. No one else was around. In a few steps he could be inside the house where, presumably, Rogan couldn't follow. But he knew, without a second thought, that the moment he did, Rogan would kill Christian.

"I don't know where your fucking amulet is, Rogan. That's what you want, isn't it? Well, I don't know."

"Pity. It would be much easier on him"—he looked down at Christian lying near his feet—"if you did." Without so much as a warning, he waved the fingers on his good hand in a small motion that caused Christian to flip onto his back. Christian stirred, then his hands suddenly moved up to this throat and began clawing at it as gasping, choking noises escaped him.

Horrified, Alec ran for him again, and was once more thrust backward by a force created when Rogan casually waved his hand at him, as if he were lazily brushing away a pesky fly.

Christian's movements were becoming weaker.

"Stop it!" Alec shouted. "Stop it, you bastard! Let him go. Your fight is with me!"

Rogan flicked a long finger and Christian gasped in a long, deep breath, able to drag in air again. But he was weak and looked only half-conscious.

"Very well. I can be a reasonable man."

Rogan smiled at him. The smile that Alec had once thought oddly charming and handsome, now only filled him with loathing.

"Let's chat, then, shall we, Ansley? You have something I want. And, clearly," he glanced at Christian again, then back up at Alec, "I have something you want. A simple trade would work quite nicely for me."

An anger such as Alec had never known before began to build deep inside him, at the very core of him, in a primal, fiery burn.

"You'll get nothing until you let me take him in the house where he'll be safe." His voice sounded deep and ominous.

"That's not the way it works, Ansley. I know from reading your beloved Christian's mind that, while you possess Ansley powers, you don't know how to focus and use them. You can't hurt me."

"You have no idea what I'm capable of." The anger continued to build in Alec, stirring to life and swirling more and more of his soul into the flames.

Rogan laughed. "I killed every one of your uncles, boy. Every one. And they *did* know how to use their powers. They couldn't stop me."

"My father did."

Rogan's eyes narrowed at that. "Your father was a sentimental fool," he spat. "I long suspected he'd set that fire himself, killing himself and, for many years, I believed you and your weak American mother as well. And all for what? To give his life to save yours? To save the world from the amulet?"

"The amulet can be used for good. He didn't give his life to save the world from it. He did it to save the world from your madness."

"I'm tired of talking." Rogan twisted his fingers and Christian began to choke again, except this time his hand movements were weak and his eyes stayed closed.

"Stop it!"

Another rush of air filled Alec's ears and before he could blink, Jamie and Bella were there.

"Careful," he shouted at them. They both, out of what looked like pure instinct, held out their hands. Sizzling streams of visible white energy flowed from them, aimed at Rogan.

He turned and, with one swipe of his hand through the air, a glimmering, iridescent barrier went up between Jamie and Bella, and Rogan, Christian and Alec. Bella and Jamie's energy hit the barrier and reflected back at them. They both dove to avoid it. One bolt hit Jamie in the gut. He yelled, dropped to the ground, and clutched his stomach.

"Jamie!" Bella shrieked and ran to him. "You bloody bastard, Rogan!"

The fury inside Alec began to bubble to the surface. He lunged for Christian again, who'd nearly ceased even trying to fight the invisible vise grip that had him in its clutches. This time when Rogan tried to thrust Alec backward, he was ready and willed himself not to move. He flinched and a ripple of pain shot through him as the energy entered him, but he kept his feet and reached Christian's side.

Rogan seemed undeterred that Alec had made some progress. He released the invisible choke-hold on Christian and let Alec touch him.

"Christian," Alec said softly, stroking his hands over his lover's face, the cold, damp skin so pallid and lifeless. Christian's lips were nearly blue from cold and lack of air for so long. "Chris, I'm here. Hang on."

His eyes fluttered open. "Alec." The word was little more than a raspy whisper.

"I'm here." He brought Christian's hand to his lips and kissed it.

"Touching." Rogan's voice was cool. "Very touching. And notice how reasonable I'm being, giving you a chance to say goodbye?"

"Shut the fuck up," Alec shot over his shoulder at the mage.

Trying to close out everything but Christian lying on the ground in front of him, Alec lowered his hands to Christian's chest and tapped into the healing energy. For the first time ever, there was no barrier blocking him and he felt the lack of it immediately. Energy rushed into him and into Christian. Even if he could only get a little into him, it had to help.

He was expecting Rogan to interfere and he did, this time grabbing Alec by the hair in a physical grip instead of a magical one and flinging him away from Christian.

"Time's up! I want my amulet, boy. And you're either going to give it to me or your lover's going to die."

Alec rose and faced the tall mage. "I told you, I don't know where it is. And even if I did, do you honestly think I'd tell you? My family's spent generations keeping it safe from pathetic, power-hungry malcontents like you!"

Alec could hear Bella on the other side of the barrier trying spells to take it down. Jamie, he saw, was conscious, but clearly in considerable pain. He was muttering spells, too, and trying different types of energy to get through.

Christian was stirring. He rolled onto his side.

Rogan held his good hand toward Christian and Christian began to rise in the air. He tried to fight it, but he was weak and it did no good.

Before Alec could react, Rogan made a motion with his other hand, the blackened claw, and Alec felt tight bands of invisible energy wrap around his body from his shoulders to his feet. His arms were locked at his sides, his legs couldn't budge. The bands were so tight his extremities began to tingle as circulation was cut off to them.

Arms stretched out as if doing a balancing act, Rogan settled his cold gaze on Alec. "Last chance. Amulet or he dies."

Energy crackled in Rogan's palm closest to Christian.

Giving up on spells, Bella began shouting and banging on the barrier with her hands. "No! You bastard, no!"

"Tell me, Ansley!"

Alec was beginning to get lightheaded from the bands that squeezed him tighter and tighter. "You want to know where the amulet is? Fine!"

"Alec?" Christian's hazy eyes settled on him. His voice was barely audible, yet Alec heard it deep inside him. "Don't tell anything. My life…isn't…worth it."

The anger that had stirred in Alec minutes before boiled inside him again, more powerful than ever, like magma creeping and churning, searching for a way to burst forth.

"You want to know, Rogan? Then come here and face me like a man. Come close and I'll tell you."

"No, Alec! No!" Bella shouted, almost in tears.

"Don't do it, Alec!" Jamie called, his voice hoarse and laced with pain. "Whatever you might remember about it, don't tell him anything!"

Rogan's eyes narrowed, but he stepped closer.

Dizziness blurred Alec's vision, and yet, a strange power seemed to merge with the fury inside him, causing it to swirl faster, burn hotter. A strange calm settled over him, like the calm before a storm.

"Closer," Alec growled.

::Alec....don't.::

Christian's voice in his mind only made him more determined.

::I love you, Christian.::

::Love you, too...::

Rogan was close enough now if Alec's hands weren't restrained he could have wrapped his hands around the mage's neck and squeezed the life from him.

"Location, Ansley!"

Alec leaned his head closer...it was the only part of his body he could move.

"No, Alec! No, no, no!" Bella sobbed.

"Ansley!" Rogan snapped. The energy in his palm facing Christian crackled louder. "You have three seconds. Two."

"Rogan..."

Rogan leaned in closer.

"Fuck you!"

The pain was instantaneous and intense, rolling through Alec like a forest fire. He screamed. But it was several seconds before he realized it wasn't his pain. It was Christian's. And with their minds linked, he could feel all of it. Intimately.

As he watched, Christian's body shook from the power of the energy that seared into him. And then, with one last shudder, he went limp.

Rogan flung Christian's body back and it collapsed in a heap on the ground.

::NO! Chris, no!::

Bella was screaming. Jamie was shouting.

Rogan turned to Alec. "Foolish boy."

The magmatic storm inside Alec burst. Power rushed through his veins, riding on his anger, his grief, all the losses he'd experienced in his life, and most of all, on the memory of Christian's pain and how the man he loved had suffered at Rogan's hands.

Heat built in his chest like a star about to explode and spread out from there, filling him, surrounding him in a pulsing halo of powerful, golden light he could see. Energy sizzled within him, his for the taking.

The invisible bands around him popped free.

"Stupid egocentric, fuck," he growled, stalking toward Rogan. The man threw up a protective shield and Alec swiped it away with barely an effort.

With one hand Alec reached out and pushed down Rogan's barrier between them and Jamie and Bella. With the other, he picked up Rogan by the neck with a strength he'd never known he possessed and let him dangle in the air.

It was almost like a dream as he watched Bella rush to Christian. Saw her check his pulse. His breathing. Saw her ashen, tear-stained face look up.

"He's dead," she whispered.

Cold, empty hatred rose in Alec to mix with the burning power, causing a churning, poisonous stew of the two. Hate. Kill. That's all he wanted. To kill this bastard who'd stolen Christian's life and so many others.

He tightened his hold on Rogan, squeezing, wanting the mage to suffer the way he'd made Christian suffer. Wanting to kill him slowly.

Rogan gasped for air and Alec enjoyed the sound.

"Holy fuck," he heard Bella say in a startled tone. Out of his peripheral vision he realized she was staring at him. So was Jamie.

Alec suddenly became aware that the pulsing golden light surrounding him moments ago had turned a deep-greenish black. He felt it eating into him like a cancer. Shocked, he looked at Rogan and realized the man was turning purple.

"Jesus," he muttered. He dropped Rogan as if he'd been burned, and focused all his energy back on the center of his power, pushing out the sickly green-black horror and letting the clean golden light fill him again.

He saw Rogan try to stand, raise his hands. But before he could call up any energy to do more harm, Alec, with only a mere thought, picked him up and flung him against the house. Again with only a thought, he surrounded the mage with golden bars of energy, then willed the bars to turn to steel.

Almost in a trance, he turned to face Jamie and Bella, who hovered next to Christian's body. Alec moved to them. It felt as if he were walking on pure energy. He couldn't even feel the ground beneath his feet. He knelt next to them, placed a hand on the blackened and bloodied wound in Jamie's stomach, and closed it.

"Sodding hell!"

"Oh, my God!"

The pair's shocked words barely registered with him. He turned to Christian, so still and pale on the ground. Moisture welled in his eyes. He picked up the man's cold hand and pressed it against his own heart.

::I love you, Christian. I'll love you always.::

"He's gone, Alec." Bella sniffled. "It's too late."

"No." Alec heard his voice, raw with pain. "I don't accept that."

"There's nothing you can do," Jamie said, his own voice thick with emotion. "We loved him, too, but there's no way to bring him back."

Bella's quiet sobs tore at Alec's heart, ripping it open to new pain…loss…and a loneliness so severe he didn't think he'd ever be able to breathe again.

Letting his love for Christian fill him and swirl together in a kaleidoscope of color with the strange rippling power, he laid his hands on Christian and let everything he had flow into the man who'd so quickly become his world.

He lost all sense of time and place. Had no idea how long he sat there, trying to do the impossible. All he knew was the giving. Giving Christian everything. Even his own life if it was required.

At last he grew so weak he could barely stay upright. He no longer had the strength to maintain the flow, and, with one last pulse, the remaining bit of energy coalesced around him, then slid back into the center of his power—the medallion around his neck.

He collapsed against Christian's body and knew no more.

CHAPTER 19

Pleasant warmth seeped into him, and his dream took him to the big meadow near the house he and his grandmother had shared for a couple of years when he was six and seven. He ran through the tall, thick green grass, loving the smell of it and the moist summer earth. Loving the feel of the sun beating down on his head as he ran…happy and filled with a contentment only young boys running barefoot and free on a hot summer day could experience.

Then the dream shifted and he was tucked against Christian's warm, muscular body in a soft bed on a cold winter afternoon. A fire blazed in the fireplace, and the reflection of the orange flames flickered and teased patterns over Chris's skin. Alec kissed each one of them, knowing he'd never be able to get enough of this man's taste, his touch. Christian's gaze was filled with so much passion and love Alec's heart swelled. This was a different kind of contentment, the kind a grown man could appreciate and lean on to get him through the days and weeks and years of his life, knowing he'd never be alone and he'd always have love and joy and fulfillment.

But a finger of dark shadow moved in at the edge of the dream, pushing at his happiness. He tried to ignore it, but it wouldn't leave. Instead it lingered and grew, trying to shove his contentment aside, and filling him with an aching loneliness in its place.

No. No! He didn't want this. It was too much…the hurt, the loss.

His breathing grew ragged. He saw the deathly pale skin of Christian's face, and those eyes once so filled with life closed forever.

"No…God. No. Christian!"

He lurched up in bed, waking at the same time he sat up, feeling the scald of tears in his eyes.

Strong, warm arms wrapped around him, pulling him close, settling his head against a solid shoulder. "Alec, I'm here," a soft voice said against his ear. "I'm here."

The voice, the heat, the familiar scent and touch filled his senses. Alec pushed away enough he could see, and discovered worried and oh-so-beloved blue eyes gazing at him.

"Chris?" He touched his palm to the other man's stubbled cheek. "I thought…I thought I'd lost you."

"I'm here. Thanks to you." Christian's voice was quiet, filled with emotion.

"I didn't think it worked."

"It did. But I was so afraid for you. You pushed yourself to the breaking point, Alec. You've been out for so long."

"How long?"

"Twenty-six hours." Moisture glistened in Christian's eyes. "Damn it. I don't know what I would have done if you hadn't ever opened your eyes again."

"I didn't know what I was going to do if you didn't either. I couldn't imagine a world without you."

Chris burrowed a hand into his hair and held him close, their foreheads pressed together. "I love you so much, Alec."

"I love you, too. God, I love you, too."

Their lips brushed, and then brushed again, and then they were kissing long and slow and sweet. Alec tasted the salt from Christian's tears. Or maybe it was from his own. They clung together, letting the pain and relief flow until, at last, they were purged.

Eventually, they lay back down in the bed and snuggled together. Alec realized he wore a comfortable pair of sweat pants and nothing else. Christian was dressed similarly. Their legs twined together, and so did their fingers as they lay facing each other

"Where's Rogan?" Alec asked.

"The Council's holding him for trial."

"Holding him how? He can't escape, can he?"

"Actually…they're holding him in the cell you created for him." A half-smile curved Christian's mouth. "No one can open it."

He lifted a hand to Alec's face and brushed his thumb over his lips. "Bella and Jamie said you could have killed Rogan. Why didn't you?"

Alec swallowed hard. "I almost did. But then I just knew, somehow, that it wasn't right. That killing wasn't what the power was supposed to be used for." He reached down and picked up the silver medallion that still hung around his neck. His gaze met Christian's. "I didn't know. I had no idea until…until he killed you and then the power just rushed through me."

"You scared the hell out of Jamie and Bella." He said it lightly, but Alec knew the truth…he really had scared them. "I guess you were pretty intimidating."

"Intimidating to myself, too. I understand now with crystal clarity how its power could very easily be used for the wrong reasons. At one point I hated Rogan, I mean really hated him with ever atom in my body. I wanted to kill him. That was all I wanted. And when those emotions took over, the power changed. It…it filled me with rage and let me believe killing Rogan was the right thing."

"Jamie said it took a damned strong person to come back from that. To master what it was doing to you."

"That's the thing…it wasn't the amulet that was doing it. I was doing it, and the power the amulet offered was too tempting. This has to be hidden away again, Christian. Forever."

Christian nodded. "You know I'll support whatever decision you make about it. It's your legacy now."

"What I want to know is how a carved stone ended up looking like this?"

"Transmogrification. That's the secret to how the Ansley family has protected it for so long. No one's ever known, but now it's clear that's how they did it."

"Transmogrification?"

"To change something from one form into something completely different. It's not a common skill. Very, very few mages have the ability to do it because it's so complicated. And even the ones who can do it can only do simple things. But apparently it's something your family mastered. The amulet could have been a rock in the yard, a candlestick on the mantle, a handkerchief in a drawer…virtually anything. It might have been in the form of the medallion you wear for a long time, or your father could have transmogrified it into the medallion right before he sent you and your mother into hiding. He also imbued it with complex protection charms that helped hide you. Sending you away saved both you and the amulet."

"Bella told you about my family, obviously."

"Yeah. You okay about it?"

Alec smiled and huffed out a soft laugh. "I guess so. It's going to take some getting used to. I mean, regular guy, American police detective versus mage from powerful magic family whose destiny it to protect the world?" He arched an eyebrow. It's a bit, uh…daunting."

Christian's chuckle filled Alec with warmth. "Yeah, I suppose it would be. But you know what I think?"

"What?"

"I think"—his hand cupped Alec's face—"that you are more than up for the challenge."

"You know what I think?"

"What?"

"I think"—he grabbed Christian's hand and pulled it down to his groin—"I'm up for something else, too."

Heat flashed in Christian's gaze, but his expression was one of concern. "Are you sure, Alec? You were out for so long, and after everything that happened…"

"I just slept for twenty-six hours. I assure you, I'm well-rested and I've never felt better. So don't go all protective on me just when I've got an ache only you can fix."

A slow, sultry smile curved Christian's lips at that, and with a soft growl, he rolled Alec to his back in the bed and settled his weight between Alec's legs.

"Hmmm," Alec said with a grin. "I can see I'm not the only one who's 'up.' Why don't you bring that beautiful cock of yours up here and let me make it feel real good."

"Keep talking like that and you might be in this bed another twenty-six hours."

"Promises, promises."

Christian's mouth came down on his and they ground their groins together in silent sensuality. Alec had just slipped his hand inside Christian's sweats and gotten his first touch of Christian's cock when a knock sounded at the door.

"Shit!"

They pulled their mouths apart and stared at one another. Christian looked torn between laughing and throwing something.

"Hold that thought," Alec said, smiling and pulling his hand out of Chris's pants.

"Bloody hell. I don't want to be holding a thought," he grumbled. "I want to be holding something else all together."

Another knock sounded. "Christian? Alec?" Bella called quietly, as if she were afraid she might wake them. If only she knew.

They heard Jamie saying, "Leave them be, Bella."

"I know they might still be sleeping, but I just want to check on them to be sure they're okay."

Christian looked at Alec and his eyes darkened with desire. "You know what?" he whispered. "I don't feel like holding my thoughts this time." He flicked a finger toward the door and Alec heard the very obvious sound of the lock clicking into place.

They heard a little gasp from the other side of the door. "Did they just lock us out?" Bella asked.

Jamie's low chuckle rumbled in the hallway. "Bella, sweet, I think it's safe to say they're just fine in there. Good night, mates," he called through the door. "May you have many hours of sweaty, kinky—"

They heard a soft grunt and Bella's exasperated voice. "Jamie!"

"Ow, Bell, that hurt."

"Serves you right, you pervert."

"Ooooh, baby, I love it when you talk dirty."

The soft sounds of Bella's laughter moved off down the hall.

"You're so bad," Alec told Christian, unable to hold back a grin.

Christian gave him a sexy little smile as he yanked down Alec's sweats and fisted his aching shaft. "That's not what you told me the last time your cock and I had intimate relations."

Alec's mouth went dry. "Jesus. Do you know how much I love you?"

"Oh, yeah. I do." Christian's voice was low and filled with a whisky-smooth warmth that sent fire through Alec's veins. Their mouths met in a slow, thorough kiss and then Christian proceeded to show him all over again just how damned right they were together.

M. L. RHODES

Award-winning author M.L. Rhodes has been writing for a living for nearly twelve years. Along with the erotic romance fiction she currently pens for Amber Quill Press, she's also published everything from poetry, to magazine articles, to traditional romance, to steamy romantic suspense novels. In her fiction works, her characterization and emotional storytelling have received high critical acclaim from such places as *Romantic Times Magazine, The Romance Studio,* and *JERR* and have garnered her numerous awards in the writing industry.

In her man-love stories, she enjoys pairing together strong, independent heroes who are open to exploring both their sexuality and their emotions. Men can and do fall in love with one another every day, and M.L. believes in celebrating that!

If you'd like to keep up with what's going on in M.L.'s world and find out about her new and upcoming releases, surf on over to her website at www.mlrhodeswriting.com. She also loves hearing from readers. You can reach her at ML@mlrhodeswriting.com.

AMBER QUILL PRESS, LLC
THE GOLD STANDARD IN PUBLISHING

QUALITY BOOKS
IN BOTH PRINT AND ELECTRONIC FORMATS

ACTION/ADVENTURE

SCIENCE FICTION

MAINSTREAM

FANTASY

ROMANCE

HISTORICAL

YOUNG ADULT

SUSPENSE/THRILLER

PARANORMAL

MYSTERY

EROTICA

HORROR

WESTERN

NON-FICTION

AMBER QUILL PRESS, LLC
http://www.amberquill.com

2203547